MINDSIGHTED

BlackWing Pirates, Book 1

Connie Suttle

SubtleDemon Publishing, LLC

To Walter, Joe, Sarah, Larry, Lee, Dianne and Mark.
Thank you.

Acknowledgements

As always, this book is the result of collaboration. If it weren't for the support of my editor, my cover artist and my beta readers, it would be less than it is. All mistakes, as usual, are mine and no other's.

About the Author:

Connie Suttle lives in Oklahoma with her husband and a conglomerate of cats. They have finally banded together to make their demands, which has proven disconcerting to all humans involved.

FaceBook: Connie Suttle Author
Twitter: @subtledemon
www.subtledemon.com

Other books by Connie Suttle:

Blood Destiny Series:
Blood Wager
Blood Passage
Blood Sense
Blood Domination
Blood Royal
Blood Queen
Blood Rebellion
Blood War
Blood Redemption
Blood Reunion
* * *

Legend of the Ir'Indicti Series:
Bumble
Shadowed
Target
Vendetta
Destroyer
* * *

High Demon Series:
Demon Lost
Demon Revealed
Demon's King
Demon's Quest
Demon's Revenge
Demon's Dream

* * *

God Wars Series:
Blood Double
Blood Trouble
Blood Revolution
Blood Love
Blood Finale
* * *

Saa Thalarr Series:
Hope and Vengeance
Wyvern and Company
Observe and Protect*
* * *

First Ordinance Series:
Finder
Keeper
BlackWing
SpellBreaker
WhiteWing

* * *

R-D Series:
Cloud Dust
Cloud Invasion
Cloud Rebel
* * *

Latter Day Demons Series:
Hot Demon in the City
A Demon's Work is Never Done
A Demon's Due
* * *

Seattle Elementals Series:

Your Money's Worth
Worth Your While*
* * *
BlackWing Pirates Series
MindSighted
MindMage*

Other Titles from SubtleDemon Publishing:

By Joe Scholes:
Malefactor
Transgressor*

*Forthcoming

Chapter 1

Prince Amlis' Castle, New Fyris
Randl Gage

"Randl, I've scheduled a council meeting tomorrow morning," Prince Amlis walked into my office. Another set of steps accompanied his—that of Amlis' guard and constant companion, Rodrik.

"I will be there," I announced as the image of Amlis formed in my mind, followed by that of Rodrik.

"This will be our first Combined Alliance Conclave, and the Grand Master will attend our council meeting tomorrow. Since he and I are expected to represent Harifa Edus, I trust you will inform me if he holds anything back that concerns New Fyris, or presents us in an unflattering light?" Amlis asked.

"As always, my Prince."

"Good. Thank you."

My official title was assistant to Prince Amlis. My unofficial work for the Prince of New Fyris was to tell him whenever something wasn't brought to light because someone didn't wish to tell him. Mostly, those things were unimportant to him and only served to cause bad feelings between the Prince of New Fyris and those who served on his council.

I disliked this addition to my duties.

Very much.

I suppose I should be grateful that a Prince would hire a blind man as his assistant—I doubted many royals would consider hiring someone like me at all.

My sight—or the physical lack of it, doesn't allow for the efficient reading of paper books or messages on comp-vids. When I place my hands on the device or physical pages, it takes several seconds for my mental vision to show me what's there.

That delay is a decided disadvantage, compared to listening to spoken words or hearing messages through a comp-vid. Most people can read much faster than the time it takes to speak the words.

I'd been shown a third system of reading—through raised dots on paper or other surfaces, but the spoken words settled into my mind easier.

A physician said it was because I'd depended upon hearing all of my life, and that my hearing was sharper because of it.

He'd also offered to replace my useless eyes with electronic ones.

I declined.

Somehow, I knew that my sightless, white eyes were a part of the gift I carried—the gift of seeing things others couldn't, and often predicting the future with great accuracy.

The mental visions are somewhat delayed—like soil that has been dry too long and is now cracked with thirst, yet unable to swallow water immediately.

Often, too, I wished for another job. Serving Amlis had become a terrible chore and one I disliked more every day. Few employers

Chapter 1

would consider a blind worker, no matter how good he might be—and especially since my blindness appeared to be a matter of choice.

I'd already decided not to reveal to a new employer my talent for detecting the animosity or ill-feelings of others toward him or her—my experience with Amlis proved that to be an unworthy endeavor.

I also knew that were I to tell Amlis that I wanted to work elsewhere, he would offer more money to keep me where I was.

I didn't want that.

Truthfully, I felt as if I'd contributed to Amlis' paranoia, simply by answering his questions. If I left, perhaps he'd gain a healthier perspective on things.

For six years after my schooling was over, I'd worked for Amlis as his assistant. My father, Brandl, also works for Amlis, and is in charge of castle schedules and maintenance. I worry that he'll lose his work if I were to leave New Fyris with little notice.

The Prince would deny any thought of pettiness in releasing my father, but he would desire revenge anyway, were I to take employment elsewhere.

In other words, I'd become Amlis' crutch, and he'd treat my father differently if I were to leave voluntarily. I could see that in Amlis as easily as I could see my father's image in the mornings, it had become so familiar.

Amlis wasn't a bad man—far from it. I'd merely made the mistake of expanding his insecurities with my visions.

"I'll have someone vid-record the meeting," Rodrik said as the Prince left my office.

"Thank you, Rodrik," I dipped my head. Rodrik wasn't only Amlis' bodyguard, he was also his cousin and first in line for the throne, should Amlis die without an heir. And, as Amlis hadn't married, there was no heir on the horizon for him.

Rodrik ignored his position as heir most of the time. He had no desire for the ornate chair Amlis occupied. I was grateful for it, too, as Amlis had asked me about that very thing only recently.

With a sigh, I turned my thoughts to the meeting the following day. I'd never met the new Grand Master for the werewolves of Harifa Edus; therefore, tomorrow would be a learning experience for me.

* * *

Queen's Palace, Le-Ath Veronis
Winkler

"Lukas asked me to attend Conclave with him," I said.

Lissa turned to look at me while putting earrings in her ears. It didn't matter how many times I'd watched her dress, it always made my blood heat. I wanted to take her straight back to bed, but she had a Council meeting scheduled.

"I have plenty going with me already," Lissa said. "You can act as an advisor for him if you want."

Lukas was Grand Master for the werewolves of Harifa Edus—for barely six months. He was as tough and as fair as they came. In fact, he reminded me of a young Weldon Harper, but I hadn't told Weldon that.

Yet.

Lukas needed experienced advisors around him, and those who'd served the previous Grand Master weren't the most reliable, since Lukas had taken that position.

The Grand Master's position now required votes instead of fights to the death; it was a requirement for admission into the Reth Alliance. Lukas had won the loyalty of most of the werewolf population; just not those who'd served the previous administration.

"I heard Lukas was meeting with Amlis for the first time tomorrow," Lissa said.

Chapter 1

"I heard that, too."

"Because he asked you to come, didn't he? Are you going?"

"Thinking about it."

"Good. He should have cleaned house the minute he walked into that position, but he didn't. He needs a steady hand on his shoulder and a strong arm to back him up," she said, turning back to the mirror so she could position the tiara on her head.

I hid a smile; she hated that thing.

"Strong and steady, that's me," I said.

"Stop grinning and let's get to the meeting," she said.

"Yes, ma'am."

"Don't ma'am me, fur-butt."

"Don't call me fur-butt, queenie-pants."

She snickered as she walked toward the door. I followed, holding back a laugh.

* * *

Amlis' Castle, New Fyris

Randl

"Pap, I don't know what to do," I admitted as I settled on a chair across the table from his. "Amlis wants me to tell him everybody's secrets, and I dislike that."

"And the new Grand Master will be here tomorrow," Pap guessed.

"Yes." I allowed my shoulders to slump.

"I wouldn't have taken him for someone who could become so paranoid," Pap said and dipped into his bowl of stew.

"I'm partly responsible," I admitted.

"Boy, you can't take the blame for everybody's weaknesses," Pap said. I envisioned him pointing his spoon at me. A few seconds later, the actual image lodged in my mind. I wanted to smile; instead, I began to eat while Pap talked.

"Amlis has access to grants and such from the Founder, but he doesn't take advantage of them. Some of his people are still depending on horses for transportation and to do their farming. He has technology freely available, and he's stuck in the before-times." Pap breathed a snort; I did smile, this time.

"Some of the crops grown here," Pap went on, "aren't available anywhere else. He could use that technology to farm those fruits and vegetables that used to grow solely on Siriaa, and sell them to Alliance buyers."

"In other words, he needs to get with the program?" I repeated a favorite phrase I'd learned from my tutor, Master Morwin. Someone had seen to it that he'd be the one to teach me, rather than the New Fyrian schools for other, sighted children.

I heard Morwin was on Avendor, now, teaching new younglings. I wished him well.

"Amlis has become so complacent—expecting you to tell him everything while everyone else does his work for him," Pap complained.

I didn't disagree—Amlis' army was headed by two captains provided by the Alliance, so the troops would be trained properly according to Alliance guidelines. New Fyris ran smoothly as a result. I sighed.

"Randl, I know you want to work elsewhere. You should have that opportunity. Don't worry about me—I can find other work if it comes down to it."

"But you like your job," I began.

"And I can like a similar job elsewhere. I went through the classes, too. I have an Alliance certified education—just not nearly as extensive as yours. By choice."

"I just feel the situation is getting more toxic, the longer I stay," I sighed.

Chapter 1

"I know. Son, you have to think about yourself, now, and not a dependent Prince or your pap, who can fend for himself."

"I just want tomorrow to be over," I said. "Amlis is worried about the new Grand Master. He was familiar with the old one, at least, even if he wasn't the best choice for his people."

"Then we'll hope the new one can settle Amlis' worries right away, since they'll be going to Conclave together."

* * *

BlackWing X
Travis Tetsuya

We were lucky to have Terrett on board with us on this flight to Pyrik. We'd found a smuggler's ship haunting the shipping lanes there, when it should have been aiming for its destination as fast as it could fly.

As it turns out, they were waiting for a passenger—who'd be smuggled to Pyrik, along with a load of designer drugs and counterfeit jewelry. Trent and I wouldn't have been so concerned if Pyrik wasn't the chosen location for the upcoming Combined Alliance Conclave.

Somebody wanted to make money off the massive meeting, whether it was selling to tourists, media, hangers-on or world leaders.

"Bro, you think we ought to back off and wait for the passenger?" Trent asked.

"Want to ask Mom, Ry or Gav?" I countered. "Terrett couldn't get anything from the crew—they don't know who this guy is, either."

"Or why he wants to go to Pyrik," Trent finished my thought for me.

"What will it hurt to stay here for a little while?" Jayna came to join us. "If he's nothing more than a nut job who can't get there through normal channels, we can send him back where he came from. If he's something more than that," she shrugged.

"We let Kooper have him," Trent and I chorused.

"Just what I was thinking," Jayna grinned.

"Terrett," I said. "Let's let these guys believe we were never here, and wait for their passenger."

Terrett, who stood in the hold of the pirate ship, watching the pirate crew while the rest of us discussed their disposition, turned in my direction. With a nod, he went back to his docile, captive pirates and began to place obsessions.

* * *

Avii Castle, Le-Ath Veronis
Quin

I'd just returned to Le-Ath Veronis after spending two months on Avendor. Wisdom and Strength had made the suggestion several years ago to leave a replica of Avii Castle at SouthStar, and place the real one where it had been before on Le-Ath Veronis. The real thing was impervious to damage; the duplicate sat in the safest place imaginable and wasn't in danger of attack.

Justis' and my daughter, Jerra, was now fourteen and deep in her studies with Master Morwin at SouthStar. I stayed with her much of the time, and she visited her father often on Le-Ath Veronis.

Father and daughter had a strong bond; Justis doted on her and smiled when she stretched her white-tipped red wings and flew with him over SouthStar's groves.

"We just received this transmission from Queen Lissa," Dena, who now worked as my personal bodyguard, brought a comp-vid to me.

"What is it?" I asked, taking the comp-vid from her hand.

"Somebody she wants you to look at," Dena shrugged.

Chapter 1

"No doubt," I said dryly, after seeing the image on the comp-vid. "Does Lissa know he holds an obsession?"

"I think she's puzzled by that," Dena acknowledged. "Terrett says the same thing."

"Remind me to have a conversation with my Sirenali," I shook my head. "He could have sent mindspeech."

"Maybe he didn't want to skew whatever you might see in this one," Dena suggested.

"Possibly," I agreed and went back to the image. "He's so heavily obsessed, I can't even get his name," I frowned. "Have they checked his prints and everything else?"

"The records indicate he's a dead man," Lissa folded into my study. "As in doornail dead. He no longer recognizes the name he was born with, either. Says his name is Vrak, no last name given."

"And no idea what the obsession is, I suppose?" I handed the comp-vid back to Dena.

"None," Lissa said. "He arranged for passage through a third party, to be smuggled onto Pyrik. We've already gone looking for that third party; he was found dead on Veechee. We wouldn't have had his name except the smugglers knew it and had taken bookings through him before."

"That doesn't sound good," Dena said. "You think this Vrak killed the one on Veechee after arranging the trip?"

"Kooper doesn't think so—the murder was too recent—as in the body was still warm when they got there, and Vrak was already aboard the ship."

"Then Vrak may have allies," I said.

"Just what I was thinking," Lissa agreed. "We now have a choice—whether to lock Vrak up or let him out on Pyrik and have him followed. Frankly, I'm concerned about that second option."

"Terrett won't be able to supersede another obsession," I said. "Vrak will remember that he was stopped and questioned. That could affect what he does after he gets to Pyrik."

"My thinking exactly," Lissa said. "Well, I'm recommending we lock him up and keep this quiet. Maybe we can send a team to Pyrik following the smugglers' ship, and see who shows up to meet them."

"I like that idea better," I said. "At least Terrett can handle smugglers. Someone who bears such a heavy obsession," I shivered. "V'ili is dead, so he can't be involved."

"Or so we think," Lissa said. "No," she held up a hand. "He's really dead, but what if this obsession was laid years ago? This man was reported dead nearly twenty years past. Nobody knows where he's been all this time."

"You're going to give me nightmares," Dena breathed. V'ili had nearly killed her in the past, along with Ardis, her husband, and their baby, Dara.

Dara was now studying with Jerra under Master Morwin's tutelage. They were barely a year apart and good friends. Dena usually went with me on my visits to SouthStar, so we could spend time with our girls during class breaks.

"Don't have nightmares just yet," Lissa told Dena. "BlackWing X will go to Pyrik to see whether they can sort this out. I'll have the ship disguised before they arrive."

That was something Lissa had come up with—a disguise and a legitimate registration for each of the twelve BlackWing ships. All of them were recognized in both Alliances, with different names, of course.

I found it amusing that Travis and Trent, Lissa's twin sons, were working on gaining their tattoos through their efforts at capturing and shutting down real pirates and their operations.

Chapter 1

Lafe did the tattoos when they were earned; that's how I knew of their progress. For now, their arms were completely covered with dragons; the chest and back tattoos would require extreme bravery to achieve.

"Will you let me know what they find?" I asked.

"Of course. In fact, stay in touch with Terrett. I think he should go with them on this mission. We merely need to come up with a legitimate reason for them to go to Pyrik, in case somebody's watching for the ASD to show up in disguise."

"What about your transport to Pyrik for the Conclave?" Dena asked.

"No, I've already said I have Larentii transportation," Lissa waved off the idea. "Quin and Justis are scheduled to come with me, since Aviaa is now a sovereign nation," she added. "But," she looked thoughtful for a moment. "Winkler is planning to go with Lukas and Amlis," she tapped her chin. "I think I can fix that up. I'll keep you posted." Lissa disappeared, leaving Dena and me to blink at her abrupt departure.

* * *

Amlis' Castle, New Fyris
Randl

I'd seen Winkler before; just not with the new Grand Master of Harifa Edus. I understood that he'd disagreed with the previous Grand Master and didn't associate with him. He'd come to New Fyris with Queen Lissa several times, however.

He was now acting as Prime Advisor to Grand Master Lukas for the Conclave, until Lukas filled that position. Winkler and Lukas stood together in the castle's vestibule, waiting for Amlis and Rodrik to approach.

It had taken the usual few moments for my mental images to adjust, but I could see those four; Amlis and Rodrik striding toward the two werewolves who stood, relaxed and ready, to greet the Prince of New Fyris.

Amlis, his body stiff with unease, shook properly with Lukas and Winkler, before Rodrik invited them to sit in the chairs reserved for honored guests.

This council meeting—a formality, really, before the trip to Pyrik and the Conclave, was going to be long and uncomfortable.

* * *

"Of course I have to go," I mumbled while Pap and I had dinner together. "I have new clothes coming, and a trunk to put them in, just to be presentable," I added.

"So." Pap buttered his bread while he considered his words for a moment. "Amlis isn't comfortable around Lukas, then."

"That's partly my fault—I didn't tell Amlis much about Lukas—or Winkler. Winkler can smell Amlis' hesitance and discomfort. While he's able to ignore it, Lukas finds it unsettling."

"You need to get away from that—it's poisonous," Pap said.

"Queen Lissa is sending a ship to transport us, so we won't have to spend the funds to pay for regular transport," I said, changing the subject. "The crew is supposed to provide bodyguards and assistance while we're on Pyrik."

"Probably some of hers, then," Pap said.

"I think that, too. I also think she may be worried about this—situation. Winkler's likely told her about Amlis by now, so it may be a way to referee without being obvious about it."

"Maybe a good idea, then," Pap agreed.

"I hope it's a good idea. I wish I could talk privately with Rodrik about this, but I fear he'd take it to Amlis, which will only make things worse."

"Then don't. If Rodrik had any sense, he'd have come to you about it, first."

Chapter 1

"I feel closed in and suffocated, here," I admitted.

"I know. Finish your dinner, son. When Conclave is over, we'll discuss where you'd like to go and see about making that happen."

"Thanks, Pap."

* * *

Avii Castle, Le-Ath Veronis

Quin

"Are you prepared to see Amlis at Conclave?" Justis asked. He, Bel Erland, Lafe, Berel, Edden and I were having dinner together.

Edden and Berel would go with Justis and me, along with Ardis, Dena, Wellend and Warlend, who'd act as our guards. Ordin and Gurnil, Master Healer and Master Librarian for the Avii, were also planning to attend.

I hadn't seen Amlis—or New Fyris—since Siriaa's destruction. Something always prevented it, somehow.

He and I—there were old wounds between us.

Rodrik too—he'd opened my back during a beating once, at Amlis' command.

I'd never really gotten a proper apology from either, and that rankled.

After all, I was no less than they; I'd come to realize that. At least the laws of the Alliances forbade the punishment of servants by beating them for misdeeds, whether real or imagined.

The Alliances called that assault, and it was punishable by fines and imprisonment, where appropriate. If it hadn't been against Alliance laws, I imagined it would be the same as it always was with those in Amlis' castle—who punished servants as they saw fit in the past.

I wondered if those nobles and such who'd made the trek from Siriaa had accepted the idea that none were beneath them, where the law was concerned. I was grateful that Ildevar Wyyld had written the clause of equality into the laws at the beginning, and that the concept was fiercely protected on every Alliance world.

"Love, you have such a sad expression on your face," Justis reached out to touch my hand.

"I know," I sighed heavily. "Too many memories, I think."

"You don't have to see him if you don't want," Bel Erland said.

"It's all right. It's time, I suppose." I waved away his offer of protection. This Conclave would be for both Alliances, after all, which Bel and his father would attend as King and Crown Prince of Karathia—with a full complement of guards, advisors and assistants following in their wake.

"Who's coming to represent Avendor?" Berel asked.

"The President and his staff," I said. "Kay told me. Ashe never participates—probably for obvious reasons."

"Merrill and Adam are going with the President—they'll talk about logging, both legal and not-so-legal, on some Campiaan Alliance worlds," Bel Erland said. "Some people think the Campiaan Alliance should allow for permits to clear out sections of rain forests. Everybody knows what that can do."

Merrill was one of Queen Lissa's mates; Bel Erland was her grandson. He'd be in possession of that information if anyone would.

"There's enough logging happening already, much of it illegally," Edden pointed out. "Those rain forests are considered public property—up to a point. They're listed as national parks and such, open for camping, hiking, wildlife observation and rafting. Cutting down those trees will only damage the ecosystem and render the area unusable and unsafe."

"It's on the agenda and they'll vote on it," Justis said. "I know how I feel—I can't say how relaxing it feels to fly over endless trees at SouthStar. I'd love to fly across a wilderness area—what better way to see the birds and animals?"

Chapter 1

"Do you think we could take Jerra and Dara sometime?" The thought of taking them on an adventure like that sounded wonderful.

"I'm sure we'd have to clear it with everyone ahead of time," Justis went back to his food.

He was right—he'd be visiting royalty and special provisions would have to be made. It made me sigh.

"What if nobody could see you while you were flying?" Bel Erland suggested, grinning.

I turned toward Justis, my eyes widening at the thought of it. If we were hidden by a spell or such, we could take the girls over any park we wanted.

"Something to consider," Justis almost smiled as he cut a chunk of steak and placed it in his mouth.

"Wellend and Warlend could fly with you, maintaining the shields," Bel Erland suggested.

"Mmmm," Justis nodded.

Wellend and Warlend had retained their abilities as warlocks; they'd merely been given red wings and were considered Avii royalty, now, instead of Karathian royalty. Avii dipped their heads respectfully to them, just as they did to Justis, Jerra and me; red wings were magical to them in that respect.

It was also Wellend and Warlend's due, for long years of faithful service to the Karathian crown and to others—although they were just as royal as anyone they'd served.

They'd developed a strong friendship with Gurnil and Ordin, and usually shared meals with them.

As for Farisa, Vorina and Wimla, they only attended certain functions, now that young Liron had grown multi-colored wings. He and I were secret friends, actually; we caught up with one another often in Gurnil's library, where he read as much as he could.

As promised, on Liron's sixteenth birthday, Daragar had taken both of us to the Larentii Archives, where Liron whooped and pulled several books off shelves to devour.

Daragar had given him duplicate copies of several things to take with him when he left, too; books that until that moment only existed in the Archives.

Gurnil had already petitioned for Liron to become an apprentice; Justis had decreed it, at Farisa's dismay.

She wanted to place the young Avii in the crafting guilds, where he would surely be as unhappy as Dena had been while working as a yellow-wing servant.

Someday, perhaps, I would ask Zaria for a favor. Liron wanted mindspeech, so he could speak with me at any time.

I wanted him to have it, too.

Perhaps Zaria would grant our wish. The last I'd heard of her whereabouts, she'd been with Tampirus, visiting the Sirenali and the Pod'l-morphs on Revalus. I realized, then, that both those races would be present at Conclave—for the first time ever.

It made me smile. No, the Sirenali had no ruling family as yet; only a Council, comprised of both elected Sirenali and Pod'l-morphs.

Their small planet was perfect for the Pod'l-morphs; much of it was covered by a rainforest near the equator. A continent that lay northward had been taken by the Sirenali, and their population had grown nicely since the occupation.

I figured Zaria had much to do with that—with help from a few Larentii, who only smiled when asked about it.

"Have your new gowns been delivered?" Justis asked, breaking me away from my thoughts.

"This morning. Don't worry, Dena will make sure the maids pack them properly," I said.

Chapter 1

"I want my Queen to be properly attired," Justis smiled. "There have never been winged attendees at the Combined Alliance Ball."

"You just want to show off your new dancing skills," I teased.

"Wellend and Warlend are good teachers," Justis chuckled.

Justis wanted to go. He'd have no trouble staring down Amlis and Rodrik, if it were necessary.

I vacillated between the desire to shout at them or withdraw and weep.

"Randl will come," Bel Erland said. "I think you and he may have many things in common."

Once again, Bel had read my expression accurately, and had given me something to cling to when I came face-to-face with Amlis again. For now, I wanted to shout at him for past mistakes and an uncaring attitude toward someone who only had his well-being at heart.

"Things will go as they will," Berel soothed. "We'll be with you, my love. There is no need to worry."

Chapter 2

New Fyris
Randl

"Transport is here." Rodrik stepped into Amlis' study, where I waited with the Prince. Our bags and trunks were already on the landing pad outside, waiting for the shuttle to arrive.

I walked behind Amlis and Rodrik through the castle, familiar enough with the structure that I could close my eyes and my mind and still navigate its halls.

My senses adjusted once we walked through the side entrance and into the sunlight; I felt the sun's warmth before I saw brighter images in my mind. Fumbling in a pocket, I pulled my dark glasses out and fitted them over my eyes.

It was a precaution, so I didn't burn what I had.

Once my vision came, I saw the shuttle was a sleek carrier, designed to carry twice our number, with baggage. The engine was strong and sturdy enough to get us past the atmosphere and to the small space station orbiting Harifa Edus.

I didn't need anyone to tell me that Lukas and his entourage were already aboard; they'd picked him up first.

Amlis wouldn't be pleased about that.

Breathing a sigh, I allowed a smiling woman to help me navigate the steps to climb into the shuttle.

Jayna. Her name was Jayna. She had a disguise shining about her, but I could see past that to the beauty beneath.

It made me want to ask her why she'd asked for the disguise—someone else provided it because she held no power to do it for herself.

She was also a member of the ASD.

Had the crew known that I could ferret out such secrets with my gift, which often felt like a curse? Perhaps that was the reason for the disguise—to fool anyone into thinking she was anything but an ASD agent.

I kept my mouth shut and that knowledge firmly lodged in my mind. Amlis would only begin to ask why he was being spied upon, when nothing would be further from the actual truth.

The ship we'd travel on needed a cover—and a reason—for arriving on Pyrik for the upcoming Conclave.

BlackWing X—that information settled into my mind. I blinked as I turned away from Jayna. A different name was printed on her name tag; I reminded myself to use that name when I addressed her.

She and others on the ship were involved in the hunt and capture of pirates in Alliance shipping lanes. It sounded like a wonderful life, far away from the insecurities of royalty and the everyday grind of life in a castle. That life limited my journeys to short walks from my home to the castle and then back again—unless I was required to visit Harifa Edus with Amlis.

Those trips were infrequent, and didn't get me away from the insecurities anyway.

Chapter 2

"It will take a few ticks to reach the space station," Jayna announced as we buckled into our seats. At least I didn't fumble with the straps; it would serve to embarrass me, and that inevitability could wait until later.

* * *

Winkler

"How goes it?" Travis set a cup of Falchani black on a small table and took the chair opposite mine in the ship's galley. I could smell the strong tea from half a mile away; his grandfather, Dragon, drank it all the time in Lissa's kitchen.

"Amlis is as insecure as they come, and that's unsettling Lukas," I said, lifting my cup of coffee for a drink. We'd only been underway for three hours and already Lukas was pacing on the exercise deck like a caged wolf.

"I just checked on Amlis' quarters," Travis nodded. "The blind assistant is attempting to settle Amlis down. I get the idea that Amlis isn't used to space travel, and that only makes his shortcomings worse."

"Where's Rodrik?" I frowned at Travis.

"On the exercise deck, using the rower machine. He's worried that space travel will destroy his arm muscles."

"Is that upsetting Lukas?"

"Not for now—they're ignoring one another."

"Good. I don't need to break up a fight on day one." I drank more coffee.

"May I join you?"

Amlis' blind assistant had come, carrying a cup of tea.

"Of course," Travis pulled out the third chair quickly.

"I know you're worried about Amlis," he said as he took the seat. I noticed he didn't have to feel his way to do so.

"I see the vision of everything," he explained. "Although it takes a few seconds. Call it a delay until my surroundings have time to settle into my mind. Randl," he held out a hand to me, exactly where it should be to shake.

"William Winkler, although everybody calls me Winkler," I took the offered hand.

"Travis," Travis held out his hand when Randl disengaged and turned toward the Falchani.

"Ah. I am most pleased to meet you, Travis. Your twin—what is his name?"

"Trent," Travis grinned. "I didn't realize you'd know that about us."

"It comes with the visions," Randl shrugged. "Do you know Quin?"

Travis froze. He did know Quin, just not as well as his father and uncle did.

"Sorry, didn't mean to pry," Randl apologized. "I was hoping she'd be at the Conclave. I haven't seen her in years and I'd like to speak with her, I think."

"The Avii Queen will be at the Conclave," I said. Travis visibly relaxed.

"Good. Very good. I will send a message when we arrive," Randl said and rose from his seat. "Thank you for speaking with me."

Travis and I watched as Randl strode away.

This one—he knew more about us, I think, than we knew about him. "I think I'll have a conversation with your mother tonight," I sighed. Travis nodded his agreement.

* * *

Randl

Chapter 2

Three days to Pyrik. My gut rumbled from the tension pouring out of Amlis on the first day.

Rodrik had escaped, at least, leaving me to deal with the Prince's insecurity. I knew something of Amlis's past—his father had gone mad and his mother appeared to do the same.

She'd chosen to stay behind on a dying planet when Amlis made the move with his people to Harifa Edus.

Word of her death came shortly after. A part of his insecurity was the fear that he'd suffer from that same madness. If he continued on his paranoid course, he'd hand it to himself.

"New Fyris is not being cheated by Harifa Edus," I said for the third time. "All transactions are conducted fairly and with just compensation, as dictated by Alliance protocol. I have gone over the agreements myself, and nothing is amiss."

"But it costs so much to import from there," Amlis whined.

"Transport isn't free," I said, a tinge of impatience in my voice. "Packaging for transport is also not free. Those who provide these necessary things are guaranteed payment, unless you wish to be brought up on charges levied by the Alliance."

"No," Amlis held up a hand. "Perhaps I should read," he said.

"Yes. Most certainly." I searched for his comp-vid while considering that he should study the agreements and cost sheets from Harifa Edus himself, rather than depending on someone else to do it for him.

I handed the comp-vid to him. "Do you wish to have dinner in the galley, or shall I have it delivered to you here?"

"Here is fine." He was already thumbing through the selections on his comp-vid. I hoped he'd take time to read through the schedule for the Conclave, too, and refresh his thoughts on how he'd like to vote on several questions.

In other words, I didn't want to be forced to whisper in his ear throughout the Conclave. He needed to know and understand everything for himself. "I'll see that your dinner is delivered, with a glass of wine," I said, heading toward the door.

"Make it a bottle," Amlis said.

"Of course."

* * *

Later, once Amlis had his dinner tray and bottle of wine, I walked back to the galley to eat.

"Sit here," Lukas pushed a chair away from his table as I searched for a place to consume my meal.

Winkler sat with him, and they were nearly finished with dinner.

Setting my tray down with a sigh, I thanked the Grand Master before taking the offered chair. I hoped they'd make small talk and stay away from the subject of Amlis and his perceived rudeness—he should have joined these two and Rodrik for dinner.

At times like these, I missed Morrett greatly; he and I would often have lively conversations over dinner, concerning this book or that topic. Unlike me, Morrett had escaped Amlis' clutches and had gone to work for the King of Karathia, as his librarian.

Amlis had plenty to say about that, and it hurt to hear so many ill-spoken words aimed in Morrett's direction for abandoning New Fyris.

Those words would never reach Morrett's ears—not from me. They were hurtful and untrue. Morrett had given Amlis his very best while employed by the Prince, and his library had grown exponentially as a result.

Too bad Amlis chose not to read the books on mental health and emotional stability; he may have gleaned vital information from those volumes.

Chapter 2

"I was hoping Amlis would join us tonight," Lukas broke my silence.

"As was I," I agreed and reached for my butter knife. It brought home images of my pap, who would do the same thing—butter his bread first of all.

"Since we'll be sitting at the same table, representing Harifa Edus as a whole, I was hoping we'd be on the same page and vote the same way—especially on environmental issues," Lukas said.

"I understand that," I nodded and cut into the fowl they'd served for dinner.

"I'd like to keep the encroaching logging industry away from Harifa Edus," Lukas added.

I felt the same way, but Amlis was looking at the money offered and not the detrimental effects of deforestation. I worried he'd choose to vote to allow logging in certain areas.

For many years, that sort of thing had been all but outlawed by the Reth Alliance, and substitutes for wood were easy to manufacture. When the Campiaan Alliance came into being, it had already been logging—heavily—on many of its member worlds. Some of that activity had been greatly reduced, but those businesses were now looking for new sources of wood, as the trade in wood products in the Campiaan Alliance was very lucrative.

Eventually, as it often happens, wood products made their way into the Reth Alliance due to trade agreements. Now, the logging industry in Campiaa was pushing to ply their trade in both Alliances.

I'd done my homework on this measure, as it would directly impact Harifa Edus if the proposal was approved. Amlis, sadly, hadn't read anything on the subject, other than the amounts of money to be earned by allowing it.

Some had suggested a counter-proposal, to grow wood on deserted worlds specifically for harvesting.

The logging industry didn't appreciate it, because that meant there were no businesses there to support the workers or to provide local crews to control the bots needed to cut and transport the logs. Additional transport from those worlds would only add to the already high cost of logging, so they'd managed to convince both sides that it wasn't a viable option.

Therefore, we were left with a simple yes or no vote—to allow logging or not. To me, it felt like a big step backward, but I had no vote in the Conclave and was never going to get one.

"The Prince is still considering his options on all questions," I said. It was the most diplomatic answer I could give. It didn't sit well with Lukas, just as the truth of the matter didn't sit well with me.

"That's a fine way to say he hasn't read it all, yet," Winkler drawled. He was right; I nodded and took another bite of my bread.

"What is your opinion on the matter?" I asked Winkler after swallowing.

"Hmmph. You're talking to a werewolf, son. We like cover—it's inborn. Downing a forest of trees goes against our nature."

"And against nature in general," I said. "Except in some cases. Parasites and such."

"Agreed. Clear what you need; leave the rest." I found I liked this werewolf, and imagined we'd agree on most things.

"I can't speak for the Prince," I reiterated. "I can only speak for myself, and I have no vote to stand with yours."

"I appreciate your candor," Lukas said, his voice calm. "Will you convey an invitation to the Prince to have dinner with Winkler and me tomorrow evening? Rodrik is welcome, too."

"I will tell him," I said.

He nodded. Winkler and he rose from the table and walked out of the galley, leaving me to my thoughts.

* * *

Chapter 2

Winkler

"Ten to one he refuses," Lukas sighed as we stopped at the door to his suite.

"I won't take that bet," I said. "He's paranoid, I'd lay a bet on that, though. I'd lay another bet that Randl knows all about it, but it's not his job to discuss the Prince's issues."

"Privacy being the main concern. I have no doubt that Randl is an exceptional employee, or we'd have learned about Amlis' troubles long ago."

"True. How do you approach a Prince and tell him he needs a therapist?" I'd already decided to fold space and visit Lissa to tell her all this, rather than sending mindspeech only. Mental instability in royalty and rulers of worlds was a ticking time bomb. "Good-night, Lukas. I have some things to do before bed," I waved and walked away.

"I imagine you do," he grinned and opened the door to his berth.

* * *

Queen's Palace, Le-Ath Veronis
Lissa

"He's paranoid as hell; I can smell it on him," Winkler said. "He wouldn't have dinner with Lukas, when he should be using every second of this trip to hammer out decisions for Harifa Edus at the Conclave. Did you know his assistant has visions?"

Winkler had changed topics so quickly it surprised me.

"Visions?"

"Well, I don't know what else to call them. He's blind, but he has mental sight, I guess. He says it takes a few seconds to form the images in his mind."

"Did you find out anything else?"

"No."

"I'll look into that," I said. "Our biggest worry is Amlis and his load of insecurity."

"Yeah."

"I'd consider asking Quin to heal him, but she may not want to get that close. They have issues from the past, and I'm not sure she even wants to see him."

"What the hell did he do to her?" Winkler was ready to slap him into next week—Quin was one of the gentle souls, and any mistreatment raised his hackles.

"Bree says he had her beaten because she spilled his food—her way of attempting to tell him it had been poisoned."

"Hmmph." Winkler wanted to growl, I could tell. "I think I could show him a bad time," he said.

"Rodrik delivered the beating."

"Two at once. Not a problem."

"Honey, you can't go around beating every ruler or politician that's fucked up. You'd never have any time off."

* * *

BlackWing X

Randl

I knew the name of the ship—its actual name. The title it bore on the outside, however, was Raptor II.

Amlis had grudgingly agreed to have dinner with Lukas and Winkler, but only after Rodrik convinced him to go. Amlis was collapsing upon himself the closer we came to Pyrik, and that wasn't a good thing.

"Can you really see the stars?" Trent took a chair at my breakfast table, a cup of hot tea in his hands.

"I see them as blurs of light," I replied.

"That's how I see them, too, at this rate of speed."

"Then my mind isn't playing tricks on me," I confessed one of my worries to him.

"No," Trent said. I turned to look at him; his smile settled into my vision of the galley interior.

"Hey, bro," Travis pulled a chair beside his brother's. "Randl," he nodded at me.

"What is that tea you drink?" I asked. "The scent is quite different from anything I've drunk before."

"Falchani black," Trent's smile widened into a grin. "It's strong enough to keep a warrior on his feet for three days, according to my dad."

I lifted an eyebrow. Same mother, different fathers, same birth date. Yes, I'd read of such before, but usually not in humanoids. Animals were generally the ones who could accomplish that feat.

"Is Amlis having dinner with Lukas tonight?" Travis asked.

"Yes, after much convincing."

"Good. I worried we'd have to run interference."

"Run interference?" I hadn't heard that term before.

"It's a term used in a game played on Old Earth, called football," he explained.

"Interesting. Can you expand on that?"

"It's when a player goes ahead of another, to smooth the way for the one behind him. Sort of an expendable, blocking for a more important player."

"Ah. I see," I nodded. "I'll remember that—for future use, you understand."

"Did you ever play sports?" Trent asked.

"No. the delay in my visions prevented it. I do play games of strategy, however."

"Do you know how to play Irzu?" Travis asked. Irzu was a game of strategy popular on Falchan. Others played it elsewhere, but the masters were always Falchani.

"I've never played that one—I had no way of getting the proper stones or a playing board or cloth," I admitted. "Imported items in New Fyris are limited to necessities, for the most part."

"I'll get you a proper set," Travis said. "I have to go; the bridge is calling my name." He slapped his brother on the back when he stood, before walking out of the galley.

"He's Captain of the Day," Trent said. "I get desk work. We switch every four days. Works out great."

"That sounds wonderful," I admitted. "My job is the same thing, every day."

"Must be tough, dealing with a paranoid prince," Trent said. "Enjoy the view. I have paperwork to deal with." He rose and stretched.

I wasn't surprised that he knew about Amlis—it was getting more and more difficult to hide the insecurities. Amlis fairly radiated with it, in my opinion.

It was one of the reasons I wanted to see Quin—or Morrett. I wished to speak with either or both in private, and ask their opinion. I could trust either, I think, not to tell anyone else about the fears I carried—and the guilt of perhaps being responsible.

More than anything, I wanted to ask Trent and his brother about their real mission. The one involving a man thought dead, who'd arranged for transport to Pyrik. That man was secretly held in an ASD facility, while the pirate ship made its way to Pyrik.

Travis and those others aboard BlackWing X wanted to see who arrived to meet that ship. They suspected treachery, and wanted the man's contacts and their motives.

Chapter 2

The ASD moved in mysterious ways—that was a common phrase everywhere in the Reth Alliance. It intrigued me. I'd never been close to anything such as this, and I wanted information.

Trent walked out of the galley, while I wondered if he knew I might be of assistance in his investigation.

My life in New Fyris was deadly dull, except for the burgeoning mental illness of the Prince who employed me.

With a sigh, I contemplated what work I could accomplish during the empty hours of the day—unless Amlis required my services.

I sincerely hoped that wasn't the case.

* * *

King's Palace, Karathia

Bel Erland

"Ready?" I asked Morrett. Dad wanted both of us with him during the Conclave. Garwin Wyatt had sent mindspeech, asking when we'd be there. He and Dormas were already at the hotel in Mer'bali, Pyrik's capital city.

We'd have three guards, Granddad and an assistant with us, to represent Karathia. People—especially those without power, generally kept their distance. Granddad could play the role to the hilt, too, as Gran often said. He'd stride through hotel lobbies and ballrooms alike, his robes billowing about him, as if he were the grandest warlock anyone would have the fortune to see.

Dad would hide a smile and follow in Granddad's wake.

I was looking forward to meeting Quin and Justis for dinner when they arrived; Mer'bali was famous for its seafood dishes and I hadn't had good seafood in a long time.

My mother, Reah, could cook seafood better than anyone, but she seldom cooked nowadays—not since she'd taken the throne of Kifirin. Dad and I were both surprised when she took the throne so willingly, after Jayd and Garde went crazy and tried to destroy the planet.

She'd named my youngest sister Lexsi as her heir, though, and that was the best choice. Lexsi was a guli, and she and her husband, Kordevik, could cut through the bullshit of any argument and hand your ass to you before you understood it had been removed.

"Ready?" Dad walked into my suite, followed by the guards and the royal scribe.

"Yeah. I've sent all the bags and trunks ahead," I replied.

"Good. Do you want to do this?"

"Sure." I grinned and folded space, taking Dad, Morrett and the others with me.

* * *

Mer'bali, Pyrik

Garwin Wyatt San Gerxon

Mer'bali stretched to the sea's edge—the sea that gave Mer'bali its name. Translated, it meant sea of harmony. In the distance, the late afternoon sun glittered on its surface, giving credence to the name.

When I turned twenty, Dad and Tybus told me what I'd known already—that there were two instead of one. If Tybus ever noticed that I'd never called him Dad before, he never mentioned it.

I called him Uncle Tybus, now, and I often acted as a diplomat for both, clearing the way with this leader or that, so the Campiaan Alliance would run smoothly.

"Do you have the contact information for Phrinnis Tampirus?" Dad strode into the room, fixing a cufflink on his shirt.

"I have the contact information for President Tampirus," I said, giving the President of the Pod'l-morphs his proper title without bothering to turn around. "And the contact information for Prime Council Derik of the Sirenali."

Chapter 2

Revalus, home to the Pod'l-morphs and Sirenali, had joined the Campiaan Alliance. This was the planet's first Combined Alliance Conclave.

"Do you have plans tonight?"

"Bel and I were planning dinner," I said. "We're both hoping Quin and a few others will join us."

"Your grandmother says that BlackWing X is following a pirate freighter. They captured a passenger making his way to Pyrik under a false identity. Travis and Trent are working with Kooper to find his contacts here."

"Can't have a conclave without intrigue," I sighed. "Who is he really?"

"Someone who was reported dead at least two decades ago."

"Nice. Where has he been all this time?"

"That's just it—nobody knows. Word has it he's obsessed and they can't get any useful information out of him."

"And there I was, hoping the word obsession had reverted to its old, standard reference to stalkers, love-struck idiots and diehard fans."

"You sound like your grandmother."

"I come by it honestly."

"Son, you're just making it worse."

"People could do a lot worse than sound like Gran," I pointed out.

"True."

"What do you want me to do instead of having dinner with Bel?"

"No, go ahead and have dinner with him. I was hoping you could meet Travis and Trent after they get in, to find out if they have new information, that's all."

"I can do that. Easy," I said.

"Good. Keep me posted. I have dinner with the Ambassadors to Venks and Benks tonight. It will probably go on forever, or I'd come with you."

"Lucky you," I said, meaning the exact opposite. Venks and Benks orbited the same star, and the leaders were so intelligent they often accused one another of stealing their sunlight. Go figure. That's why Dad was meeting with the ambassadors instead of both leaders; they couldn't stand to be in the same room.

"Are you sure you can handle this on your own?" I turned to tease my father.

"The ambassadors aren't quite as stupid as both Presidents, thank the gods," Dad grinned. "I think I can make it through dinner and drinks without killing one or both of them."

"Are you sure you can't employ compulsion?"

"I can't tell you how many times I've wanted to," he said and lifted his jacket from the sofa. "I'll have my usual CSD guards and Dormas with me. Tell Bel I said hello."

"Thanks, Dad."

"If you happen to see your mother, tell her I'd like to see her while she's here."

"I'll do that. Maybe we can have a family dinner or something."

"I wish I could get a home-cooked meal, but asking a Queen to fix fish for dinner just sounds crass."

I laughed, which was what Dad was hoping for. "See ya," Dad turned toward the door. "Send mindspeech if you hear anything new."

"Will do."

Just after the door closed behind Dad and his guards, Bel Erland sent mindspeech. *We're here*, he said. *Room 17895.*

I'll be down in a sec, I told him and turned to mist.

* * *

Chapter 2

Quin

Lissa's suite was next to mine at the hotel, and after receiving mindspeech from Bel Erland, discovered he was just down the hall.

Want to come over? Bel asked. *Garwin Wyatt is here. He and his dad have a top floor suite.*

As the founder of the Campiaan Alliance, I wasn't surprised that Teeg San Gerxon had a top floor suite.

If Ildevar Wyyld came, he'd have a massive, top-floor suite, too. Ildevar seldom attended functions such as this, preferring to remain in contact via live vid-feed during meetings and votes.

"Dena, I want to go down the hall to see Bel Erland," I called out.

"Not without me," she appeared in my doorway.

"Then let's go," I said.

"You're in a hurry. You'd think you hadn't seen Bel Erland for years," she teased.

"Sometimes it feels that way," I retorted. "Tell Ardis where we're going, so he and Justis won't have heart attacks."

"Ardis," Dena called over her shoulder. "Quin and I are going down the hall to see Bel Erland."

"All right. Tell her to send mindspeech to Justis regarding dinner plans."

"Will do."

"Come on," I headed toward the door. "Bel says Garwin Wyatt is there, too. I haven't seen him in two years."

Dena and I walked as fast as we could down the hall toward the Karathian suite and knocked on the door.

I was surprised to see Erland, Bel's grandfather, at the door instead of Bel Erland. "Travis and Trent just arrived, Quinnie Bee," Erland ushered us into the suite quickly. "That pirate ship they were following was blown up the second it entered Pyrik's atmosphere."

Chapter 3

*M*er'bali

Garwin Wyatt

There's evidence that the ship was scanned, I informed Dad in mindspeech. *The ASD is working on the source of the scan, but haven't come up with anything yet. Travis said someone aboard BlackWing X suggested that the pirate ship was scanned for the passenger who was removed days ago, and when he wasn't located on the ship, it was hit with laser rockets.*

I'd like confirmation on all counts, Dad returned. *Keep me advised.*

I will.

Who? Dad thought to ask. *Who made that suggestion? Is he or she a suspect in all this?*

Not likely, I replied. *This is Prince Amlis' blind assistant. I think he's some sort of clairvoyant.*

I'd like to meet him, Dad said. *Let Travis know, and clear it with the Prince.*

All right. I'll let you know where and when.

Good. Thanks. Gotta go—the ambassadors are glaring at each other.

* * *

Randl

I knew bare seconds before the ship exploded, and cried out with the vision of it. Someone hadn't found what they sought aboard that pirate vessel, and all those aboard died because of it.

Trent, who'd been close by, heard my shout first, and then his brother's report of the destroyed ship seconds later.

He'd asked me what happened afterward. I didn't lie; I told him what I knew of the matter.

He was surprised that I not only knew he worked for the ASD, but that I was aware of their mission—tracking the pirate ship.

That's how I found myself on Pyrik, inside a richly-appointed suite belonging to the King of Karathia, where Morrett waited to greet me. Travis and Trent, as it turns out, could fold space. Several things were locking into place, like pieces of a puzzle, where those two were concerned.

Then, Quin entered the room and rushed forward to embrace me. I was so happy to see her, I trembled with joy.

"This is Garwin Wyatt San Gerxon," Quin pulled away to introduce me to another man. "He is Teeg San Gerxon's son and serves as a diplomat for the Campiaan Alliance."

"Happy to meet you," Garwin Wyatt held out a hand. After my vision of his hand cleared, I accepted it.

"Thank you," I dipped my head to him.

"My father wishes to meet you, to discuss your theory that the pirate ship was scanned," Garwin Wyatt told me. "And please, call me Wyatt. All my friends do."

"It isn't a theory," I said. "I know it's difficult to believe, but I sensed it."

"You should believe Randl," Quin came to my defense. "He knew his village and others like it on Vogeffa II would be attacked, long before it actually happened. He and his father were waiting for Lafe, Terrett and me when we rode into that small town to warn them about Cayetes' attacks."

"Vogeffa II?" Wyatt asked.

"Yes. That was our home, until Quin called for help to rescue us from Vardil Cayetes," I said. "We are grateful for her compassion as well as her connections. We were settled in New Fyris afterward, because their population needed a boost."

I didn't add that I was dissatisfied with my situation in New Fyris. Many who work are dissatisfied. They go to work anyway, to feed their families. I doubted I'd ever get a family, since Amlis normally demanded so much of my time.

Randl? Morrett's mindspeech reached me first.

"Morrett?" I turned toward the doorway while my mental sight adjusted.

Believe anything Randl tells you, Morrett declared in mindspeech. I blinked sightless eyes at him as he strode forward and pulled me into a tight hug.

"That's not an endorsement or anything," the Crown Prince of Karathia laughed.

"All here have mindspeech?" I knew the answer but asked anyway. I couldn't send, but I could hear it if it were directed at me.

Randl can't return your mindspeech, but he can certainly hear you, Morrett's mental chuckle made me smile. I'd missed him when he left New Fyris. I was learning that he enjoyed his work for the Karathian King.

I could never joke or tease with Amlis. I imagined it would be the equivalent of hurling a live cow at a threshing machine—its landing and the aftermath wouldn't be pretty. Rodrik—I doubted he'd have the wisdom to buy a sense of humor, because he'd certainly been born without one.

"Terrett says that the Prince and the others have been safely delivered to Pyrik, although the Prince is complaining that you're not at his side," Trent informed me. Someone on the ship had sent a mental message to him, advising him of that.

My shoulders slumped before I thought to stop the gesture.

"What's wrong?" Quin asked.

"May I speak with you in private? You and Morrett?" I asked.

"Send them into my suite," Bel Erland said. "We'll give you privacy."

"Thank you, Prince Bel," I bowed to him.

"Call me Bel, or Bel Erland. It's easier." I caught his smile before it disappeared.

"Of course, Bel," I agreed. Quin, Morrett and I followed the Prince as he led us toward his private suite.

* * *

Quin

"It's Amlis, isn't it?" I couldn't stop the words from tumbling out the moment Bel left us alone and closed the door.

"He's—unstable," Randl dropped his head and admitted reluctantly.

"It's hereditary," I said. "You never met his father. He was in charge of Old Fyris, and he almost destroyed everything."

"What can I do?" Randl begged, turning his face toward mine. "I want to find another job. He's become so paranoid, and I feel I'm to blame. He asks what this one or that thinks of him, and my answers only make things worse."

"Randl, no," I reached out to take his hand. "He shouldn't be asking those questions of you. No sane person would. His instability is goading him in this, and, as you work for him, you cannot refuse a direct command."

"I want to find another job, but Pap works for him, too. If I leave, Pap will suffer."

"If we can't find something suitable, I'll hire you both at Avii Castle," I said, suddenly determined. Amlis and his family had cost me too much already. I wasn't about to allow him to ruin other's lives, too.

Morrett had stood back, listening to our conversation and nodding his head. *Randl would be a godsend to the ASD,* he offered. *I know this. Look what he just told them, when it would have taken them hours or even days to discover the same thing.*

"That's true," I turned back to Randl. "I know Kooper Griff. While we're here, I'll arrange a meeting."

"What about Pap?" Randl wouldn't budge unless he knew his father was taken care of.

"What does he do for Amlis?" I asked.

"He runs the castle," Randl sighed. "He likes his job."

"I think I can find something similar," I said. "If not at Avii Castle, then surely on Le-Ath Veronis somewhere." It concerned me that Randl was so troubled. Amlis was truly over the edge if a normally calm seer was this upset.

Will you not consider his healing? Morrett asked.

"Morrett," I sighed before covering my face with both hands for a moment. "He and his family tried to kill me," I said after dropping my hands. "Several times. It would be an unwilling gesture on my part, although I should be less selfish than this. For the people of New Fyris, if nothing else."

"How do I avoid answering the Prince's questions while we're here on Pyrik?" Randl asked. "He'll want to know about everyone who approaches him, and many who do not."

He can't ask you if you resign, Morrett patted Randl's shoulder. *If Quin can't find you and your Pap a job, I'll ask King Rylend.*

"I'll get Lissa to send mindspeech to Kooper," I said. "Just give me time to get this done. I'll ask her to have your Pap notified, too, in case things don't go so well with Amlis."

"Thank you. This means more than I can say," Randl breathed.

"Come on, we'll find some excuse not to send you back; I think we can improvise until Kooper is notified." I hugged Randl, who wrapped his arms about me in gratitude.

* * *

Travis

"Director, he knew it before it happened," I said. Kooper arrived minutes after Quin and Morrett left with Randl.

"Your mother says Randl's not happy in his job—that Amlis is turning paranoid." Kooper settled his long frame into a chair at the hotel bar. "It's never good news to hear one of your rulers is losing it, either. Bad things happen in their wake."

"I can verify the crazy," I offered. "Trent, too—and Winkler."

"I'll hire the young man," Kooper nodded at a waiter to take his order. "We need him and dozens more just like him."

"He may be one of a kind," I pointed out. "Word is that his mother was one of the mutants—their words, not mine—from Gungl, who fled the city once Cayetes got his hands on everything. She died shortly after Randl was born, I think."

"Did your homework, I see." Kooper nodded his approval.

"Trent and I went looking for his records the minute he boarded ship. It's almost unheard of for a blind man to be working in close proximity to royalty. He's refused the procedure that could help him see, too."

"Probably worries it'll interfere with his seer's ability."

"It could be," I agreed.

"Two bourbons," Kooper held out his wrist for the scanner.

"Right away, sir." The waiter walked away from us.

"How do we get him away from a paranoid Prince at a Conclave?" I asked.

"Inform the Prince in question that the ASD requires Randl's assistance. I'll have a contract drawn up, if necessary, to wave in the Prince's face."

"You know that won't go well."

"I'll provide temporary assistants, if it's necessary. It'll take a couple of mine ten minutes to read Amlis' schedule and record his voting preferences."

"Except he hasn't made up his mind on most of it, yet," I countered. "He's refusing to even look at the topics for discussion—Winkler told me that after he and Lukas had dinner with him. Rodrik knows more than the Prince, at this point."

"Who's next in line to the throne?"

"Rodrik. He's Amlis' cousin."

"Did he inherit the cray-cray, as your mother says?"

"Doesn't look like it. He does have the same sour mood, though, if what I've seen so far is accurate."

"Must be a ton of laughs in New Fyris, then. Thank you," Kooper accepted his glass of bourbon. The waiter lifted my glass from the tray and set it down in front of me.

"Thank you." I nodded at the waiter, who left to deliver other drinks.

"To Randl, who saved us time on figuring out what happened to the pirate ship," I held up my glass.

"Second that," Kooper lifted his glass, then drank. "Now, all we have to do is look for the source of the scan and the laser rockets."

"Piece of cake," I replied with a shrug.

* * *

Winkler

Lukas' suite was directly across the hall from Amlis'. I understood that accommodating hotel employees thought it a good idea and it would have been for most presidents and monarchs representing the same planet.

Amlis had thrown a tantrum after receiving the message that Randl's talents were required by the ASD in searching for criminals in the pirate ship bombing. He hadn't been given details, but everyone aboard BlackWing X knew a ship exploded.

Hell, the entire planet of Pyrik held its breath until they learned the ship wasn't carrying a royal, president or ambassador to the conference.

So far, the ship hadn't been officially identified, although Travis, Trent and most of the crew knew all there was to know about the pirate vessel.

I figured it was only a matter of time, too, before Kooper realized he ought to take Randl to visit the prisoner they'd taken. Quin couldn't read a thing about him. If it were me, I'd see what a talented clairvoyant could do.

Kooper, I sent, *you ought to take Randl to visit your prisoner.* He'd know what I meant.

Good idea, although we don't even have a uniform for him yet.

I'd do it, I pointed out. *Doesn't make a damn bit of difference how he's dressed, if he can deliver information.*

True enough. I'll send some of mine to collect our seer. Want to go with them?

I would, but I'm babysitting.

Amlis?

Yeah. He wanted to hit Lukas, when we went to tell him Randl wasn't coming back.

Let me know if he gets violent. We don't need that at Conclave.

Chapter 3

Tell me about it.

I already did.

You really ought to study Old Earth idioms and colloquialisms, I pointed out.

I'll do that on my next tea break. I'll keep you informed on the other.

Kooper was a sarcastic bastard. I liked that about him.

* * *

Randl

"How much do you know about our mission?" Travis asked. I was back aboard BlackWing X, with Trent, Jayna and a few other crew members.

"I understand there was someone who arranged to be transported to Pyrik," I said. "I think that's why the ship was destroyed. I hope that information doesn't get me in trouble."

"Not a chance, unless you say that to someone outside the ASD, or who doesn't need to know inside the ASD," Travis said. He and I sat in the Captain's cubby, located behind the bridge.

Trent, who sat beside me, swiveled his chair in my direction. "We want to take you to see the prisoner," he said. "Kooper suggested it, in case you can see what Quin can't. So far, we haven't gotten any useful information from him. It's almost as if he doesn't know himself—until an opportunity presents itself or he meets a contact who knows more than he does."

"That's frightening," I said.

"Welcome to the world of obsessed minds," Travis sighed. "We haven't seen many in the past fifteen years or so, but this one is certainly obsessed. Quin says so."

"Quin can see so many things I can't," I admitted. "Why would I have anything to add to her assessment?"

"Because your talent may work differently," Trent suggested. "We'll give it a try anyway. Don't worry if you don't see anything—it won't place your new job in jeopardy, and we'll still be right where we were before. This isn't a test—it's an experiment."

"That I can do," I said, turning my vision away from Trent to study Travis. "When are we going?"

"Now, if you're up for it. Kooper is still working on a uniform, and, as you're sort of special, the usual physical training will be waived. We may teach you how to handle weapons, but that's only for extreme emergencies. The rest is just studying and memorization of Alliance laws and ASD procedures. Shouldn't be difficult for you."

"I enjoy studying—well, reading, actually, although it takes longer for me to do it, with my condition. It doesn't matter what the reading material is. I have a good memory, too."

"Good. We'll be taking you to an ASD holding facility on Refizan." Travis rose and stretched. Trent and I stood, too. For them, this was routine. For me, it was all new.

I'll get used to it, I reminded myself. I'd gotten used to change from the moment I foresaw danger for my father when I was young.

I hoped my new colleagues wouldn't fall into the paranoia trap, like Amlis did. It would be much more difficult to tear myself away from their clutches if that happened.

* * *

ASD Holding Facility, Refizan
Travis

At times, it was easy to forget that Randl was blind. His mind vision worked so well, and he'd become so adept at covering the slight delay in his visions that he appeared sighted.

Until he pulled out his dark glasses when we landed in a shaded courtyard adjoining the holding facility.

He'd been advised to wear the glasses outside, no matter how much light there was. The darkness provided by the glasses didn't impede his visions at all.

"This way." Trent touched Randl's arm after waiting a few seconds. Randl nodded and followed in Trent's wake.

I walked behind Randl as we strode down wide halls to reach the prisoner's cell. Two guards walked toward us. I saw Randl's shoulders stiffen. I went on alert, but both guards nodded as they passed and moved on.

Perhaps they thought Randl another prisoner to be locked away. Trent and I weren't strangers, here—it was Kooper's location of choice to haul in pirates we'd captured, before questioning them and setting up necessary trials and more permanent accommodations.

Refizan had a close working relationship with the ASD Director, and was quite discreet in all matters.

What's wrong? I sent to Randl.

His steps faltered, then stopped. When he turned to face me, I saw he'd gone pale.

"Those two—they'll die. Many will die. The prisoner, too," he whispered.

Kooper, we need to evacuate the holding facility now, I mentally shouted.

* * *

Queen's Palace, Le-Ath Veronis
Randl

"How often do you watch news-vids?" Travis flopped onto a chair nearby and flipped his long, black braid over a shoulder.

I sat on a comfortable chair in Queen Lissa's library, watching the news reports generated by a local news facility.

I watched as security feeds from cameras close to the Refizani Holding Facility showed the explosions. Deaths were reported, although there hadn't been any, thanks to Travis and Trent's swift actions.

The prisoners from the cells were now housed in Queen Lissa's dungeon, and Trent told me they were shielded in some way, so nobody would know they were there. I still hadn't visited the prisoner in question, although I felt it likely that he'd drawn the would-be killers to him, somehow.

"I watch them sometimes," I answered Travis' question. "I've never been directly involved in what is reported, or in this case, not reported."

"Welcome to the ASD," Travis snorted. "Mom says she'll go to the dungeon with us, when you're ready to take a look at our prisoner."

"Queen Lissa is your mother." My words were flat, as I'd already known this about him. He and Trent were Princes of Le-Ath Veronis. At least they weren't like the Prince I'd been employed by before.

I found myself grateful I no longer worked for Amlis, even with the terror generated by probable deaths and the subsequent destruction I'd witnessed as a new employee of the ASD.

"Come on, you already knew that," Travis teased.

"Yes," I admitted. I almost smiled, too. It was nice to have colleagues who appeared to be of a similar age and had a sense of humor.

"Come on. Let's raid the kitchen, then go to the dungeon. Kooper wants us back on Pyrik tonight. This whole thing is deeper than we thought, and he wants all hands on deck."

All hands on deck. That was a new phrase for me, but I understood its meaning. I tucked it into my memory, in case there was an opportunity to use it sometime.

"I am hungry," I admitted. Travis laughed and folded me to the palace kitchen.

* * *

"I had no idea that a Queen would cook," I admitted after cutting into what Travis said was chicken-fried steak, which Queen Lissa made for us. She'd joined us for lunch, which happened outside normal kitchen hours since Travis and I were still on Pyrik time.

"This is delicious," I added, after consuming my first bite.

"You haven't lived until you've had Mom's cookies and her chicken-fried steak," Trent declared.

"Hmmph," Lissa said, a smile in her voice. "You should visit Kifirin. You'll get a meal fit for any king—or a god or two—if Queen Reah or Princess Lexsi cook."

"I love Reah's fish," Travis nodded while cutting another piece of steak.

"Everybody does."

"Have you seen the prisoner?" I asked Queen Lissa.

"Not yet. We'll size him up at the same time."

"I admit, you have many phrases I've never heard before," I said. "Size him up. All hands on deck. I like them."

"Stick around, you haven't heard anything, yet. Mom can teach you how to curse, too, if you don't know how already," Trent snickered.

"Trent Tetsuya," Lissa warned. I imagined she'd frowned—insincerely—at her son. The expression was gone before my vision adjusted.

"These potatoes melt in my mouth," I said. "They're wonderful."

"I don't think they've been feeding you properly," Lissa said. "If you haven't had good potatoes."

"I never ate at the palace in New Fyris," I confessed. "Too much drama in the kitchens, so I walked home for meals instead. Home was a few minutes away from the palace, but Pap and I aren't the best cooks."

"Your father has two job offers," Lissa said. "I had them delivered earlier today."

"Amlis has already dismissed him, hasn't he?"

"Well, I don't consider a tantrum thrown by an affected Prince to be anything official, but your father was happy to receive the offers. He's considering both."

"Can you tell me what the offers are?"

"I could use someone to manage my palace on the light half of Le-Ath Veronis, and Justis and Quin would like someone to coordinate their palace schedule for equipment, rooms, meals, meetings, banquets and so forth."

"Pap does have a good mind for schedules," I nodded. "And for details."

"He'd be welcome either place." Lissa's smile stayed in place long enough for me to see it.

"He could probably do both, with a good comp-vid and transport when it's necessary," Trent suggested.

"What a great idea," Lissa said. "I'll make that suggestion, and he can stay at whichever location he wants. They're really not that far apart, and a short boat ride will get him back and forth. I'll have Renée send him a message, and let him know we can pick him up any time he's ready to come to Le-Ath Veronis."

"I'll send a message and tell him to come tomorrow," I said. "It'll be good to get him away from that mess."

"Sounds great. Finish your meal; we have a mess in the dungeon to visit," Travis said.

* * *

Chapter 3

Lissa

Randl stood outside the prisoner's cage, silent and still for so long I wondered if he were awake.

I had no idea how his talents worked, but after ten minutes of silence, he turned toward me.

"We must go," he said.

His words sent a shiver through me. I folded the four of us out of the dungeon immediately.

Once we were inside my study, I thought I'd have to call Karzac; Randl looked as if he were about to lose everything he'd eaten. Terrified, I watched him struggle with nausea as minutes ticked by. Travis and Trent were worried about their new friend—that was obvious, but they also had no idea what to do for him.

"He—has been changed," Randl finally sat down on the sofa across from my desk. "It isn't only the obsession," he added, holding up a hand while he fought another wave of nausea.

"Bro, what are you saying?" Trent asked, his voice calm.

"I've never seen anything like this before," Randl whispered. "Every cell in his body—feels like a recording device to me. Someone very powerful did this to him, and I can't figure out how, or why he was chosen."

"You mean somebody is on the receiving end of this?" I asked.

"I think so, although he's never been informed of who that is. Someone was supposed to find him on Pyrik—as you've already surmised. All of us have been recorded and noted in every particle of his being. If he meets with his designated contact, that information will be transmitted."

I understood now why Randl hadn't said anything in front of the prisoner. Images were one thing. Words were another. Randl hadn't wanted to reveal to the prisoner that he understood any part of how he'd been altered.

"You say this is at the cellular level?" I couldn't imagine anyone other than a god or a Larentii who could do that.

"Yes." Randl looked queasy again.

"How do we get rid of it?" Travis asked. He was having mindspeech with Kooper; I understood that.

"You have to burn him to destroy it."

"Oh, my gosh." I rubbed my forehead with trembling fingers. "Renée," I called out. She was vampire; she'd hear me through the closed door.

"Yes?" Renée opened the door and peeked inside.

"Tell Gavin and Tony to have the prisoner transferred to a privacy cell. Right away."

I had three privacy cells—concrete and titanium all around, and only a small door at the center of a larger, solid door, to pass meals in and out.

The prisoners there were in isolation from all, so those cells were seldom used.

This prisoner—after Randl's explanation, I was terrified.

I needed Bree or Zaria to talk to, and had no idea where either were.

"What does Kooper say?" I turned to Travis.

"He's on his way," Travis replied. "He's not happy, either."

* * *

Randl

It was embarrassing to appear so weak in front of Queen Lissa and her sons, but I'd never been affected by anything like this.

Why had this been done? Who would receive the information?

I still felt nauseated, but refused to let it show. Kooper Griff arrived and began pacing between the sofa and Lissa's desk, after she'd told him the prisoner was now in isolation.

Chapter 3

"Where did this man work—before he was reported dead?" I asked suddenly, interrupting Kooper's limited journey across an expensive carpet.

Kooper went still. "Travis?" he turned to Travis.

"I have it here, on my comp-vid," Travis pulled the device from a pocket.

"May I see?" I asked.

"You're first in line." Kooper took the comp-vid from Travis and handed it to me.

"He worked for a company that manufactured optical lenses, for powerful telescopes and such?" I struggled to read as fast as my vision would allow. "Until he disappeared twenty years ago."

"That tells us nothing," Lissa grumbled.

"Vrak Falken ran one of the robotic machines that measured and polished lenses," I shook my head and handed the comp-vid back to Kooper. "He was an amateur astronomer in his free time. Had two wives. No children. Official records say he was found dead after a fall from his rooftop observatory. Nothing noteworthy there, and the body was cremated, so we have no idea who was actually reported dead at the time."

"That's just what I thought," Travis agreed. "Nothing to warrant selecting him from a room full of strangers, except that somebody else died in his place and nobody knows where he's been for the past twenty years."

"My worry is this," Lissa said. "How many more like him are out there? How many are reported dead or missing, who've been selected because they don't stand out? What is their purpose? This is terrifying—that we know next to nothing about them."

"Perhaps when I return to Pyrik, I can look for others like this?" I suggested.

"I think you may be the only one who can see this," Lissa confirmed. "Quin couldn't, and she's the best I know, next to Bree and Zaria."

"Randl Gage, you just became one of the most important hires the ASD ever made," Kooper sighed. "Come on, let's get you decent clothes and take you back to Pyrik. You and the crew of BlackWing X are going undercover."

Chapter 4

Mer'bali, Pyrik

Quin

Kooper Griff joined Justis, Bel, Wellend, Warlend and me for breakfast. He looked as if he hadn't slept. Actually, I could see in him that he hadn't slept. The prisoner, whose image I'd studied, greatly worried the Director.

Randl had seen something I hadn't. I went still. My talent ensured that I could see someone's mind, history and intentions, provided they weren't obsessed.

Randl had read the man's entire body, right down to its cells.

Yes, I could sense illness, but what I saw in Kooper—the information he'd gotten on the prisoner—I'd never have seen that. Randl's talent was formidable.

"Quin, I was hoping you'd be available for a special assignment," Kooper said after breakfast was served by hotel employees.

Kooper's words drew a frown from Justis, but he didn't object.

"What does it involve?" Bel asked.

"Mostly looking at images and vids—of the Conclave attendees. Just to see if anyone carries obsession. Once that's been determined, I'll ask Randl to take a look."

"I can do that easily," I said.

"It'll pay well," Kooper offered a wry smile. "I know you haven't gotten paid in the past. That will change."

"That sounds reasonable enough," Bel reached for the small plate of butter pats. He was warming his waffle with a spell so the butter would melt quickly before he poured syrup.

I patted his leg under the table. He grinned and dumped three butter squares on his waffle. Just as I'd thought, the butter melted immediately.

"Warm syrup?" Bel held up the small pitcher and offered it to me after pouring a generous amount on his waffle. I squelched a laugh.

"I'll send vids and images this afternoon," Kooper promised. "Will you pack this to go?" he asked a waiter after pointing to his plate.

"Of course."

Kooper left a few minutes later, his breakfast packed in a warming box.

* * *

Randl

We looked much like any other swarm of assistants and clerks who'd come to the Conclave, ready to work for their attending royal, ruler, president or prime minister. Only a handful would be allowed inside the meetings, but those would be armed with multiple comp-vids, ready to share pertinent information with their co-workers, who'd then disseminate it to a waiting planet or kingdom.

Official badges were woven into our Conclave-approved uniforms, proclaiming us assistants to Queen Lissa's entourage.

Chapter 4

Every badge was coded with a specific sequence, which meant our individual DNA would be matched with that sequence in the badge whenever we passed a security station. We were dressed in Queen Lissa's traditional black-and-silver, although we wore short sleeves as opposed to the long-sleeved uniforms worn by her guards.

It wasn't our job to disseminate information; it was our job to look for anyone who could be connected to Vrak Falken.

With all the clerks and squads of assistants roaming the host hotel complex, we'd disappear into the crowds easily enough.

We'd also been disguised by Erland Morphis, King Rylend's father, who, like his son and grandson, was a strong Fifth-level warlock.

A massive courtyard and park lay at the center of the hotel complex, which contained trees, a small lake, flower beds and trimmed lawns. Walkways looped across the area, along with regularly-spaced benches.

That's where we were now, having tea at an outdoor table and watching everyone who wandered in and out of the hotel facility that housed the meetings.

You'll find it completely boring most of the time, until something happens and sends you into high-gear-panic mode, Trent informed me. *It's one or the other—no in-between.*

I saw right past his disguise—he and Travis no longer looked like twins to everyone else. I dipped my head to acknowledge his sending, then sipped tea that had gone cold.

Winkler says Amlis is having another meltdown, and doesn't want to go to the meet-and-greet dinner tonight.

My shoulders sagged. I had no healing ability; if I did, I'd be tempted to heal Amlis just for the benefit to those around him. I couldn't imagine that Rodrik was enjoying this, and if he couldn't control Amlis, then nobody could.

"I'd like to research the information on unseating a royal, according to Alliance guidelines," I said softly. "Something has to be done."

"We know that. The Director's already looking into it," Travis replied. "Lukas is the Primary ruler for Harifa Edus, and his position and testimony will carry a lot of weight. I think Ildevar and the Council of Twenty will have the final say, though."

We stopped talking as a group walked past our table; it included one harried Princess and six gabbling assistants.

Nobody in the group was affected like Vrak, and there were no obsessions. I discreetly shook my head once they were away from us.

This is getting us nowhere, Travis sent.

Agreed. Let's check in with the logistics team, to see whether they've pinpointed the source of the laser rocket. Trent was just as bored as I was. *We can check with Quin after that, to see if she's found anything in the images Kooper sent her*, he added.

Travis stood first, and stretched. Three women ogled him as they passed; the twins were well-muscled and worked out regularly to stay that way. It didn't matter that Travis' face was different; the three who watched were looking at everything except his face.

Trent and I rose from our seats to follow Travis, as he walked toward our hotel across the quad.

* * *

Quin

Dena set a plate of food at my elbow as I thumbed through the comp-vid sent by Kooper. All the Conclave attendees, including assistants and guards, were listed, with an image and a brief biography.

So far, I'd seen many things, but obsession wasn't one of them.

Chapter 4

A hard knock on the suite door startled Dena and me—Justis and the others had gone out and had a key to get in.

"Who in the name of," Dena muttered as she stalked toward the door. "Fuck," she breathed after checking the vid-cam image.

"Who is it?"

"Rodrik."

I wanted to say fuck. I didn't.

"I need Quin," Rodrik's voice came through the comm. "Now."

The word *fuck* may have left my mouth as I rose and hurried toward the door. "Why do you need me?" I demanded after Dena pressed the comm button.

"It's Amlis. Something's wrong with him."

I wanted to ask what was wrong with him, other than the family penchant for paranoia and mental illness. I also wanted to tell Rodrik to leave and not come back.

"Let's go," I turned to Dena, who frowned. She didn't want me to leave the suite, and especially not with Rodrik.

"Fine," she grumbled and opened the door.

* * *

We're going to Amlis' suite, I informed Justis as we followed Rodrik down a long hallway. *Rodrik says something's wrong with him.*

Quin, I forbid it, Justis' sending was terse.

We're already there, I replied.

We're on our way, he snapped. *Winkler and Lukas are with me.*

Then ask Winkler to fold space, I said and walked through the door of Amlis' suite.

"Oh, no," Dena breathed. At least she could speak; words—and my breath—caught in my throat.

Amlis sat on the floor of the suite, his wrists bearing jagged cuts from a steak knife he still gripped in one hand. Blood covered most of his body, as well as the carpet beneath him.

Only the dullness of the knife and Amlis' poor knowledge of how to effectively commit suicide had saved him. With light forming about me, I almost fell on him to perform a healing, while Dena, behaving in a more practical fashion, removed the knife from Amlis' hand.

* * *

Winkler

The fool tried to kill himself—with a steak knife, no less. If he'd known to make the slashes vertical instead of horizontal, he'd be dead.

As it was, I'd been forced to contact Kooper and transport Amlis to a private facility for a blood transfusion, to replace what he'd lost. His wrists, however, showed no marks of the suicide attempt after Quin healed him.

Justis, Quin, Dena and I stood outside the hospital room while Amlis was examined by Karzac, who'd answered my call. Rodrik was in the room with Amlis, vibrating with anxiety.

If Amlis weren't healthy enough to attend Conclave, Rodrik would be forced to act in his stead.

"He should rest for an eight-day, and be re-evaluated during that time," Karzac said. "They'll give him more blood today, until his tests yield better results."

"What about Conclave?" Rodrik said. Honestly, Rodrik should learn to keep his mouth shut—well everybody should—around Karzac.

"If New Fyris is to be represented, I suggest you begin your study now," Karzac growled at Rodrik. "This one was in no shape to come and you knew that. How long, Master Rodrik, has the Prince's mental health been on the decline? How long ago should you have requested help? There are methods to do so—discreet methods—in which therapy can be provided to those who rule in the Reth Alliance."

Rodrik wasn't used to being reprimanded. At least he knew better than to argue, because he didn't have a legitimate excuse. He was Amlis' heir, until Amlis could produce his own. As such, he had the authority to approach the Reth Alliance to present evidence and ask for an evaluation.

Discretion would be employed, and if the request were fraudulent, that would be determined. If it were legitimate, then the ruler in question would be approached. If they refused the offer of help, then the process to remove them from their office would begin.

Mental instability in a ruler was trouble, and the Reth Alliance knew it. It was a relatively new determination, too, and was often referred to as *Kifirin's Rule*, passed after the King of Kifirin lost his mind and attacked his own people.

Karzac, who wasn't in the mood to suffer Rodrik's presence any longer, folded away. Another physician walked toward the room as if he'd been called, and shouldered his way past those of us in the hall to enter the room.

Rodrik walked toward us, then, stopping in front of Quin.

"I, ah, am grateful," he began uncomfortably, his words sounding foreign and awkward. Quin, faster than he expected, punched him in the face, then swept out a wing and knocked his feet off the floor. He fell with a grunt and a curse.

I stifled a laugh as Quin stalked away, Dena right behind her.

* * *

Randl

"Quin punched Rodrik." I blinked; my delayed vision almost missed the high slap of hands between Travis and Trent.

"On another note," Travis turned to me, a wide grin on his face, "Amlis tried to commit suicide, but Quin saved his ass. We don't know yet whether he's of sound mind or if Quin left that part of him alone."

"Suicide." I ducked my head. A feeling of guilt overwhelmed me for a moment—if I'd been there, I'd have seen this before it happened.

"Stop worrying about it, bro—his physical health is fine, thanks to Quinnie. He just won't be attending Conclave—Rodrik will have to fill in for him. Doctor's orders."

"That's for the best," I sighed. "Amlis wasn't stable enough to make important decisions."

"We know. We've had plenty of conversations with Winkler. Lukas has asked to meet with him, to go over the agenda again and discuss the votes from New Fyris."

"I hope Rodrik has a conscience, then, and considers the people and not the Prince's treasury."

"I heard from Mom," Travis turned to Trent. "She says that with all that's going on with the prisoner, she doesn't want Lexsi or Kay near him."

"Who are Lexsi and Kay?" I asked.

"Lexsi is our cousin. Kay is—well, she's pretty special. They're the only ones who may be able to reverse an obsession."

"I had no idea it could be done," I confessed.

"Just keep that to yourself," Travis cautioned. "Those two are the only possibilities we have, and should only be approached in extremely special cases."

"I can understand why," I agreed. "Besides, whoever would normally receive information from the prisoner shouldn't know that. It could place both women in terrible danger."

"That's what Mom said," Trent agreed. "Would you like to have dinner with the family tomorrow night? You can meet Lexsi and Queen Reah then."

So many questions crowded my mind. Who was I to be invited to a family gathering that included Queens, a King, and the Founder of the Campiaan Alliance? "I know your brother is Teeg San Gerxon," I blurted.

Travis guffawed. Trent grinned and slapped me on the back.

"He wants to meet you," Trent said. "He's been in contact with his son, Garwin Wyatt. Wyatt informed him the pirate ship was scanned before it was destroyed, and that you reported it."

"I should learn to keep my mouth shut," I mumbled. Travis laughed again and slapped me on the back, like his brother. "Come on, Teeg's not so bad. He just looks intimidating to everybody else."

"Jayna says that David reached the ship," Trent pulled a comp-vid from his pocket to check a message.

"David?" I asked.

"David Hiboux. He's our engineer and mechanic. The ship developed a hiccup, so he's checking on it."

"Ah. What should I wear to the family dinner?"

"Something nice but comfortable," Travis said. "Come on, let's go see Quinnie. She can update us on Amlis and Rodrik."

* * *

Dena, Quin's bodyguard, opened the door to Quin's suite, once Travis let her know we were at the door. Her multi-colored wings were held tightly against her back as she led us to the room Quin chose as a temporary study.

We found Quin there, royal-red wings draped casually around her as she thumbed through images on a comp-vid.

"Randl," she stood and sounded genuinely glad to see me. "Travis, Trent, good to see you."

"Good to see you, too, wingy-woman," Travis chuckled.

"No respect," Quin turned her gaze on me and waited until I saw her smile. I understood she was teasing, however, and smiled back at her.

"Want to take a break and tell us about Amlis?" Trent asked.

"Sure. Dena, will you order tea for all of us?" Quin asked. "Order for you, too."

"Of course," Dena said and walked from the room to place an order. There was no doubt that Dena was still angry with Amlis and Rodrik, and wanted to do to both what Quin had done to Rodrik.

It wasn't her place and she could be charged with assault against a royal if she did. Therefore, she had to hold her anger in check.

I'd known she was furious the moment she answered the door, and my vision enabled me to see why.

I didn't blame her. Quin had confided in Dena, and Dena's outrage at a long-ago beating at Rodrik's hand for saving Amlis' life was justified.

Quin, though, hadn't harmed Rodrik enough, in my opinion.

Randl, the matter is closed, Quin's voice filtered into my mind.

"What is a life worth, Queen Quin?" I asked and bowed to her. "You gave a gift beyond price, and the response was to harm you for it."

"People are weak at times," a hand dropped onto my shoulder. King Justis of the Avii had joined us.

"Your Majesty," I turned and bowed to the King.

"You don't have to do that," Justis said. "Here, you're considered family. I know how you and your father helped Quin on Vogeffa II. Between you, you saved many other lives. Your father now works for the Avii and Queen Lissa. You should be hearing from him soon, once he's settled at Avii Castle."

Chapter 4

"Thank you for providing a home for him," I dipped my head in respect.

"It can be your home, too," Quin offered. "Whenever you have time off from your new job."

"I would like that very much," I said. How wonderful would it be to watch the Avii in flight whenever I wanted?

"Tea," Dena walked in, followed by a hotel employee carrying a heavy tray of cups, tiny cakes and a large teapot.

"I was hoping for a snack," Justis said. "Sit, everyone. Let's have tea and talk."

* * *

Varok of Pyrik

Lee'Qee was a secret the President of Pyrik kept hidden. That's why I and those who came before me made a home there, among the abandoned factories and crumbling infrastructure.

Long ago, it had been the hub of Pyrik's industry, until an accident involving the nuclear energy used to power Lee'Qee forced all to abandon it three centuries earlier.

Pyrik was forced to adopt solar energy afterward, and the many, many deaths attributed to the leaking poison were hidden from the history books by presidential command.

The current president had nothing to do with that, of course, and back then, Pyrik hadn't been a member of the Campiaan Alliance. In fact, the Campiaan Alliance was relatively new, compared to the Reth Alliance.

The nuclear accident that devastated Lee'Qee was old news when Pyrik was invited to join the newly-formed Campiaan Alliance.

For clicks surrounding Lee'Qee, there was nothing except tree-covered forests, a few hills, and wide meadows, which served as home to many species of birds and animals. Pyrik now referred to it as an animal sanctuary, provided to rebuild those species. Residents weren't allowed to go there.

Nobody said it was for their own safety.

I and my crew live here. Others have been sent elsewhere, as needed. We have a mission.

That mission is to destroy Pyrik and every royal, president, prime minister and head of state with it, during the Conclave.

Once that is accomplished, every member planet of both Alliances will become acquainted with the might and firepower of the Ke'Leru Pirates. We were currently in the process of adding to our fleet and recruiting members to our cause—whether willingly or otherwise, it mattered not to me.

Lee'Qee can be seen from space, but the official story is that it was abandoned once solar power became the preferred power source. Many worlds had something similar; those merely didn't have numerous deaths from a nuclear accident associated with them.

Those who came before, and now my crew and I—we'd adapted to the area. I often joked that we thrived on the poison leeching from the ground, when it would kill anyone else.

As for the ASD and CSD—we had plans for them, too, beginning with the assassinations of their Directors.

"Still no concrete evidence that our contact was killed on Refizan," my brother, Perill, set a comp-vid in front of me.

"Hmmph." I lifted the device and studied the report. "What about those containers of remains? Have the forensics reports been released?"

"Not yet," Perill said. "Our people on Refizan are waiting for that information."

"You can't deny that our connection disappeared after the explosion," I pointed out.

Chapter 4

"Yes, I know. The ASD has been quite sly in the past, though. I told you to allow the ship to dock so we could ask questions. The ASD has ramped up their presence here, because you chose to destroy the ship instead."

"Remember, brother, we all came to the same, hasty conclusion—that they'd killed our contact during the journey."

"We know that wasn't true," Perill argued.

"Now we do, after we consulted our Prophet. Don't worry, brother, they won't find us; everybody will consider it an act of revenge by another criminal element and all will go back to sleep."

"That's exactly what it is," Perill grumbled. "An act of revenge—by us."

"Except nobody knows about us. They'll look elsewhere for a scapegoat. Stop worrying."

"As you say, brother," Perill replied and stalked away.

* * *

Randl

BlackWing X

"Naturalized Amterean," David Hiboux grinned and held out a hand. I knew that about the dwarf engineer before he told me, but I smiled and shook hands with him without saying so.

He'd recently been to Avendor; I could almost smell the fresh air and gishi fruit about him. "Normally he's with us, but he takes vacations once in a while, to spend time with his wife," Travis said. "What's up with the ship?" he turned to David.

"Cooling system glitch. Need to replace it," David said. "I wouldn't recommend going into hyperdrive the way it is."

"How long?" Trent asked.

"Maybe a day, at most, once I get the replacement parts."

"I'll see about putting a rush on that," Trent said. "What are you doing for dinner, Dave?" His voice sounded robotic.

"Funny," David sniffed. "I haven't made plans," he added.

"There's a restaurant about half a click from the hotel. Serves a decent facsimile of a burger," Travis explained. "Want to come? We're taking Randl with us."

"Damn, I haven't had a decent burger in months," David said. "I'll go. Decent beer, too?"

"Good enough," Trent shrugged.

Two hours later, we walked into Flipper's, an upscale version of a sandwich shop, which served beers from both Alliances. I wasn't a heavy drinker, but I enjoyed a beer with Pap now and then.

"Beef patty sandwich, with mustard sauce, onions, pickles, tomato and cheese," Trent told the waitress when she arrived to take our orders. I could tell by the deep frown as she tapped the order into her comp-vid that she didn't find Trent's choice palatable.

"I want the same, with crispy potatoes," David said. "And a Refizani Blue-label."

"Add crispy potatoes and a Refizani Blue to mine," Trent said.

"I want what they're having," I said.

"Make that four," Travis grinned and tapped the tabletop menu display to shut it off.

"Want an appetizer out first?" the waitress lifted an eyebrow at Travis. She only saw his disguised face, but his physique didn't fail to catch her eye.

"Batter-fried onions?" Travis asked me.

"Sounds good," I said.

"Two orders," Travis told the waitress. "We're hungry."

"I'll have your beers and appetizers out soon," the waitress gave Travis one last look and walked away, her hips swinging an invitation to him.

"You can have that if you want it, bro," Trent teased.

"No, thanks," Travis said.

Chapter 4

Only a few stray crispy potatoes lay on plates as we drank a third beer. The food was very good; I could see why Travis and Trent liked the restaurant so much. I was beginning to wonder if being drunk affected someone's ability to fold space, as it did when driving a vehicle, until two men and one woman followed the hostess past our table.

They'd stopped briefly to allow a server to pass carrying a laden tray of food. That's how my vision adjusted well enough in my inebriated state to see them clearly.

"Travis, may I borrow your comp-vid?" I asked as the group moved past our table.

"Sure." Travis wasn't as affected as I by the consumption of three beers, and pulled his comp-vid from a pocket with steady hands.

I took it and tapped my message carefully into it, before handing it back to Travis, face-up.

* * *

Travis

I though Randl wanted to contact his father or something. That wasn't the case. He'd written a message to me.

The three who passed our table have the same affliction as your mother's guest.

In three blinks, I'd transferred the message to Kooper.

* * *

"Those three." Randl pointed to the group in question, who sat at a corner table at the restaurant. We were tucked inside a disguised hover-van three blocks away, while a micro-drone recorded images of the three targets.

"We can follow them," Kell Abenott offered. He and Opal, his mate, had joined Kooper after I'd sent the message.

"Mist only—we don't want a repeat of what happened last time," Kooper huffed while staring at the three people. His comp-vid buzzed while we watched the targets eat their meal.

"No identification on any of them," Kooper said after reading the message. "Probably from outside the Alliances. Without getting closer, there's no way to determine their true origin."

"I can't see it, either," Randl said. "There's something blocking that vision in them, too."

"But you can see the same thing here that you saw in Vrak?"

"Yes. Something in their cells, just like the one called Vrak," Randl confirmed.

"Send a copy of these images to Quin," Kooper barked at his comp-vid. "Maybe she can tell us something we don't know, yet."

"Right away, Director," someone on the other end replied.

* * *

Randl

Travis folded the four of us back to the ship; Kooper thought it better if we stayed aboard the docked vehicle. I didn't mind; seeing the three at the restaurant had unnerved me. Whatever affected them was new to the ASD Director, too. During my life on Vogeffa II, I'd seen plenty of the unusual as far as mutations went, but nothing like this.

"Here," Travis handed me a bottle of Refizani Blue. "Mom sent us a case after she heard about the encounter."

"It raised the hair on my arms," I admitted and accepted the beer.

"Didn't do much for me, either," David took a bottle. "Man, those unmarked hover-vans give me the willies."

He was teasing; I understood that and laughed at his words.

* * *

Kooper Griff

"We don't have good news, I'm afraid," Kell said. Opal, who'd sat next to him at the breakfast table in my suite, appeared angry and frustrated.

"You lost them?" I could tell by Opal's resulting stiffness that they had. These two were the best trackers in the ASD, and they'd lost the three we'd found the night before.

"They have a disappearing trick," Opal growled. I'd never heard that sound from her before.

My hand stilled in its journey to lift my cup of tea. "What sort of disappearing trick?" I asked after a moment. Opal and Kell had been mist. They should have been able to float right on top of their quarry, if necessary.

"It's not what you're thinking," Kell said. He was an ancient vampire and could read my body language if not my mind. "They didn't disappear down a rabbit hole. I wouldn't call it folding space, but it's similar. They were walking along the street, headed who knows where, when suddenly, all three stopped—as if they'd been halted by a giant hand at the same moment. I'd call it eerie, and I don't often use that word," Kell shook his head. He still didn't believe what he'd seen.

"Then what?" I asked.

"Then poof," Opal tossed out a hand. "Gone. All three, with not a puff of smoke left behind."

"We searched the area and found nothing," Kell went on. "Once they disappeared, even their scent faded at the location. I couldn't detect anything of them after a while."

I'll admit, that worried me. If a vampire or werewolf could no longer scent these people moments after they disappeared, we could be fucked and not in a pleasurable way.

"Are there images from nearby security cameras?" I asked, lifting the cup of tea to drink.

"None. We've already checked. They knew what they were doing, I think," Kell grimaced.

"I can provide projected images," Opal said, her voice stiff. She didn't utilize her abilities as anything other than a talented shapeshifter while in ASD employ, but this had her worried and baffled enough to skirt that rule.

"Then let's see it," I leaned back to give her room.

Opal's eyes lost focus, then a three-dimensional image floated over the small table. I blinked as I watched the two men and their female companion walk along a narrow, deserted street.

Just as Kell said, the three of them stopped abruptly. In moments, they were gone.

"Rewind, please," I breathed.

Opal replayed the image.

"Stop," I commanded. The image froze. "There—it looks as if they're listening," I pointed. All three had their heads cocked to one side, as if they'd heard something. A warning, perhaps?

"Fuck. This is crazy," I mumbled, raking fingers through my hair. "Can you give me those images?"

"On comp-vid?" The image disappeared above the table.

"I don't care if it's written in pencil, I need it," I said.

"I'll place it on your comp-vid," Opal agreed. This was so important, in her mind, that she'd expend the power to do it.

"Director, I have no idea what it is we're dealing with," Kell said. "But it scares me."

I was beginning to agree with him.

Chapter 5

B*lackWing X*
Randl

"They traced the origin of the scan, but there's nothing there now," Travis informed me at breakfast.

I had a slight hangover from drinking more beer after boarding the ship the night before, but I didn't tell Travis that.

"Are we going?" I asked. I wanted to see the location myself, in case I could sense anything.

"Yep. Right after breakfast. Here," he set two pain-kill tabs in front of me, then pushed a glass of water in my direction. "Drink up. It'll help."

"How?" I asked. I didn't have to finish the question; he understood what I meant.

"I've been drunk enough times to recognize a hangover when I see one," he said. I imagined a grin accompanied his words, but it was gone before my mental vision adjusted.

"Does your mother know?" I asked.

Travis laughed.

An hour later, we wore disguises provided by Bel Erland and were on our way to a location on Pyrik's surface, on the outskirts of Mer'bali. The ship's hover-shuttle parked outside a concrete building that bore a holographic *For Sale or Lease* sign above the door.

"Kooper's already checked the records; nobody's leased or bought it, and it's been on the market for two years," Trent said as we climbed out of the shuttle.

"I wouldn't buy it, either," I said, after mentally studying the exterior. Parts of it had crumbled away, revealing steel bars beneath the concrete. It likely had foundation problems, too. "Too many things to repair," I shrugged when Trent turned toward me.

"Bro, do you think they had a portable scan unit on the roof?" Travis asked as we walked toward the door.

"Could be. Let's go inside, first, so Randl can get a feel for the place."

Travis had a key-scanner, which he pointed at the door. I heard the old-fashioned lock click and the door creak open before I saw the actual images.

"Power isn't on," Travis informed me as he stepped inside. "Kooper says it's been off since the building was listed."

"Another point in its disfavor," Trent said and followed his brother inside.

My skin prickled as I walked through the door. "Travis, I forgot something in the shuttle," I said. "Will you and Trent come help?"

Code, bro? Travis' mental voice asked.

"Please," I said, with a nod.

Both followed me to the sidewalk, then to the shuttle. Travis opened the door; I climbed inside, then motioned the brothers to follow.

Once the door was shut, I sighed. "We're being watched inside the building," I said.

"Fucking hells," Trent cursed.

"We have to go back, or they'll suspect we know," I said.

"Damn," Travis whispered.

"I'll take this," I felt for the jacket I'd brought with me. "Let's go back. Just—guard your words, all right?"

"Sure."

"I've never been so grateful for a disguise in my life," Trent added as we clambered from the shuttle a second time.

Whatever watched us caused a buzzing in my mind as we traveled through the deserted space. Once we reached the top floor, we knew what had happened. A huge hole in the roof had recently been repaired. There were no records of repairs done; Travis told me as much in mindspeech.

So the ones who scanned the ship did the repairs, after knocking a hole in the roof to begin with, Trent said.

Looks that way, Travis agreed.

"Well, we've found what we came for," Travis said aloud.

"I want to go to the roof," I said, surprising both brothers.

"Sure," Travis shrugged and led us toward a stairwell in an empty corner. The key scanner got us through the locked door at the top, and we stepped onto the flat roof.

The buzzing stopped. Whatever watched us inside the building didn't cover the outside of it.

Once my vision of the rooftop cleared, I walked toward the patched hole. Crouching down, I placed a hand on the patch.

"Three here, to make the repairs," I said after a moment. "None of them the ones we saw last night. All male, and all with the same affliction."

"Fuck me running," Trent sighed.

* * *

Travis

"So there are six, at least," Kooper didn't sound happy when I delivered Randl's news. "Six who can possibly disappear without a trace," he added, his frustration evident in his voice.

"Here's my question," Randl said. He and Trent were with me for the debriefing; Kooper requested it.

"What's that?" Kooper turned toward Randl.

"You say the three last night disappeared. What has kept the one in Queen Lissa's dungeon from disappearing, if they can do this on their own? Surely he'd have escaped the cell in the Refizani facility if he could do so."

Kooper drew an audible breath.

"I think," Randl said, "that something pulled them away. I don't think they disappeared on their own."

Kooper blew out the breath he was holding. "That makes sense," he growled and pulled his comp-vid from a pocket. "Randl, can you see well enough to look at these images?" He held out the comp-vid.

After only a moment's hesitation, Randl took it. Kooper tapped the screen, so the vid-images would play. Randl blinked, then nodded as the vid ran. "Yes," he said afterward, handing the comp-vid to Kooper. "I believe my suggestion is correct. It appears that they were waiting or listening for a signal, before someone or something pulled them away."

"Thank the Mighty," Kooper breathed before pocketing the comp-vid. "I had terrifying visions of a new race that could fool us all."

"They're still fooling us—for now," Randl pointed out.

"You're right," Kooper admitted. "We have to figure this out and fast. The Conclave starts tomorrow. Unless I'm badly mistaken, that's why we're seeing all this here and now."

"You think they'll strike on the first day?" Travis asked.

Chapter 5

"I sure as hells hope not," Kooper replied.

* * *

Randl

Terrett and Jayna went to dinner with us; Quin invited them, as Jayna was a good friend and Terrett was one of Quin's mates. They'd stayed aboard the BlackWing X up to that point, watching the ship and restocking supplies while the rest of us worked on the planet's surface.

David joined us, too, and appeared genuinely excited about it.

"He's friends with Uncle Perdil," Travis grinned, which brought a frown from David. "Perdil and I see eye-to-eye," David said, causing Travis to bark a laugh.

"Come on or we'll be late," Trent said, attempting to hurry us along. He transported us from the ship to the massive suite atop the hotel; the large space was needed to accommodate so many, I discovered.

∗ ∗ ∗

"Teeg San Gerxon," he introduced himself and held out a hand. I took it after the usual delay in my vision.

"Very pleased to meet you, Founder San Gerxon," I said, employing the courtly skills Master Morwin taught me.

"Oh, good—you found each other," Wyatt appeared at his father's side.

"Hello, Wyatt, good to see you again," I nodded in his direction.

"Wyatt tells me there's a slight delay in your mental vision. Is that correct?" Founder San Gerxon asked. "And please, call me Teeg."

"Yes," I said. "It's only a short delay, as if my brain has to adjust when things change around me. Small things I often miss— such as a quick smile or swift gestures."

77

"Understandable," Teeg agreed. "It's astounding that you can process the images at all."

"I've gotten better over the years," I admitted. "At first, images were very slow to appear in my mind."

"What about the clairvoyance?" Wyatt asked. "Was that slow, too?"

"No," I confessed. "That has always been sharp and immediate."

"I believe his clairvoyance may have trained his brain to operate along new pathways." Someone new had arrived.

"Physician," I bowed to him as the information slid into my mind ahead of his image.

"Randl, this is Karzac Halivar," Teeg introduced the man.

"You're Refizani by birth," I said, holding out my hand. "I must say, the beer from your home planet is quite good, Doctor Halivar."

"Astonishing," Doctor Halivar whispered and clasped my hand in his.

"What can you tell us about the building where the portable scanner was placed?" Teeg interjected.

"Ah. The scanner was placed there, certainly. I believe the hole was torn in the roof to fire the rockets, if it were necessary."

"That would make sense," Teeg breathed a sigh. "The scanner would work without the hole, if it were a relatively new device."

"Have you not determined the source of the rockets, yet?" Karzac asked.

"The general area," Teeg replied. "Randl just pinpointed their location. These new rockets apparently sent out shadow lasers, which makes it difficult to determine which blast actually hit the ship."

"Isn't that the new technology being designed by Kend Industries?" Karzac asked.

"Yes, and the designer has no idea how it was stolen. We've checked all the records—nothing has been taken or copied, so we have no clue how it ended up here. Kend is sending the designer to review the images from local sat-bots, to attempt to sort this out."

Ruther Kend. I turned that name over in my mind. He'd been kidnapped shortly after my rescue from Vogeffa II. Someone had wanted his expertise, then, to repair faulty technology.

In fact, his entire family had been kidnapped, and his captors threatened Kend's family if he didn't cooperate.

"You're sure he isn't being threatened again?" I asked. "Ruther Kend, that is."

"We're sure," Teeg said. "ASD and CSD checked everything, and just for good measure, Quin confirmed it."

"Discussing family secrets?" Kooper Griff had arrived; I recognized his voice before the image cleared.

"Just Ruther Kend's technology, which was apparently used in the destruction of the pirate ship," Wyatt said. "Want something to drink, Director?"

"Sure. Bourbon on the rocks, if they have it."

Wyatt walked away to find a server; I turned to Kooper. "Who will Kend be sending?" I asked.

"He said he'd send his best designer—the one who worked on the new technology involved," Kooper shrugged. "They'll be here tomorrow."

I could tell he wanted them here sooner than that, but he didn't say it. "Did you get through any of the vids I sent?" Kooper redirected my attention.

"Yes. I'm grateful for them—I can stop and go back to any part I may have missed with vids. It's easier than sitting in a classroom, in that respect."

"You have the comp-vid code for questions, correct?"

"Travis gave it to me," I said. "So far, I haven't needed it." The code would allow me to send questions to the instructors at ASD Academy. I didn't tell Kooper, but after my visions of the instructors cleared, my clairvoyance enabled me to answer the questions on my own.

"You'll be tested on the courses," Kooper reminded me. "Do you want a verbal test, or by comp-vid?"

"Comp-vid is fine," I shrugged. "As long as I get sufficient time to read and respond."

"You'll have it," Kooper said. "They'll extend the time to accommodate the circumstances."

"Thank you."

"There's something else," Kooper said, suddenly uncomfortable.

"What's that?" I knew already, and it tied my guts in a knot.

"Amlis wants to see you. I'll send Travis and Trent with you, if you want. Winkler, too—he's volunteered to go in case Amlis gets out of hand."

"Yes, Travis and Trent's presence would be much appreciated. Please tell Winkler yes, too," I said. The werewolf could stare anyone down, if it were necessary.

"I'll arrange it for tomorrow morning, before Conclave starts," Kooper said. "When registration begins at ten bells, I expect you, Travis and Trent near the entrance."

"Of course, Director."

* * *

Space-Yacht Mindbender

Sabrina Kend

Tell him to screw himself, I'm done, I tapped on my comp-vid. It was bad enough that Fergue and I had split up three months earlier. *He's a lying, cheating tree-weasel,* I added to the previous message.

My best friend, Lorvis, sent the message a day after I'd boarded ship for Pyrik. It had taken almost another day for me to calm down enough to send a reply. It was probably a good thing I hadn't been at home when Fergue asked Lorvis to send a message, telling me he wanted to get back together.

I might have asked Gord to punch him.

Gord, my bodyguard, looked up from his comp-vid as if he knew I was thinking about him.

Just once, I'd like to go somewhere on my own, without a bodyguard. Daddy was paranoid ever since we'd been kidnapped fifteen turns earlier. Nobody in the family went out unguarded.

He'd hired people, too, to teach us self-defense.

Fergue had gone through a vetting process, although he belonged to a wealthy family on Jaledis and should be above reproach. I wished they'd checked his loyalty meter, too, because it was on empty.

The whole time we'd been together, he was secretly seeing someone else.

"Calm down—you'll be meeting with the ASD Director tomorrow, and likely the CSD Director, too. You need to be composed when you see them. Your father's biggest contracts are with both agencies, you know."

"Thanks, Gord, for stating the obvious," I grumbled and switched off the comp-vid. Just seeing Fergue's name brought out the worst in me.

You have a job to do, I reminded myself. I had vids to review, to see how well they matched the laser rocket tests I'd run with my own designs. Leaning back in my seat, I closed my eyes and blew out a breath. There wasn't any way someone could have gotten my technology; it was too carefully guarded.

"I'm going to bed," I announced. Gord barely looked up from his comp-vid. On my father's private ship, I was safe enough. Leaving Gord to whatever game he was playing, I gathered my things and headed for my cabin.

* * *

Randl

"Welcome to the land of the dead." Amlis' greeting made me step backward. I didn't want to be here to begin with; his words increased my desire to get away.

He wasn't in bed; he stood before the wide window in his room, gazing at the gardens below the hospital, his back toward us. Travis and Trent had come with Winkler and me—as guards or witnesses, I suppose.

"What does that mean?" Winkler asked Amlis, his voice a low growl.

"They won't let me do anything except talk to the doctors. I may as well be dead," Amlis turned toward us briefly, before showing us his back again. "Rodrik is acting in my stead, I hear."

"He is," Winkler agreed. "He and Lukas met for breakfast, this morning. It'll help to have a clear strategy when the votes are cast."

"And I didn't have a clear strategy, did I?"

"No," I said. "You did not."

"Ah. The traitor to New Fyris speaks."

"I suggest you review the definition of traitor," Winkler snapped. "Randl accepted a more lucrative offer, that's all. If you only wanted to see him in order to abuse him, we'll go, now."

"Take him," Amlis waved an arm in dismissal. "It won't be long before the Reth Alliance news vids are filled with reports of the blind man who unseated the Prince of New Fyris."

Chapter 5

Winkler didn't bother saying good-bye. We were whisked away by the angry werewolf, and landed outside Kooper Griff's suite.

"Kooper wants you to see the representative Kend Industries sent," Winkler said quietly. "I hope you're up for this."

"We're with you," Travis whispered as Winkler knocked on Kooper's door.

* * *

Sabrina Kend

The balcony outside Director Griff's hotel suite was where I sat, patiently waiting for the CSD Director to arrive.

That's when four I hadn't expected arrived. I blinked.

The first to take a seat was tall, dark-haired and moved with an easy grace. Two more were Falchani—twins unless I missed my guess. Both were well-muscled, with long, black braids swinging at their backs as they took seats.

Last of all was one I didn't expect. While not as tall as the first, he was almost of a height with the Falchani. He wasn't as muscular in build, but he wasn't displeasing to look upon. Light brown hair lifted in the morning breeze, blowing away from his forehead and revealing eyes that were nearly white.

He was blind.

My breath caught—I'd never seen anyone who'd refused to have their eyes repaired. Surely this was a refusal, too; he was dressed well enough, in black trousers and boots, topped by a wine-colored shirt.

He turned toward me, his eyes unblinking for several moments.

"Tell her what you see," Kooper Griff said, lifting his cup of tea and drinking.

"Are you sure, Director?" The man asked.

"I'm sure."

"It is a pleasure to meet you, Sabrina Kend," the man dipped his head to me. "I've heard many things about your father. When they told me that the rocket designer was coming to review what was fired from here, I had no idea it would be Master Kend's daughter."

"Your man has done his research," I turned toward Director Griff.

"He hasn't read a thing about you until now," Kooper set his teacup down. "Randl, can you see anything else?"

Kooper Griff wanted to know if I'd betrayed my father as well as my own designs. I stiffened and considered calling Director Griff several names.

"She knows nothing of this subterfuge or whether industrial espionage is involved," the one called Randl informed Director Griff after only a few moments passed. "She does wish to call you an asshole, however."

My anger resulting from that private revelation was dispelled when Griff and the Falchani began to laugh. Somehow, Kooper Griff had found a clairvoyant to employ, and a very good one, too. The only ones in my experience were either charlatans or their gifts weren't nearly this precise.

That's when Jett Riffler, Director of the CSD and a native Avendoran Fi'Gu, walked onto the balcony.

"Jett," Kooper rose to his feet and offered his hand. "Good to see you."

"And you as well," Director Riffler beamed, his teeth a gleaming white against mahogany-colored skin. An elaborate tattoo ran down the left side of his face; if I were to see his arms and legs, the left ones would be covered with the same tattoos. The right side of a Fi'Gu's body was never tattooed—to honor their gods.

"May I introduce Sabrina Kend, Ruther Kend's daughter?" Director Griff turned in my direction.

Chapter 5

"Ah, Ms. Kend," Director Riffler turned his smile on me. "I hope you will help us with this conundrum we face."

"I hope so, too," I stood and held out my hand to him. "If they have my designs, I certainly want to know about it."

* * *

Travis

"I haven't seen Kooper laugh that hard in ages," Trent said as we took our positions near the reception desk outside the meeting hall. We were now dressed as hotel guards, with restored disguises—Trent, Randl and I.

Another set of actual hotel guards were on the other side of the reception area; Randl had already checked them and reported them safe.

"At least we got breakfast; this looks to be a marathon," I said as the doors opened and attendees crowded the desk area.

"The royals, presidents and leaders were pre-checked last night," Trent agreed. "The common herd is huge."

Randl blew out a breath at the sudden onslaught of people crowding into the foyer. There was a designated order for their arrival, but somebody always missed the memo, as Mom would say.

You're having a hard time with so many at once, aren't you? I sent to Randl. I caught the brief nod of agreement as he struggled to keep up with the constant movement before us.

Kooper, I sent, *Randl can't deal with this many people at once; they're moving through too quickly for him to get a decent lock on any of them.*

I was afraid of that, Kooper replied. *Look, I'll put him with Teeg inside the meeting hall. He can act as an extra guard on the Founder's private balcony and study the attendees as they sit at their tables.*

That sounds better, I agreed.

I'll send someone to get him, Kooper said and cut off mindspeech.

Kooper's *someone* ended up being Winkler.

* * *

Randl

Winkler came for me, leading me through a private, locked entrance to an elevator. The tall werewolf grinned as he scanned his wrist to open the elevator doors.

"You'll be with Teeg," he explained as we stepped inside the car. "This way, you can take your time looking at everyone at the tables."

"It was overwhelming, so many at once," I admitted.

"We should have thought of that, but at least we know now," Winkler said. "Kooper says to report anything you see to Teeg, Dormas or Wyatt. They'll get the message to him."

"Thank you," I said. "I hope this doesn't alter my employment with the Agency."

"Son, you're already a star," Winkler laughed. "Don't worry, Kooper's happy enough with you already."

I was grateful; I'd felt inadequate with the press of bodies crowding into the foyer. My vision couldn't clear fast enough to get a feel for any of them.

"Coffee or tea?" Wyatt held his grin long enough for me to see it when I stepped inside the spacious, private balcony reserved for the Campiaan Alliance Founder.

"Tea," I said. I had a cup in my hands quickly as I scanned the tables below; they were already occupied by the royals, presidents and such, along with a bodyguard, while assistants and advisors filtered in.

At least the enclosed balcony provided some relief from the noise of everyone talking at once. That had overwhelmed me, too.

<h1 align="center">Chapter 5</h1>

As yet, Teeg hadn't arrived; only Wyatt and Dormas occupied the balcony with me.

"Where is the President of Pyrik?" I asked while studying table after table below, looking for anything out of the ordinary.

"He'll probably wait until the last minute, to make a grand entrance I'm sure," Wyatt replied. As yet, there wasn't anyone at his table. "I heard he had a quick meeting scheduled with Jett Riffler, after Riffler met with Kooper this morning."

"I didn't see that in the CSD Director," I said absently. "Maybe they set it up after I left with Travis and Trent."

"Hmmm," Wyatt mumbled. I knew then that Wyatt had heard about the meeting from President Bargel himself the night before.

Except Bargel hadn't informed Jett Riffler.

"Wyatt," I turned swiftly in his direction. "I think Director. Riffler may be in trouble."

* * *

Sabrina Kend

Director Riffler was bleeding heavily as I glared at President Bargel. I'd been with Riffler when the President of Pyrik and three bodyguards approached, asking for a meeting.

Riffler was escorting me to his suite at the time, so I could study the laser rocket blasts fired from the planet's surface.

President Bargel and his guards waited outside the door to Riffler's suite.

Once Riffler invited them inside after unlocking the door, things became chaotic quickly. Riffler shoved me out of the way as one guard fired a laser pistol at the Director, hitting him in the shoulder.

The other two would have finished the job if I hadn't shot the one who'd fired first.

We were now at a standoff, as I pointed the illegal ranos pistol I carried at them and President Bargel.

I could only hold them off so long, I figured, before they understood that I was one person while they were three.

The other guard was already dead at their feet, his head blown apart and gray matter splattered on his companions.

Ignoring the nausea that threatened, I glared at these would-be assassins, waiting for my life to end.

Gord was supposed to meet me at Riffler's suite. Where was he?

"What are you doing, Bargel?" Riffler hissed from behind me. His voice would have been calm, I think, but he was in too much pain and losing blood swiftly.

"What I've wanted to do for a long time," Bargel growled. "Get rid of you and your digging into my records."

"Anomalies," Riffler snapped.

"Right. Anomalies. Fuck you and your anomalies. Kill them both," Bargel ordered his companions.

Both glanced at one another—probably deciding which one was going to take the hit for the team, because I'd kill at least one of them before I went down.

A fleeting image of my arrival on a penal planet somewhere went through my mind as I leveled my weapon at Bargel, who stood between his remaining guards.

He swallowed with difficulty. No matter which guard fired, he'd be the one to die. "Let's talk about this," he held up both hands.

"It's too late to do that, don't you think?" I demanded, struggling to keep the wobble from my voice.

I shrieked when the room suddenly boiled with people. Riffler used his good arm to pull me against him as the guards' heads were lopped off by the Falchani I'd seen earlier.

Chapter 5

Another man—I realized it was Teeg San Gerxon, Founder of the Campiaan Alliance, threw Bargel hard against a wall, then shouted for a physician.

I remember blinking into sightless eyes before darkness came.

Chapter 6

*T**ravis*

"It pays to be paranoid enough to carry an illegal weapon," I said, settling at a galley table aboard BlackWing X. "Kooper says the shield on Sabrina's weapon is a work of genius, because it sailed through all the security stops without a hiccup."

"How is she?" Randl asked. "Is Director Riffler all right?"

"They're both fine—Quin took care of Riffler. Sabrina Kend just needed to wake on her own. Kooper's asking her questions now."

"All three bodyguards were affected," I sighed. "How could that happen?"

"You recall that Bargel has been noticeably absent from all the pre-meetings," Trent pointed out. "These three were new hires, if the records are correct."

"What about Conclave?" I asked. Today's meeting had been canceled—by Teeg San Gerxon after the events in Riffler's suite. News vids across both Alliances were playing the images from inside Riffler's suite—Teeg released those vids so there would be no question that Bargel was not only attempting murder, but was guilty of something else, too. Just what that could be was a matter of speculation at the moment.

"No word on the Conclave yet," I said. "There could be a delay, though."

"At least we don't see Sabrina in the vids—the camera was pointed at the door, where Bargel and his thugs were," Trent said. "The news stations are being told that Riffler defended himself, although he was wounded."

"I see you have your mother's claws," Randl hid a grin. "Nice job of beheading."

"We found out about them when we were twelve," Trent laughed. "Our dads were teaching us how to defend ourselves against a knife attack. We weren't allowed weapons. Bro, here, sliced Great-uncle Crane's practice knife in half."

"They just popped out," I shrugged. "They're a weapon of last resort, too. Don't want the enemy to know we're never without weapons."

"I'm grateful the beheadings aren't all over the Alliances," Trent said. "I need a beer or ten."

"I'd take one, too," Randl said. "We almost didn't get there in time."

"I hope Sabrina Kend knows how to keep her mouth shut," I said. "Come on, let's go find a beer somewhere."

* * *

Sabrina Kend

"How did you know Riffler was in trouble?" I asked. Director Griff sighed at my question. My money was on the blind man, but I didn't say that. I was in enough trouble as it was, although packing a contraband ranos pistol had saved Jett Riffler's life and my own.

Chapter 6

When I realized Director Griff had no intention of answering my question, I asked another. "How much trouble am I in?"

Nobody except ASD and CSD were allowed to have ranos pistols. I'd built my own, with an additional shielding device to keep it hidden from even the most sensitive scanners.

"Young woman," Director Griff's eyes were lit with restrained laughter, "You're in trouble for sure. I'd be willing to look the other way on—certain charges—if you agree to work for the ASD."

"Now that was unexpected," I blinked at him. "My father," I began.

"Your father will be apprised of all the charges leveled against you if you don't," Griff's eyes turned hard. "And there's a substantial list, I assure you."

I wanted to curse. I held it back. "Fine. How long? I have things to do, you know."

"Tell me you need your father's money."

"I don't need anything from anybody," I snapped. "I have money of my own. I'm sure you've had my information on your comp-vid since the moment I arrived on Pyrik."

"Maybe."

"How long?" I repeated my question.

"Three years. Better than spending thirty in prison for carrying an illegal weapon, manufacturing an illegal weapon, firing an illegal weapon, killing someone with said weapon," he lifted an eyebrow at me.

"Fuck." I did curse, then. "What about saving Riffler's life?"

"I knocked off the last fifty years for killing with an illegal weapon, for saving his life," Griff shrugged. "We have your images from another camera inside Riffler's suite. We can show those to your father. It's a prison sentence for sure, if those get out. It wouldn't have been so bad if it were only a laser pistol," he added. "Ranos technology warrants a stiffer penalty."

"Nobody was supposed to find it," I hissed, staring down at my hands.

"And that's why I want you in my employ," Griff sat back in his chair. "We won't demand you give your technology away while you work for me," he continued. "I'm willing to pay for the shield design you used. The ASD only wants the option of a first chance at anything you produce while you're with us."

"That's something you already get from my father," I grumbled.

"But you know how to defend yourself in an emergency," Griff was smiling again. "I like that. I have a special assignment ready for you, too, if you agree to work for me. If not," he tossed out a hand.

"Prison." I spoke the word as flatly as I could.

"Your choice," he slapped a knee and stood. "In the meantime, I want you to review those images we brought you here to see. I'll drop you off with my team, and they'll handle it. I have a few things to tie up tonight."

"Your team?"

"Oh, they're having a beer in the bar downstairs. I'll leave you with them."

"Do I get a beer, too?"

"You can have as many as you want, as long as you're sober enough to review those images tomorrow morning."

"Right." I was under the long thumb of the law already.

"Come on, it won't be horrible unless you want it that way," Griff was grinning again. He was enjoying himself; I wasn't.

"What about my things? Where's Gord?" I asked.

"Oh. Gord was Bargel's first victim, I'm afraid. He's recovering in the same hospital as Director Riffler."

Chapter 6

"Thank the gods he's still alive," I mumbled. I realized how tense I was when I stood stiffly to follow Griff from his suite.

* * *

Randl

I was drinking my second bottle of Refizani beer when Kooper arrived with Sabrina Kend. "She needs a beer," Kooper said. "Travis, you'll be in charge of getting her together with the laser rocket images tomorrow morning. Unless she has a change of heart, I believe she may be working for the ASD for the next three years."

"Take a seat," David said. He'd come with us and pointed Sabrina toward the empty chair around our low table.

"Amterean?" Sabrina pointed her question at Dave.

"Close enough," he said. "What do you want to drink?"

"I'll have what you're having," she said.

"Bring another round, and add one," David waved at our server. Soon enough, we all had a fresh beer in front of us.

"Long day," Travis held up his bottle.

"You can say that again," Sabrina agreed. "Fucking, bird shitty, horrible day." She tipped the bottle to her lips and drank.

"She knows how to curse—I like that," Trent chuckled.

Sabrina's dark hair was pulled back and tied neatly at her nape, otherwise it would have hung long past her shoulders. She wore few cosmetics; she didn't need them and wasn't insecure about her appearance.

Kooper had all but blackmailed her to join the ASD, however, and I could tell she was inwardly fuming about it.

"Three years isn't so long," I said.

"Yeah." She drank again, nearly emptying her bottle. I pushed my fresh beer in her direction.

"Thanks."

"Not a problem."

She snorted at my response, but didn't say anything. So far, I hadn't seen her smile. I hoped that was a possibility, but the way things had gone for her this day, it could be long in coming.

"So, what do you guys do for the ASD—besides lop heads off bad guys?" Sabrina pointed her second bottle of beer at Travis and Trent.

"She saw that?" Travis and Trent said at the same moment. When my vision of them cleared, I found them staring at one another.

"You should ah, keep that to yourself," Dave said and helped himself to the small dish of nuts on the table. "It's a big, hairy, ASD secret, you know."

"Hairy secrets?" I could hear the frown in Sabrina's voice.

"No worries," David said and crunched on a handful of nuts.

"What the fuck is he talking about?" Sabrina turned to me.

"You wouldn't believe me if I told you," I replied. David burst out laughing.

* * *

Sabrina

"Here it is—home sweet home," Travis swept an arm out when we landed in the galley aboard a ship—Raptor II.

"You live on a ship?" I blinked at Travis.

"Most of the time," he shrugged and grinned. "Trent will show you your quarters—you'll be bunking next to Jayna. Don't worry—she doesn't bite. Much."

"Your bags are already in your cabin," the one called Jayna walked into the galley. "I can take you. I was ready for bed anyway."

"Breakfast is at six bells," Travis said. "Don't be late. We have an eight bell appointment with those vids."

Chapter 6

"Right." I wanted to wrinkle my nose at him, but thought better of it. So much for sleeping in after a fucking long day. Breakfast at six? Ewww.

"When's the last time you had self-defense lessons?" Travis asked before I could turn to follow Jayna.

"The day before I left to come here," I said.

"Good. Beginning the day after tomorrow, either Jayna or I will take up where your instructor left off."

"My day couldn't end any better, could it?" I said.

"How your day ends is up to you," Travis said. "You can be pissed if you want. It won't change anything."

"Oh, so now you're a philosopher," I tossed up a hand.

"Come on, you don't want to get into a shouting match with him," Jayna took my arm and steered me toward the door. "He's the Captain, in case you haven't guessed already."

* * *

Randl

"She's used to being her own boss," I said. "She works in her father's facility, but her designs are separate from his. She doesn't need his guidance or his money any longer."

"Then she'll have to get used to this," Travis sighed. "It wasn't my choice to sign her up. I suggested hiring her as a consultant. Kooper had other ideas."

"When will you tell her she's officially a pirate?" I asked.

"In a few days—if we don't kill each other, first. We'll inform her of the whole situation, too, if things work out. Kooper says the Conclave has been postponed for five days, due to the need for a replacement for President Bargel. He has four Vice Presidents who preside over different sectors, and one will have to be chosen to replace Bargel."

"Sounds like fun," I said.

"You know, I like your sense of humor," Travis sighed.

"I never got to use it around Amlis."

"I got that idea after we met with him."

"I'm grateful I don't have to listen to him any longer," I confessed.

"I would be, too. Go to bed—we have an early day tomorrow. Besides, Jett Riffler owes his life to you. He won't forget that."

"His life is his own," I said. "Good-night, Captain Travis."

* * *

Quin

I'd seen images of everyone except the President of Pyrik and his new bodyguards. I was looking at him now, via live vid-feed.

"There's an obsession," I told Kooper, who sat beside me in an interrogation room as we watched the vid-feed from Bargel's cell.

"That's what I was afraid of," Kooper frowned. "Riffler says the anomalies he spoke of are in accounting and the atmospheric measurements from around Pyrik."

"Planning to question the people who took those measurements?" I asked.

"Tomorrow. Was hoping you could watch while one of mine questions them."

"I will, but what if they're obsessed, too?"

"I'll ask Randl to take a look. If he can't determine anything, we're back where we started on this. Either way, I'll have a new team taking the planet's temperature tomorrow, and going over the books."

"The planet doesn't carry the poison from Siriaa, I know that much, but something has bothered me since I got here," I admitted.

"Any idea what that is?"

"Not yet. Get your people on it, and I'll work from another angle."

Chapter 6

"Sounds good. Anything else you can tell me about our murderous President?" Kooper jerked his head toward the vid-screen.

"No. Sorry."

"I'm sending Kell into that building tomorrow as mist, to see if he can find out who's watching and listening, and how they're doing it."

"Where the rocket was fired?"

"Yes. Randl says somebody's watching the inside, but Travis and Trent couldn't locate what or where it was."

"What if it's a scry?" I asked. "Bel Erland can do that sort of thing long distance."

"That's frightening," Kooper said. "I'll check on it, though."

"Send Wellend with Kell, then. Maybe he can determine whether a spell is involved."

"Good idea. Will you ask him to meet Kell in my suite tomorrow morning at seven bells?"

"Of course."

* * *

Sabrina

I dressed with my eyes half-closed, thinking all the while that I wanted to go back to bed and sleep for a week.

Jayna was dressed and looked far too wide-awake so early in the morning when I answered her knock on my cabin door.

Fergue would have called her homely.

Fuck Fergue, I reminded myself. All he was concerned about were his looks—and how other people looked. Jayna was perfectly fine, in my estimation. Certainly she was fit enough and wore her uniform well.

I followed Jayna to the galley, where two crew members were busy serving breakfast.

"Try the bagels and cream cheese," Randl suggested as he joined me at the end of the serving line. "Do you need something to settle your stomach?"

How the fuck did he know I had an upset stomach? After a moment, I realized it was a useless question.

"I think it'll be all right, once I get some food," I said. "I didn't eat dinner last night."

"You should have asked for something while we were at the bar," Randl observed.

"Yeah." I did as he suggested, however, and went for a bagel and cream cheese in all its blandness—with tea, of course. No need to vomit on the Captain's shoes or the vid-console while studying rocket blasts.

* * *

Randl

"Hey bro," Trent dropped his tray opposite mine at the table I'd chosen. Sabrina selected a tiny table near the wall, indicating her desire to be left alone.

I didn't bother her and went to a table three over to give her privacy. After all, her life had changed dramatically in the space of a few hours. She was unsettled, just as her stomach was.

"Good morning, Captain Trent," I grinned at him. No need for him to know I was worrying about Sabrina.

"Travis and I came up with an idea last night," Trent said. His spoon rattled inside his mug—he was stirring honey into his tea.

"What idea?" I asked. I could have used my vision to see, but I chose to let him tell me instead.

"We know you don't see stuff immediately, so it wouldn't do any good to teach you how to fight."

"Very true," I agreed. Trent sipped his tea for a moment. "What we came up with is this—how about learning to break out of a hold if somebody grabs you? We can cover all sorts of scenarios, and teach you what it will take to get away from that kind of thing."

"That's—that has possibilities," I said, mulling over the idea in my mind. "Yes—I would very much like to learn that."

"Good. You start tomorrow. Jayna will be training Sabrina; Travis and I will work with you. Today, Trent and I will see what Sabrina can tell us about those rockets, and sort through whatever Kooper sends us from the building and the air and soil quality surveys he's conducting. You, you lucky dog, get to go with Quin to take a look at the former President and some of his scientists."

"Are they studying the bodies of the affected ones?" I asked.

"I heard that they were. Why?"

"I think it's dangerous," I said.

"Again—why?"

"I can't pinpoint a reason; it just makes me uncomfortable."

"Feel free to say that to Kooper, although I can't guarantee what his reaction will be to the term *uncomfortable*."

"I was afraid you'd say that."

"Go do your part for the ASD today, and try to figure out why the forensic exams make you uncomfortable."

"Right."

* * *

Sabrina

"This is and isn't my technology," I said when Travis came to check on me mid-morning.

"What's that supposed to mean?"

I wanted to thump my forehead on the desk. If I explained the design, fabrication and testing of the technology in layman's terms, it would take forever and I wasn't really in the mood.

"What it means," I said as patiently as I could, "is that they have the beginnings of my design, but not the latest results. Look," I tapped the screen on my left. "That's what was fired at the ship. Here's the actual laser rocket," I pointed to the blast line that destroyed its target. "You see how it looks solid from the sat-bot's vantage point?"

"Yes."

"Now look at the six other shadow blast lines," I moved the image with a pointer. "They look hollow—you can tell they're fake from outside the planet. On the planet, and viewed from a horizontal position, they look like the real thing. Here," I pointed to the right screen, "Is the latest test after I improved my design."

"All of those look solid," Travis blinked at the images.

"Yes—from above and below. They're supposed to be exact duplicates, so you won't know which blast line is the real one."

"Tricky," Travis breathed as he looked from one screen to the other.

"This means that if they stole my design, they had to steal it nearly a year ago, if you compare the records of my test results to these."

"Then we need to work backward, to see what was going on in your father's research facility at the time."

"Right."

"I'll get Kooper to ask for employee records and security vids," he said. "That's just—well, genius," he shook his head at the images.

"Right." I wasn't about to disagree with him. I was confident in my designs, if nothing else. What troubled me most was that I was now sure someone had stolen what I'd created, and in the wrong hands, it could become a terrible weapon.

As it had already, I reminded myself.

* * *

Randl

Chapter 6

"How did he get elected?" I asked. Bargel was far from eloquent, and had only dim recollections of the actual laws governing his planet.

Quin and I sat in a small room connected to the interviewing space, watching a live vid-feed of the questioning performed by one of Kooper's skilled operatives. A fog covered his mind, true enough, but there was enough of his regular personality there to make a judgment in the matter.

"It's as if the fog is slowly enveloping his mind," I added, watching Bargel fumble another answer.

"I get the same feeling," Quin nodded. "And that's really strange. I've never seen anything like this before."

"How does an obsession work?" I asked. "I've had no experience with them until recently."

"The obsession is immediate and absolute," Quin said. "It can only be removed by the one who laid it, or, in extreme circumstances, by one of two people."

"Don't let them near him," I pointed at Bargel's image. "I don't know why I think that, I just do."

"Do you think Bargel may have some resistance to the obsession?" Quin asked. "I've never seen anyone do it before, but then I haven't seen everybody who's ever borne an obsession."

"I don't know." I wanted to shiver and forced myself not to. David's phrase about getting the willies came to mind. The term seemed appropriate for this situation.

Quin rustled her feathers as she stared at Bargel. "This really bothers me," she said. "And I can't explain that."

"I said the same thing this morning. Trent told me to come up with a better term and a reason for feeling uncomfortable about this before telling Director Griff."

"Kooper does love his concrete answers," Quin acknowledged.

Kooper walked into our tiny room at that moment, as if he'd been called. "Wellend says there was a heavy spell on that building, so your hunch was a good one," he told Quin. "The thing is, it disappeared almost the moment he discovered it—as if they were afraid he'd track it back to the one who cast it."

"So that's what a spell feels like," I said.

"What did it feel like?" Quin asked.

"Like a buzzing in my head," I explained. "It wasn't comfortable."

"I'll get the reports on soil and air quality this afternoon, to compare to the ones Bargel has distributed in the past ten years. We'll see how that matches up. Unfortunately, going through the books will take longer, but we've got the best account-bots working on a preliminary report," Kooper said.

"Will you notify us on the findings?" I asked.

"Sure. Plus, the three killed yesterday weren't any of the ones we've seen before, so who knows how many are out there?" Kooper complained.

"I can't see anything in Bargel about them," Quin said. "I doubt he saw any difference in them and anyone else."

"I want both of you to look at all his employees tomorrow," Kooper said. "To make sure there aren't more of them he hired."

Quin and I watched Kooper leave, closing the door firmly behind him.

"Let's see what we have," Quin said. "First, it looks like these affected people want to destroy the Conclave—whole or in part we don't know, yet. Second, they wanted to kill Director Riffler. They almost accomplished that. If it hadn't been for you and Sabrina Kend, he'd be dead. Three—there's something Bargel wants to hide, but we don't know for sure what that is. Is there anything I missed?"

Chapter 6

"Four—what do they ultimately want?" I asked. "Going to this much trouble goes far beyond the usual, doesn't it? Even with a desire for revenge of some sort, does that encompass every leader in both Alliances? That would be some plan of revenge, all right."

"I've seen a plan for revenge that stretched that far, but it was eventually destroyed, along with the ones who planned it. But," Quin held up a hand, "We're forgetting V'ili, I think."

"V'ili?"

"I need to tell you about V'ili," Quin said. "Do you have plans for lunch?"

"Not yet."

"Good. I'll see if my mother can join us."

"I didn't know you had a mother."

"Wait until you see her," Quin smiled.

* * *

Amlis

They thought I was still crazy. Some of them, anyway. Rodrik treated me as if I were made of glass.

I missed Randl. Anyone would, but he'd become a crutch for me. I understood that, now—after it had been carefully explained.

My meeting with the white-winged woman—after Quin healed me of everything including my mental issues—hadn't gone very well.

"Randl has more important things to do," intense blue eyes had gazed into mine. "It's time you set him free."

"And how do you propose I do that? I need him to train his replacement, at the very least," I'd complained.

"Any assistant worth his or her weight in breakfast cereal will figure things out fast enough," she snapped. "Let Randl go, and don't make him second-guess his decision to leave your employ."

I'd done exactly that, and felt like an ass for doing it. If Randl ever spoke to me again, I'd be much surprised. Perhaps not as much as learning that New Fyris had a Guardian, but I'd been warned not to tell that secret. It would only add to the already low estimation of my mental stability.

I considered that Rodrik and I had made an enemy of Quin long ago—it merely had taken years for her to feel confident enough to express her anger.

She'd healed me first, before giving Rodrik a black eye and bruises. Both of us should feel grateful, I think, for the compassion she bore for any living thing that needed her help.

Time for the Prince of New Fyris to stand on his own, the winged woman said. *Make your country self-supporting and happy.*

I turned away from the window in my room and stared at the comp-vid in my hand. Lists of programs to improve New Fyris with funding from the Alliance required my attention.

* * *

Randl

"She'll be here," Quin said as a third place setting was added to the table. Quin chose the balcony outside the suite she shared with Justis, to have our midday meal.

"Does she have wings?" I thought to ask.

"When she wants them."

Who had wings when they wanted them? You either had them or didn't, in my experience.

"Depends on the person."

She'd appeared in her seat as if she'd been there all along. I drew in a breath, waiting for my vision to settle. I saw her image.

Nothing else came.

"It's all right," Quin patted my hand. "You won't see anything, either. Randl, this is my mother, Zaria."

Chapter 7

*Q*uin

Randl had such a look of wonder on his face, once his mental vision picked up the sparkle of gold on Zaria's skin and wings.

"Mom, Randl needs mindspeech," I said as Randl continued to stare.

"I know." She turned a smile in my direction. "I have something else for him, too, plus gifts for a few of his friends."

Randl expressed his confusion with a perplexed frown.

"Don't worry," I reached out to pat his hand. "Mom knows more about people than I do."

"We'll eat first," Zaria declared. "Then we'll look into Randl's lack of mindspeech."

* * *

Randl

"How does this work?" I couldn't help but feel worried as Quin's mother, Zaria, placed her hands on either side of my face.

"It's completely painless," she said with a smile in her voice. "Close your eyes." *There. You have mindspeech,* she informed me. *As for your mind vision—it was already working on making the visions come faster. I just hurried things along. Open your eyes.*

"I didn't feel anything," I said and blinked. Yes, I was waiting for my mental vision to clear before seeing what was before me.

I found Zaria's face close to mine—immediately.

"Your brain was rewiring the pathways, I just accelerated the process," she smiled at me.

"How?" I breathed, blinking at her again. I'd never been conscious of my blinking before. Emotion welled up and my subsequent breaths were shaky.

"It's a gift," she patted my cheek and moved away. "The how doesn't matter, just that it is. Now, here's this." She lifted a fine gold chain from the table and held it out to me. Hanging from the chain was a small, gold medallion.

"It has your name on it," she said and dropped it over my head. "It will only work for you. Never take it off—even while bathing."

"What is it?" I dipped my head and lifted the medallion with shaking fingers.

"A good luck charm," she laughed. "I have one for several others, too—the boxes here are marked with their names. When Miss Sabrina complains that she doesn't want gifts from strangers, tell her Zaria says that Fergue is the biggest asshole in the universes."

"I'll uh, remember that," I floundered.

"Good."

"I put the boxes in a small case for you," Quin said. She'd been watching her mother work with me and now smiled as she lifted the small satchel. "Keep the case—it's the kind businessmen use to carry comp-vids and such."

I was overwhelmed for a moment, by the generosity of the two women. Zaria had given me gifts far above anything offered to royalty.

Does it work? I sent mindspeech to Quin.

It does, she laughed.

"Thank you, Zaria," I stood and bowed to her. "I cannot repay you, except in gratitude."

"From you, that is more than enough," Zaria said. "Just keep doing what you're doing. I think those gifts will pay for all." *Keep your vision adjustment to yourself*, she added in mindspeech. *Except with Kooper, Travis and Trent. Ask them to teach you how to shoot a pistol.*

I will, I replied. In some ways, it could give me a decided advantage.

* * *

Quin and I spent the afternoon listening to Bargel's scientists, who knowingly altered information on their reports in exchange for money and favors for their research facilities.

At least none of them bore obsessions, like Bargel did.

"We'll see the real information later tonight," Quin said after the last scientist was led away in shock cuffs.

We already knew some of what would be found—certain areas of Pyrik had radiation poisoning. Most of the land was designated as wildlife refuges, where the population wasn't allowed to go. The excuse was that certain animals were breeding there to increase their populations.

I doubted many of those animals actually existed, because the same scientists who'd been paid to alter reports had likely fabricated information on the animals in question.

"Both Alliances have rules regarding cleanup of old nuclear waste sites," Quin stretched her arms over her head and yawned. "It was probably hidden when Pyrik joined the Campiaan Alliance, because of the expense involved."

"And then it was just left there, because nobody wanted to deal with it or pay for it," I agreed. "I can't believe the answers we want are this simple, though," I said.

"I was thinking the same thing. Something else is going on; we just don't know what it is, yet. According to these scientists, there were six dump sites, all designated as wildlife refuges and closed-off from the public."

"They didn't talk much about the old city where the nuclear plant was, but they all said it was clean. Only the dump sites were the areas of concern."

"Pyrik will have heavy fines levied, at the very least, unless they can find a way to wriggle out of it," Quin observed. "Let's go—I can get someone to take you back to the ship after we get to my suite."

* * *

Travis

"Six dump sites, all leaking radiation," Kooper blew out a breath and dropped a comp-vid in front of me. He'd come to the ship's galley to give me an update on the questioning, and information on the new soil and air analyses. In return, he expected a report on Sabrina's findings regarding the sat-bot images.

"Turns out," Kooper went on, "It's much cheaper to pay off scientists than clean up the mess. At least they were honest about the manipulation of their reports. Saved me plenty of time and trouble. Quin and Randl say they were telling the truth and none were obsessed."

"I can't believe this is the whole of it," I said. "Why would they destroy a ship, if this is all it is? Sure, it explains the attempt on

Riffler's life, but that's it. Why was Vrak so important? What is it that's affecting Vrak and the others we've seen?"

"I have no idea. The forensics specialists are still examining everything there is to examine on those bodies. I won't get a report until tomorrow, at the earliest."

"Here he is," Trent folded into the galley, with Randl at his side. Randl carried an expensive, leather valise.

"Sit down," Kooper gestured. Trent and Randl joined us; Randl shoved the valise beneath the table before sitting in the chair beside mine.

"Where did that come from?" I asked.

"Quin gave it to me."

"Ah."

"She said I could carry my comp-vid and other things in it."

"Nice."

"What's the word from Sabrina?" Kooper asked.

"She says the technology is identical to hers—from a year ago. She's made improvements since then, so if it's industrial espionage, the theft took place around that time. She showed me how the two designs are now different, by showing me the laser echoes from the sat-bot images. From above, the echoes look hollow. Her improvements show the echoes appearing solid. It would be very difficult to sort out which was the real laser blast until you were hit with it. Certainly not enough time to employ counter measures."

"Spooky," Trent wiggled his fingers. Randl laughed.

"It's still good enough to have everybody fooled from the surface," Kooper grumbled.

"It does that well enough," I agreed. "What are they going to do about the dump sites?"

"Teeg hasn't made a decision, and probably won't until Bargel's successor is in place. They'll have to hammer out a plan for cleanup, but that could take a while. I'm sure a fine will be levied, too, but the amount will have to be determined. Pyrik could be placed on probation, as a result."

"And here we are, having a Conclave," Trent shook his head. Randl forced back a snicker.

"What's the word on the scry spell on the building?" I asked.

"Nothing. Since it disappeared so quickly, there's no way to track it to a source."

"So they could be spying from long distance, and know about everybody who went in and out," Randl said.

"Your disguises would hold," Kooper reassured him. "They don't have your real images."

"That's something, at least," Randl sighed.

"You're worried about this, aren't you?" I turned toward him.

"Very much."

Kooper's comp-vid squawked before I could ask Randl a follow-up question.

"Holy fuck," Kooper was standing the moment he read the message. "Come with me. We have something to sort out."

* * *

Randl

Three forensic physicians and one assistant physician were in holding cells, after they'd attempted to kill Jett Riffler in his hospital room.

"These are the ones assigned to examine the bodies of those affected, aren't they?" I asked the moot question. I knew who they were. I also knew what the danger was that I'd worried about for two days.

"What do you know?" Kooper demanded. He, Travis, Trent and I stood at high windows overlooking the prisoners' cells.

Chapter 7

"I think the act of examining those bodies unleashed something that is now affecting those four," I said, touching the glass. "They have the beginnings of the infection, for lack of a better term. If Quin were here, she may tell you that they carry the beginnings of an obsession. That obsession may have been to kill Director Riffler."

"Are you saying that the obsession can pass from one to another, like a virus?" Travis sounded incredulous.

"I can't say that for sure," I hedged. "It's so cloudy to me—their minds and my vision of them."

"Travis, Trent," Kooper turned to them, his voice stern. "Did you clean your claws using power after you beheaded those two in Riffler's suite?"

"Yeah. Our clothes and shoes, too. Why?"

"We need to quarantine everything in that room. Anything their blood touched, everything," Kooper snapped. "I'm sending mindspeech to Quin. I hate to pull her in so late, but there's no help for it, I'm afraid."

Bel Erland transported Quin into the facility. She hugged me immediately before turning to the four prisoners in the rooms below.

"This is awful," she breathed after a few moments. "These—they feel exactly how Bargel did to me—with his obsession. Like it was growing."

"Fucking hells," Kooper swore before lifting his comp-vid and tapping on its surface. "Bloody, fucking hells."

* * *

Kooper Griff

"Jett, did any of them touch you?" I demanded.

I stood at his bedside, after having him moved to another room. Quin and Randl were busy examining the hospital staff, to ensure they were unaffected by whatever was eating away at former President Bargel and four forensics specialists.

"No, I threw my dinner tray at the first one when he lifted a knife and came toward me. The guards grabbed all of them, then."

"I've spoken to the guards. They're unaffected."

Quin and Randl said so, after I'd pulled them all out of bed for a quick examination. I didn't say how grateful I was that the forensics specialists weren't practiced in sticking a knife in a body that could move on its own.

Randl had been right to say the examination of those bodies made him uncomfortable. I made a mental note to pay special attention to his feelings from now on.

"Care to explain that? How the physicians were affected and the guards weren't?" Jett scooted into a more comfortable position on his bed. "I'd like to get out of this infernal bed, too, if you don't mind. I feel perfectly fine."

"I know," I waved off his request. "Maybe tomorrow. Keeping you here keeps the population misinformed about your miraculous recovery."

"Yeah. I appreciate that, by the way."

"Thank Quin, not me."

"That winged woman is quite talented."

"In many ways," I agreed, "And I can't explain what I don't fully understand, yet," I told him. "When you're moved away from this facility, I'll give you what I have."

"Good. I hope it's tomorrow."

"I'm looking for a secure place for you, now. When I find it, I'll have you moved immediately."

"I suppose I should say thank you, but it won't be sincere," Jett complained.

"Thank me later. I don't give a damn about sincerity."

"I understand that about you."

* * *

Chapter 7

"For now, Kooper's considering it similar to a virus—a slow-spreading one," Travis said.

We'd been up most of the night, going from one hospital employee to another, ensuring that none of them had been infected by whatever the four forensics physicians carried.

Those four were now quarantined and their cells off-limits to anyone not wearing biohazard suits. Quin and Bel Erland went back to their suites at the hotel when we finished our examinations; Travis, Trent and I sat at our favorite table in BlackWing X's galley, having a beer before going to bed.

"Activities canceled until noon," Trent yawned before taking another swallow of beer from his bottle.

"Yeah. Thanks, Captain Trent," Travis said.

"Oh. I forgot," I said, pulling the case from beneath the table, where I'd left it earlier. "I have something for you. From Zaria."

Travis and Trent froze.

"Zaria?" Travis whispered after several moments passed.

"Yeah." I dug around in the satchel, searching for the boxes with their names printed on them. "Here." I set the appropriate boxes in front of them. "I have one, too. She said not to take them off, not even in the shower."

"Holy shit, bro—Zaria is trying to tell us something," Trent breathed as he lifted his medallion from the box.

"She said they'll only work for the person whose name is on the medallion," I added.

Without another word, both medallions were placed around their necks and hidden beneath shirts. "What did you mean, Zaria is trying to tell us something?" I thought to ask. These two knew who Zaria was.

"What did she look like when you saw her?" Travis asked a question of his own.

"Dark hair, intense blue eyes, white wings," I shrugged. "Quin says Zaria is her mother."

"For all intents and purposes, Zaria *is* Quin's mother," Trent said. "She's also Larentii—whenever she feels like it."

I stilled. "Huh?" was the only thing I could articulate past that.

"Don't worry about it. If Zaria gives you something, it's time to sit up and pay attention," Travis said. "Who else has a box?"

"David, Sabrina and Jayna," I said. "I have a message for Sabrina. Zaria says she could balk at receiving a gift from a stranger."

"If Zaria says so, then you can take that to the bank," Travis said.

"Why would I take it—wait, that's another of your strange phrases, isn't it?"

Trent choked so hard on a laugh, his brother had to slap him on the back.

* * *

Sabrina

Something had happened the night before, I just didn't know what it was. I'd be damned if I'd ask what it was, too. Determined to learn what it was on my own, I faced Jayna in my first self-defense lesson aboard ship.

"That's good," she said after I managed to break out of her hold on the second try. "You should work on your strength, though. I believe Travis and Trent want Randl to work out with weights. You can do that together. In a few weeks, we'll see about training you with weapons."

"My aim was good enough to take down an attacker," I grunted as she came at me again.

"From close range," Jayna reminded me and knocked me flat on my back. "Come on, you need to keep your feet under you. Standing with your feet together guarantees that somebody can knock you down with little effort."

"Great," I hissed when I got my breath back. Rolling over, I pulled myself to a standing position as smoothly as I could.

"I'll get Travis or Trent to teach you balance," Jayna added. "You'll come up from a fall easier and more gracefully than you ever imagined possible. The Falchani have a knack for it."

"And there I was, thinking I'd done a good job," I deflected her next strike.

"You're not bad—at least you've had some training and only picked up a few poor habits along the way. I knew nothing when I started, and was clumsy as all hells."

"For all of five minutes, probably," I grunted as she hit me with a follow-up blow to the shoulder. I hadn't been ready for that one, and only managed to turn my face away in time.

I was beginning to realize how quickly I'd go down if faced with a trained, experienced fighter. My training would only protect me against an average, uneducated attacker. My resolve to learn everything I could from Jayna solidified in fierce determination.

If I could honestly protect myself after three years with the ASD, then I'd suffer through it gladly. There'd been a time when I'd felt more helpless than I'd ever felt, when my family and I had been kidnapped by one of the worst criminals the Alliances had ever seen.

We'd been separated, too, and I found myself herded onto an abandoned outpost, amid many strangers. The outpost had failing life support systems and, as we were useless as hostages in the kidnappers' eyes, we'd been left there to die.

If I hadn't employed everything I'd learned from my genius father to divert energy to a distress call, we'd have died.

I will forever be grateful to those who hadn't ignored the weak signal and strayed from their shipping route to investigate. That act had saved many lives—mine included.

It was an arm of the ASD that saved my father, too, although the full story of how that happened would probably never be explained to me.

Too many closely guarded secrets and a mountain of classified information was involved, no doubt.

"I think I've beaten you up enough for today," Jayna said. "Come on, clean up and we'll go to breakfast. I hear they're making omelets."

* * *

"Here." Randl slid a small box toward me. I'd chosen my usual table and ate alone in the galley—until Randl set his tray on the other side and pulled the box from his pocket.

"What's that?" I asked after I swallowed what I was chewing.

"It's something Zaria sent for you," he said and pulled out the chair opposite mine to sit down. "I have one, too. Zaria says that if you have a problem accepting gifts from strangers, to tell you that Fergue is the biggest asshole in the Alliances."

"She sent the same thing to Travis and me," Trent said, setting his mug of tea on the table and pulling in another chair. "Trust me, Zaria is trying to protect you in some way. David and Jayna got one, too, and the rest of us are already wearing them."

I snorted a breath before reaching out to lift the lid from the box. Inside was an elegant gold chain with a beautiful, gold pendant hanging from it. My name, in lovely script, was engraved on one side.

"She says to always wear it, even in the shower," Randl said.

"Who is Zaria?" I thought to ask as I held the pendant in my hand, examining it closely.

"Quin's mother," Randl shrugged.

"Quin. Queen Quin, of the Avii?"

"Yes."

Somehow, she'd been involved in the rescue of my parents—they said so. "I'll wear it, then," I said and pulled the chain over my head.

"Good." Trent released a sigh, as if he were worried that I wouldn't accept the gift. "Now," he said, more business-like, "Who is Fergue?"

"A lying, cheating asshole," I said. "Any other questions?"

"No." Trent shrugged and sipped tea to hide his grin.

"What's on the agenda for today?" I asked.

"A trip to your home world, for some investigative work and to test the hyperdrive after I repaired it," David said as he ambled up to the table. "I think you need to homestead on a bigger table," he said, dragging another chair in and sitting between Randl and me.

"Hmmph," I said and cut another chunk off my omelet. The food was good and I wasn't about to let them keep me from eating.

"We have ASD vids for you to study while we're on the way," Trent said. "There'll be a test later to ensure you learn your lessons."

"They're interesting," Randl said. "You'll be able to ask questions, too."

"How long is the course and when will the tests be given?" I asked.

"If you attend the classes, six months. With the vids—as quickly as you finish them and declare yourself ready for testing." Trent grinned.

"When will we get underway?" I asked, pointedly ignoring him.

"When David and I make it to the bridge—less than an hour," Trent replied. "Dave is our engineer and after every repair, he's always on the bridge to see how things go."

"Because long-distance finger-pointing is never as much fun as doing it in close quarters," David said. "Captains Trent and Travis prefer the short-distance method."

"There'll be things to sign on your comp-vid, too, before you get started on the lessons," Trent said, rising and stretching. For a moment, I wanted to reach out and pull the end of his long, black braid.

Since he was one of my new bosses, I didn't want to spend time in the brig for assaulting the Captain's person, or whatever the legal, ASD-ish term was.

"What sort of things?" I asked instead.

"Confidentiality agreements, permission for extensive weapons training, that sort of thing. Basically, you're telling Director Griff that you won't get in trouble, or get the ASD in trouble, and you'll keep secrets, as a working member of the ASD."

"Right."

"I'll let you play with an ASD-issued ranos pistol if you sign those agreements and mean it," Trent said.

"Seriously?"

"Yeah. Kooper says to let you examine the real thing after you're officially signed up, and compare your design with it and send him a report on potential improvements. After that, bro and I will teach you the proper way to use it."

I watched him walk away, only a slight swagger in his walk. David walked beside him, already discussing what he'd done to repair the hyperdrive.

"How long do you think we'll be gone?" I turned toward Randl, who'd just finished his food.

"I think we'll be back when the Conclave is set to start again," Randl shrugged. "Until then, we'll be hunting for the one who stole your designs, if what I can read from Trent and Travis is correct."

"Then that's what we'll be doing," I blew out a breath. "I really wasn't ready to face my father so soon after breaking Alliance laws." I couldn't contain the shiver that shook my body. Dad wouldn't be happy about this—I could almost hear him shouting that I'd placed myself in much more danger than usual.

"There are worse places to be," Randl said, his voice soft.

"You're right," I agreed. "I've been to some of those."

"Me, too."

* * *

Turbak, Jaledis

Fergue Biing

"You really fucked the reptagator when you let Sabrina go," my best friend, Akrinn Lemm, slid onto the chair opposite mine at the best coffee and tea shop in Turbak.

"What makes you say that? She's not set to inherit the business, you know." I toyed with the mug in front of me, considering a refill of my favorite coffee drink.

"Hmmph. It's because she has her own business, separate from his. If Kend dies, then Sabrina's mother and her two little brothers inherit that part. She doesn't need it. Is that why you got caught cheating on her? I know you're better than that," Akrinn sniffed.

"Look, it cooled off between us, mostly because she's stingy with her—ah—affections."

"Then why get caught getting what she's not giving out? Man, I thought you were smarter than that."

"Maybe, maybe not." I lifted my mug to tell the server I wanted another cup. The coffee-bot made the familiar sound of steaming milk almost immediately. "Look, I like Ula a lot more than I ever liked Sabrina. You're the one who suggested I go out with Sabby. It was all right at first, until she wouldn't give me the goods."

"So Ula gives you the goods, as you put it."

"Sure does. All the time."

"Fergue, you're the sixth son of a politician, and your inheritance will be pitiful. If you don't marry well, you'll be stuck on some backward planet as an ambassador or something."

"I won't. Ula and I have plans. If those don't work out, we'll find something else."

"You're really that stuck on Ula, aren't you?"

"We get along really well. Sometimes, that makes a big difference. Sabby was always talking above my head, with designs and schematics and shit to save the Alliance or something."

"Well, you have been schooled as a third-generation politician or ambassador. Why wouldn't she talk that shit with you? You could be in a position to employ those ideas someday."

"I told you that's not what I want to do."

"That's what your father wants you to do."

"Don't remind me."

"Maybe I'll ask Sabrina out, then, when she gets back."

"You do that," I grumbled. "Just leave me out of it, all right? I tried to make it up with her at your suggestion. She called me names and says she'll never see me again."

"Then I'll ask her out," Akrinn rose from his seat and nodded at the server who set my fresh drink on the table. "See you around."

I barely acknowledged his exit—Akrinn always had somewhere else to be nowadays.

* * *

BlackWing X

Travis

Jaledis is less than two day's journey from Pyrik, and a perfect run to test David's work on the hyperdrive. So far, it was working perfectly. David sat on a chair at the communications console with an I-told-you-so expression on his face.

I'd forwarded Sabrina's signed agreements to Kooper already, and only waited for word back from him before telling her she was a part of the BlackWing Pirates network. Sure, we'd keep the Raptor II logo and call sign up as long as we were working this case—unless we were called out unexpectedly.

I heard from Mom, too. She said Uncle Karzac was working on a way to remotely examine the afflicted bodies, so that no contact would be made with actual humanoids—only robots. It was time to see if anyone could decipher what the affliction actually was and how dangerous it could be.

If we were looking at an epidemic, the sooner we knew that, the better off we'd be. I told Mom about the medallions sent by Zaria. She'd gone silent for several seconds, before speaking again.

"If she says wear them constantly, then make sure that happens," was all she'd told me.

Mom was powerful in her own right.

Zaria—who knew what her limits might be?

"How close are we?" Trent folded onto the bridge and dropped onto the chair next to mine.

"Another hour and a half before we dock," I said. "Want to eat in Turbak?"

"Sure. Sabrina can show us around, I think."

"I'll give her the good news," I said and stood. I'd been sitting too long watching stars flash past us. Mom always says it's like watching stripes on the highway fly by. I'd had to ask Winkler what the hells she was talking about.

Chapter 8

abrina

An alarm sounded throughout the ship when we approached Jaledis' space station. If we were selected for inspection, we'd be required to stand outside our quarters while the port authorities walked through the vessel.

Only the Captain and the bridge crew were allowed anywhere else, and they'd be on the bridge and approached first.

"We're cleared," Travis' voice announced moments later. "Stand down." Only a few seconds later, he added, "We'll have dinner in Turbak on the company tonight. Sabrina's picking our restaurant. Make it a good one, Agent Kend."

I went still.

I *was* Agent Kend—the forms I'd signed said so. *After* I'd pledged all but my newborn children to the ASD.

I knew a really good steakhouse in Turbak, too, but you'd need reservations—unless your name was Kend. I lifted my comp-vid and tapped in a code. Travis and Trent should like it—they cooked in the Falchani style, or so they said.

It was owned by Falchani, too, or they bore a good enough resemblance to pass for Falchani. Either way, the food at Cedar Falls was excellent and a favorite of mine.

Reservation confirmed—S Kend and up to ten guests in the River Room, flashed on my comp-vid.

I wished for mindspeech, then, so I could inform the swaggering captains that I had a decent reservation for all of us, including the cooks, if they wanted to come.

Instead, I sent Travis a message by comp-vid, and included a copy of the reservation for Cedar Falls.

Good choice, his mindspeech sounded in my head.

I considered asking him if he'd been there before, but held back. Finding something appropriate to wear for dinner was now my top priority.

* * *

Randl

"I don't think I've ever eaten Falchani-style," I admitted as we walked toward the security gate at the space station. A scan of our wrist-chips was required to get onto the planet, after the ship had docked and the crew approved by the Port Authority.

We'd get a shuttle to the surface, once we passed security. The same shuttle would take us to the restaurant, too, for an extra fee.

I realized then that I'd never be forced to answer security questions for Amlis again, and it made me feel so free I felt I could fly.

Would I have alternative identification, like many ASD agents had? Travis would know, I suspected. I'd ask when we were aboard ship again. My case was a special one, after all, and I had no idea whether other identification was necessary.

"Is he blind?" The security agent asked Travis, who led our small group through security.

"Yes, but he's quite talented in making his way," Travis replied smoothly.

"I don't think I've ever seen someone who stayed blind," the guard said.

"He hears very well," Trent said while holding his wrist over the scanner. "And he's very intelligent, too. Randl, tell this man something he doesn't know."

"He has a winning lottery chip in his pocket," I said.

"It's a winner?" The man blinked at me in surprise. "Wait, please," he held up a hand, preventing David from passing through the gate. "I have to check this." Pulling out his comp-vid, he tapped it, then waved the lottery chip over the scanner. His eyes became huge—as they should—the winning numbers had been released less than an hour before.

"Oh, my—I've won ten thousand credits," he whispered, staring at his comp-vid and then at me.

"I'd suggest never telling anyone that he saw this in you," Terrett moved forward and locked eyes with the man. "Now, we're hungry, and we'd like to move along, please."

Until then, I'd barely heard Terrett say three words—as if he preferred not to speak.

"Of course." The security agent stuffed the comp-vid and chip in his pocket and watched as we walked through, scanning our wrists as we went. Soon enough, we were at the outer gate and looking for a shuttle.

* * *

"If I set my mind to it, I can see all sorts of things," I explained to Sabrina as the shuttle carried us toward the surface and the city of Turbak. "Usually, I try not to pry too much, because it's an invasion of privacy. I see things on the horizon—mostly those that place people in danger." I shrugged. It was something I'd always had, and was normal to me.

"That is some gift you carry," Sabrina shook her head. "No, I don't want it," she laughed and held up a hand. "I'm better off not knowing, I think."

To be honest, I was fascinated by the gift Terrett carried. That was certainly useful, in my opinion, as long as it was employed in an ethical fashion.

"We're here," Travis announced. He and Jayna climbed out of the shuttle first, followed by Trent and David, then Susan and Bekzi, the cooks, and then James and Nathan, the pilot and navigator. Sabrina and I got out last.

The sound of a waterfall greeted me the moment I stepped out of the shuttle—I suppose it was to simulate the Falls in the capital city of Falchan.

"Come on, I'm starved," Travis motioned for us to follow.

"He won't get in unless I'm there," Sabrina grumbled beside me. When we made our way inside the restaurant, we found Travis hugging another man—a Falchani, I could see it easily.

"Trent, you rascal," the man let Travis go and turned to hug Trent.

"Hello, Uncle Turtle," Trent slapped the man on the back.

"Uncle Turtle?" Sabrina blinked at me in confusion.

"Not his real Uncle, but someone he grew up calling Uncle, so almost the same thing," I reported what I saw in the Falchani man. "He's a real Falchani warrior, too, and can slice someone in half before they have time to blink."

"And there I thought I was giving them something they might not ordinarily get," Sabrina fumed quietly.

"I think you made them very happy," I said. "Stop worrying about it."

Chapter 8

"I really should stop worrying about it?"

"Yes. They're all happy. You did a good deed. Let's eat."

She turned away from me for a moment, but when she turned back, I saw her struggle not to laugh.

"Go ahead," I told her. "It's good for you."

I smiled as Sabrina giggled all the way to the River Room.

* * *

Trent

I'd begun to think Kooper had a devious way of torturing Travis and me. I didn't miss the looks Sabrina sent our way now and then. According to ASD rules, superiors didn't date those under their command.

Three fucking years before we could step forward and say anything to her other than what would normally pass between Captain and crew. The reasons were obvious—you have a falling out—you're screwed. You make the crew think there's favoritism—you're screwed.

Any way you looked at this, we were screwed.

Sabrina sat cross-legged on her cushion at the low table, talking and laughing between Randl and Jayna. Travis and I sat opposite those three, with Uncle Turtle and Uncle Flyer, who'd joined us for dinner.

Travis and I thought Turtle and Flyer were crazy for opening a restaurant here, but they'd done exceptionally well with it. In fact, it was one of the most exclusive restaurants on Jaledis.

Why did you choose Jaledis? I sent mindspeech to Uncle Flyer. He'd made the best noodles on Falchan after serving in the Falchani army for decades. Turtle had run a bar that had excellent food after his stint in the military.

They'd parlayed their cooking experiences into a successful restaurant in the oddest place you'd think to find it.

It was a suggestion—from Zaria, Flyer returned.

I held my breath for a moment before releasing it. Yes, he and Turtle had worked with her before. That had slipped my mind.

Of course, Zaria would send them where they'd do some good—and serve excellent food at the same time.

You can stay with us while you're here—the compound is big enough for two large families, Turtle's mental voice contained a smile.

Sounds tempting, I said. *Travis and I will discuss it and get back to you.*

"The steak is wonderful," I nodded my appreciation to Turtle and Flyer.

"I like the noodles," Jayna said. "I've never had noodles this good."

The meal was served family-style, and there was plenty of everything. Steaks were cooked table-side and served straight from the portable grill. Randl had never used chopsticks before, but he was a quick study and now employed them easily to eat his meal.

Bro, you want to stay at Turtle and Flyer's compound? Travis sent. Looked like Uncle Turtle had been working on him while Flyer worked on me.

I'd like to—you think the ship will be all right?

I can ask Kooper for a shield, Travis replied. *We'll know for sure if anybody comes close that shouldn't.*

Then ask. You know Turtle and Flyer's compound will be heavily shielded. After we start poking around, we might need that.

I was thinking the same thing.

* * *

Sabrina

Chapter 8

I worried that I'd have to call my father after dinner to let him know I was back. A reprieve came in the form of Travis and Trent's Uncles offering a place to stay while we were in Turbak.

Their compound was huge—larger than what Dad built near the research facility, and that was enormous.

I learned that one uncle lived in the west side of the compound, while the east side was occupied by the second uncle. A large courtyard separated the two. Travis, Trent, Terrett, Randl and David had rooms in Turtle's half, while Flyer's side housed the rest of us.

Travis and Trent shut down the ship and brought bags back for the rest of us. I had mixed feelings about them collecting clothing for me, but didn't say anything. I didn't have to; the heat of my face probably told them everything they wanted to know.

Snatching my duffle from the pile in the courtyard, I marched toward Flyer's compound, my back as straight as I could keep it. At least nobody laughed—while I could still hear it, anyway.

* * *

Randl

She's embarrassed, I informed Travis, whose left eyebrow lifted as his eyes followed Sabrina's stiff walk across the courtyard.

I know. It's kind of hot, Travis replied while a grin spread across his features.

I sorted out that he wasn't referring to the heat rising in Sabrina's face. He'd voiced something I'd already suspected; I'd merely avoided it until now.

There was a great deal of attraction between the brothers and Sabrina. It crushed the small bit of hope I'd held that she might look my way at times.

It's nothing more than I've seen in hundreds of faces in hundreds of places, I reminded myself. People pining after what they couldn't have. I hadn't thought I'd join their ranks—until now.

Stop setting your sight so high, I chided myself. Who'd want a blind man who could see everything else? In Amlis' case, it had been a disaster. Perhaps I was destined to be alone—for the sake of anyone I might come to love.

Or already loved—at least a little.

"Come on, bro," Trent slapped me on the back. "We have training early in the morning. If you want a beer before bed, follow me."

"Yeah. Beer." I turned to follow Trent's broad back, well-muscled from years of training. I wasn't foolish enough to think that was all Sabrina found attractive about him. *Fuck being a realist*, I decided. *I'll have two beers.*

* * *

"Where did the weights come from?" I asked. On a flagstone-covered square at the center of the courtyard lay several racks of weights. Travis and Trent hadn't wasted time calling us out of bed, either. At least the courtyard was shaded; the sun would have blinded the others. I already had that affliction, but it could still damage what I had.

"From the weight store," Travis laughed at my question. "Come along, my lazy crew. It's time you discovered the pleasure of aching muscles."

"I have some from yesterday," Sabrina grumbled behind me.

"No complaining," Trent barked. "First, we'll stretch, to keep the aches at a minimum. Then we'll start out light and work our way up. You need arm strength and upper body strength if we're expected to turn out a fighter who can take down something stronger than an eight-year-old."

"An eight-year-old what?" I heard Sabrina's soft mumble.

"Straighten up and pay attention," Travis snapped. "Do what I do. No talking."

Chapter 8

The stretching exercises turned into something that resembled a dance. The movements were slow and deliberate; I could feel my muscles complaining after only a few minutes of activity.

This was payment for years of walking as my only form of exercise. My legs felt better than my arms for a while, until both began to ache.

"Sit," Trent said. "Cross-legged, with your hands resting on your knees." He dropped gracefully to the flagstones and was in the required position swiftly with no wasted movement.

This graceful, efficient way of moving was from the Falchani; that was easy to understand. I imagined he'd rise the same way—with smooth grace and a minimum of effort.

I found myself wanting to do it, too.

"Close your eyes and empty your mind," Trent instructed. "If your thoughts intrude, shove them out as many times as it takes."

For me, that was easy. Bright stars invaded my mind and I focused on the emptiness between them. Yes, they'd appeared in my dreams since I was a child, but I had no idea of their meaning.

I'd always felt more rested after a star dream, however, and welcomed them when they came.

After a while, the stars gathered close—as if they wanted me to reach out mentally and touch all of them at once.

A soft snore woke me from the trance; Sabrina had fallen asleep behind me.

* * *

Travis

Trent fell over on the flagstones, squelching laughter when Sabrina's head drooped and she snored.

It wasn't unusual for someone to fall asleep the first time or three, although the snore was a decided plus. Until that happened, I'd been watching Randl, whose face bore a look as if he were in heaven.

He really was a quick study.

"Up," Trent called, once he was sitting upright and could maintain a straight face again. He and I were standing first, with Bekzi, David, Terrett and Jayna right behind us. Susan had been working on her stance and posture—with great improvement, I noticed. Nathan and James rose with Susan; Randl and Sabrina scrambled awkwardly to their feet, their muscles stiff.

It would happen for a while, until they were used to this.

* * *

Randl

"Start at the low end," Trent advised as he pointed at smaller weights at the end of the rack. "We'll do arm curls, first. Take your weights," he tapped the two near the end. "Now, hold them at your sides. Keep your body loose—don't tighten up," he instructed.

"Then, keeping your elbows locked in place at your side, bring the weights up while turning them toward you, until you feel it, here," he tapped my upper arm. "Breathe out on the way up, in on the way down. Don't let the weight drop to your side; maintain control on the way down or you'll defeat the whole purpose. This strengthens upper arms, forearms and wrists," Trent added.

I did as he instructed while he watched. Behind me, I could hear Travis telling Sabrina the same thing. Trent was saving a guffaw for later, when Sabrina wouldn't hear. He'd found it quite humorous that she'd fallen asleep during meditation.

"When we're back aboard ship, we'll work out with the machines in the exercise facility," Trent said. "They'll tone the muscles we can't deal with using free weights. I'll put you on the treadmill, too, to get those legs in better shape."

Chapter 8

He wanted me to run. Before, when it took time for my vision to adjust, running wasn't an option. It could be now, and I'd only realized that after Trent's suggestion.

Running. During my childhood, I'd wanted that more than anything. Childhood for me had been anything except normal. I could see intentions behind children's faces. At times, I considered it a cruel joke played on me.

Eventually I'd learned to block what was unimportant, but that talent had come too late for me to make childhood friends.

"That's good," Trent laid a hand on my shoulder. I'd been lifting weights while my thoughts strayed and I'd lost count. "You'll be really sore tomorrow if you keep going," he grinned. "I will have no sympathy."

"Are you being sympathetic now, or is that a dire warning?" I asked, replacing the weights on the rack.

"Both. Come on, bro, breakfast is waiting."

* * *

Sabrina

Travis' touch had been purely professional when he showed me the proper way to do arm curls. My previous instructor was clearly of the lazy sort—he hadn't watched me carefully to ensure I wasn't moving my elbows.

As a result, I hadn't gotten much benefit from his instruction. Travis never said a word about that, either, but his mouth tightened when I'd pulled up both elbows the first time. After that, I was doing proper curls and could feel the burn every time I lifted and lowered.

As for falling asleep during meditation, I considered that embarrassment could be a constant during the next three years. I sat at breakfast, consuming my food in silence and wondering what else I'd been doing wrong for years.

"What's on the agenda for today?" Jayna asked. I turned my attention toward her, rather than stealing another glance at Travis and Trent.

"Well, Sabrina, here, is going to introduce us to her workshop, and allow us access to all her records of visitors and suppliers," Travis grinned in my direction—I'd jerked my head around the moment he said my name.

Yeah, embarrassment for three years.

Definitely.

* * *

Randl

Her desk was covered in comp-vids and schematics on larger, drawing comp-pads. The rest of her workspace was decidedly neat— as if her design process was delightfully unpredictable, but the application process was determined and well-considered.

Ruther Kend, her father, was on his way as we stood inside Sabrina's laboratory; Travis and Trent were already searching through her records at the appropriate stage of development for her new technology.

"Fergue and friends?" Travis straightened from bending over the desk to stare at Sabrina.

"They brought me lunch." She sounded defensive.

"Are there images?" I asked.

"Yeah, come look," Trent said. I walked toward Sabrina's desk while she stepped aside. I could tell that she was suddenly afraid.

Afraid that I would discover something she'd never suspected of good friends.

Betrayal.

Four had come—I could see the images in the vid Trent displayed for me.

Chapter 8

"Fergue Biing," I pointed at the image of a handsome man who stood beside Sabrina's desk, his hands in his pockets. "He's all right—for being a cheating asshole," I amended.

Sabrina snorted at my words.

"Ula Karn," I pointed toward the young woman who stood on the other side of Sabrina's desk. "Cheating with said asshole," I said. That resulted in Sabrina's indrawn breath—she hadn't known those two were together—she'd only known Fergue had been hiding another woman behind her back.

"Lorvis Verll," I hastened my next assessment. "Wait. Something is off about her." I considered that for a moment when the fourth person walked into the camera's field of view.

"Oh, no," I whispered.

"That's Akrinn Lemm, Fergue's best friend," Sabrina snapped. "What's wrong with him?"

"It isn't what's wrong with him—well, it is. He just killed Fergue."

* * *

Travis

Whoever Akrinn Lemm really was, he had a devious, criminal mind. If we hadn't sent the local police to Fergue's home, then the first person who'd walked through the door would have been killed by the gun rigged onto Fergue's hand.

A spell had been laid on the corpse's hand to activate and shoot, once the door opened. The police had sent a 'bot to open the door. The thing was nothing more than a useless pile of junk, now, thanks to the blast that greeted it.

The most damning evidence of all, perhaps, was the comp-vid lying near Fergue. The last message sent from it had been to Sabrina, telling her that he'd accidentally taken something from her lab and that she should come pick it up immediately.

Somebody knew she was back on Jaledis. They also knew that she'd be looking into the theft of her design upon her return from Pyrik. They probably didn't know that she'd have ASD agents coming back with her, or that she was now an ASD agent herself.

Fergue would have taken the blame for the theft instead of Akrinn Lemm, had Randl not seen Lemm's involvement.

I had suspicions of how Lemm had gotten the information on Sabrina, but that could wait until later. For now, the ASD knew that Akrinn Lemm was guilty of industrial espionage, murder, and could have ties to the events on Pyrik.

Fergue's parents were on the way, but they'd been on a nearby planet when they received word of Fergue's death.

There was the problem, too, of Lorvis Verll, Sabrina's supposed best friend. Randl indicated her as a person of interest, and the local division of the ASD was now tracking her.

My suspicion was that she and Lemm were together—wherever that was. I think Randl was convinced of the same; he merely hadn't said anything to spare Sabrina's feelings.

There is a connection between Lorvis and Akrinn, Randl confirmed my guess.

I'm grateful Zaria gave you mindspeech. Is there anything else you can tell me?

I don't think those two are on Jaledis any longer. We should probably look at ships leaving the space station shortly after Fergue was killed.

I've got the locals working on that already, I told him. Fergue died too easy—a clear indication that he knew the killer and wasn't expecting this.

Fergue's bloodied body had a hole the size of a grapefruit in its chest. Akrinn Lemm had aimed for the heart at close range. I doubted there was anything left of that vital organ for the pathologists to examine.

Do you think Akrinn has the same thing affecting him as those on Pyrik? I thought to ask.

I can't tell that without seeing him in person, Randl gave a half-shrug. We stood against the wall in Fergue's foyer, watching while the ASD investigators did their job, cataloging evidence and recording images of the crime scene.

Trent had taken Sabrina and the others outside—it was just as well that Sabrina wasn't seeing this, I think. I had no idea how intimate she'd been with this man, but even without that sort of contact, they'd been close at one time—close enough that she'd find this intensely disturbing.

How's she doing? I sent mindspeech to Trent.

She looks green, bro, Trent replied.

Get her out of here, then. If you need to, call the local department physician.

Will do. I'll take them back to the compound, first.

Good idea. Randl and I will be along after a bit.

Is he green?

Nah—looks to have a better stomach for this stuff.

Good. I'll keep you posted if we call for a doctor.

Thanks, bro.

* * *

Sabrina

More than anything, I wanted to vomit after seeing Fergue's body, a huge, bloody hole blasted where his heart should have been.

Don't think about it, I scolded myself. I appeared weak enough in front of the others. No sense in making it worse.

"Come on, I'm taking you back to the compound," Trent announced. He'd probably held a mental conversation with his brother before making that decision. I was grateful, to be honest. If I could only make it to my room, I could curl up in the shower and scream or vomit. Maybe both.

Lorvis.

How long had we been friends?

How long had she and Akrinn—I couldn't finish that thought.

They'd brought lunch for me, that day. I'd left to wash my hands, thinking my lab was safe.

With my friends.

Who hadn't really been my friends, as it turned out.

"Baby, no."

Was that Trent's voice? Blackness came before I could sort it out.

* * *

Travis

"We have Ula Verll in custody," the local Chief walked up to me as Fergue's body was loaded into a hover-van. "She swears she knows nothing, and is having a meltdown over Fergue Biing's death."

"I'd like to take my associate to see her," I said, jerking my head toward Randl.

"If I hadn't heard the same thing from Director Griff a few moments ago, I'd be asking why," he shook his head. "Come on, you can ride with me."

Randl and I climbed into the back seat of the Chief's hover-car and buckled in for the ride to his office.

* * *

Randl

She's not affected, I informed Travis.

"We'd like to interview her, if you don't mind," Travis told Chief Markus.

"I'll come with you," he said and walked us toward the interview room where Ula sat, wiping her eyes with tissues.

"Let me talk to her," I said.

Chief Markus frowned but didn't say anything. Instead, he allowed the scanner to read his right retina before allowing us inside the room.

"Hello, Ula," I said, pulling out a chair to sit across from her. Travis and the Chief stood against the wall behind me. I hoped they didn't look too intimidating.

"You blind?" Ula hiccupped.

"Yes."

"That's fucked up."

"It can be," I admitted. "I see that Mr. Biing's death is a terrible blow for you, and that you genuinely cared for him," I said.

"I loved him," she wiped away more tears. "Still love him. Wait, how can you see that, when you're blind?"

"Call it a gift. You last heard from Fergue this morning, didn't you? He asked you out to dinner, is that correct?"

"Yes. How do you know this?"

"We'll discuss that later. Did you know that Akrinn Lemm was going to visit Fergue after the two of you talked?"

"No. He never said that." She reached for more tissues.

"Were you aware that Akrinn stole something from Sabrina Kend's laboratory last year? Do you remember that day when you, Fergue, Lorvis and Akrinn took lunch to Sabrina?"

"That was a long time ago. Did Akrinn take something?"

"He did. Now, did you also know that Akrinn was the one who urged Fergue to ask Sabrina out?"

"Yes, but it was just—Fergue didn't really feel anything for her."

"He was thinking about the money, wasn't he?"

"I don't feel comfortable talking about that."

"All right. What about Lorvis—are she and Akrinn together?"

"They've been seeing each other on the sly—Lorvis didn't want Sabrina to know about that after Sabrina broke up with Fergue, because Ferge and Akrinn are best friends."

"Do you think that could just be an excuse? Do you think Lorvis could have been distracting you and Fergue while Akrinn took what he wanted from Sabrina's lab?"

"I suppose that's possible, but what does that have to do with Fergue's death?" She covered her face with both hands to muffle a sob.

"Akrinn killed Fergue this morning, shortly after you spoke with Fergue," I said. Ula dropped her hands and stared at me in horror, her mouth working with no sound passing her lips.

"Akrinn set Fergue up to take the blame for what he stole from Sabrina," I went on. "Akrinn then sent a message to Sabrina from Fergue's comp-vid, telling her that Fergue had taken the designs she'd been working on. Those designs, by the way, were recently employed to fire on a ship approaching Pyrik. The ship was destroyed and the crew was killed. Sabrina's comp-vid received the message sent by Akrinn. A spell was laid on Fergue's body, and a laser pistol was placed in his hand. The spell activated when the door opened and the pistol fired."

"Oh, gods, is Sabrina dead, too?"

Chapter 9

*S*abrina

"Take it easy, you've had a trying day," someone said when I jerked awake. When had I gotten on a bed? I couldn't remember that.

"I'm the local agency physician," the man said. "Your Captain called for me right after you fainted. How are you feeling?" he thought to ask.

I felt awful, but didn't want to tell him that. "All right," I croaked. "Can I have water?"

"Yes."

I blinked as Jayna came into view, carrying a water bottle. "Need help sitting up?" she asked.

"Maybe. My head is swimming," I confessed.

"Just as I suspected," the physician said. "Give her water and whatever she can hold down. If things get worse, let me know."

Jayna helped me sit up; I slurped as much water as I could before lying down again and closing my eyes. Maybe meditation would keep terrible thoughts from overwhelming me again. I started by shoving everything out of my mind and thinking about nothing.

* * *

Travis

What do you mean she fainted? I sent.

Physician says she's fine; she was overwhelmed, that's all.

Is she all right now?

Jayna says Sabrina's meditating, probably to get this shit out of her head. Lorvis was her best friend since primary school. That's a big betrayal, bro, laid on top of seeing an ex killed like that. Kooper says he's notified her father.

You think her parents can help?

No idea. When she comes out of her funk, I'll ask.

We're almost done, here. If we don't leave soon, Chief Markus may grab Randl and never let him go after watching him question Ula.

I hope Randl knows how to refuse politely, Trent observed.

Chief Markus doesn't stand a chance against Kooper. Kooper has plans for Randl, and Markus isn't a part of that.

My worry is that Randl would feel smothered in a smaller environment, just as he was in New Fyris. Somehow, I get the feeling that he was made for bigger things.

Yeah. Look, Randl and I will be on our way in a few. We'll talk when I get there.

* * *

Sabrina

I did and didn't want to see my parents. They'd liked Fergue. I'd liked Fergue, until he went behind my back. If you wanted someone else, it was courtesy to notify the one you were already with, so they could make a decision to welcome another into the relationship or walk away. After all, multiple mates were a common thing in both Alliances.

Now I knew how bad the betrayal was—not just by Fergue, but by Lorvis, and that was so much worse.

"Sabrina?" Travis' voice was followed by a tap on my door, which stood slightly ajar.

"Yes?"

"We'd like to come in."

"That's fine." I didn't ask who *we* were—it didn't matter.

He, Randl and Trent walked in together. I drew a breath and let it out slowly. "May I have your personal comp-vid?" Travis held out a hand once he reached the side of my bed.

I knew this was coming. All along, Lorvis and I had a connection application on our comp-vids, so one would always know where the other was. She also suspected the reason I'd returned and passed that information to Akrinn the moment I reached Jaledis.

Fergue and I were both supposed to die, with Fergue taking the blame for industrial espionage.

Without Randl's gift and my conscription by the ASD, I would be dead. I'd have marched right into Fergue's home demanding answers, and I'd have died.

Simple.

Easy.

Lorvis didn't care that I'd die. Those words echoed through my mind as I handed my comp-vid to Travis.

"This it?" Director Griff appeared inside the room and lifted the comp-vid from Travis' hand.

"Yes." I hung my head. How had I been so blind? I then reconsidered my phrasing. Randl was blind, and he could see better than I. I was gullible—something Randl had never been.

"You had no reason to suspect them," Randl said. "Stop beating yourself up about it. What you can do now is tell the Captains what you know about Akrinn and Lorvis. Knowing their habits, food preferences and such may help us track them."

"You'll have a new, untraceable comp-vid by the end of the day," Kooper Griff informed me before disappearing.

"Is that our new mission?" I asked, refusing to look at Travis or Trent. "To find Akrinn and Lorvis?"

"For the next few days, at least," Trent said. "Conclave is set to begin in five days unless it's delayed again. We have a lot to do between now and then. I suggest lunch with your parents, then we'll be on our way. We're still looking into which ship those two could have escaped on, so it'll take about that long to determine which one to follow."

"Randl, want to go look at manifests, to see if you can tell something from any of them?" Travis asked.

"Yes," Randl said. "I hope I can get an idea of where they are."

"Me, too. Sabrina, Trent invited your parents here for lunch. Clean up, all right? We'll catch these assholes, and you can be a part of that."

* * *

Trent

Jayna, Sabrina and I had lunch with Ruther Kend and his wife, Barra. Sabrina was crumbling inside—I could see that easily. As a result, she was pushing food around her plate, drinking too much rice wine and not talking much.

"I'm part Falchani," I answered Ruther Kend's question. "The Falchani genes run strong in my family."

"Is your mother or your father of Falchani descent?" Barra asked.

"My father," I said, offering a smile. "My mother has Karathian and Elemaiyan ancestry."

"That's a strange mix," Ruther observed and dipped noodles expertly from his bowl with chopsticks.

"It seems to work, though," I shrugged.

"What's your father's name?"

"Drew Tatsuya."

"What about your mother?"

I was afraid he'd ask that question. Well, there was nothing for it, I suppose. "My mother is the Queen of Le-Ath Veronis."

Ruther Kend went still. Sabrina's mother stopped chewing. Sabrina's head snapped up and she stared at me in shock.

"Pardon me for being blunt, but what the hells are you doing working for the ASD?" Ruther demanded.

"My family has a strong work ethic," I said and reached for the bottle of rice wine. "My father and grandfather insist on us making ourselves useful. My father and his brother run the Queen's army on Le-Ath Veronis. Travis and I have extensive training on and off the battlefield. Working for the ASD is a very good fit for us."

"I think that's outrageous and wondrous at the same time," Barra admitted. "An actual Prince is my daughter's boss."

"We don't prefer that title—it makes us sound like more than we are," I confessed. "We're regular ASD, nothing more."

Sabrina choked on her rice wine. *Eat*, I told her in mindspeech. *If you don't, you'll pass out before lunch is over.*

An angry frown was her answer, but she lifted noodles to her mouth as instructed.

* * *

Sabrina

I didn't appreciate Trent telling me to eat and stop drinking so much, but he was right. Already I felt dizzy, and wouldn't be particularly coherent if Daddy asked me anything.

The rice wine was taking the edge off my misery, though, and that's why I was drinking so much of it.

"I hear Akrinn and Lorvis stole your work," Daddy leveled a gaze on me. I almost choked again.

Why is it that whenever you want to be alone or unconscious to drive away your troubles in your own way, that's when people tend to crowd around you?

"They did. I only found out this morning."

"Did both kill Fergue? I'm sorry to bring this up, sweet thing, but I need to know," Daddy said.

"Maybe. I know Akrinn was there for sure," I said. "Lorvis— it's so hard to believe." My last words had turned into a choked whisper. We'd confided in one another. Told each other everything.

Had her part always been a lie—even in primary school?

"Word is that both sets of parents are being questioned," Mom huffed. "I hope they didn't know anything about this, or they'll be in prison before the day's over."

"That's routine, Mrs. Kend," Trent interjected smoothly. "It's my guess that their parents knew nothing of this. Akrinn and Lorvis lived separately from their parents, and it isn't unusual for criminals to hide this sort of thing from family members."

"Right under our noses, and we knew nothing about it," Dad shook his head. "I always considered myself a good judge of character. Those two had everybody fooled."

My stomach rumbled after I swallowed a second mouthful of noodles. Trent was correct—I needed to eat. I just hated to give him the satisfaction of being right.

* * *

Chapter 9

Travis and I studied seventeen ships that had cleared Jaledis' orbit after Fergue's murder. My senses tingled every time I saw the *Strafer*. Travis sent all the images to Quin, for a second opinion. We now waited for a reply.

All look normal except the Strafer, came her reply. *Not that it doesn't look normal, too, it's just that it feels—empty.*

Travis was in silent communication with Kooper immediately, and three ASD ships, including BlackWing VII, were sent after it.

"Tell them to approach with caution," I said. After the way Fergue died and the spell that was laid on his body to kill another, I was wary.

"Will do." Travis wore a grim expression as he relayed the message to Kooper. Afterward, Travis and I turned our attention to the vid-camera images at the dock where *Strafer* was berthed before she left Jaledis.

"Here," I pointed at the images of two who walked toward the gangway leading to *Strafer*.

"That's not them," Travis said, zooming in on the images.

"You say that, because you can't see past the spelled disguises," I sighed. What I saw was an outer shell, covering Akrinn and Lorvis. Both appeared to be males and taller than they actually were.

"That has to be a really good spell," Travis whispered and ran the images back so he could look again. "I'll ask for the local office to run a recognition program, to match movements instead. I've already requested a manifest for passengers and cargo."

A few moments later, we had the records Travis wanted. I went over the manifest while Travis reviewed images taken of Lorvis and Akrinn, while the ship's comp compared them to the two I'd pointed out near *Strafer*.

"May I send this to Quin?" I asked after leaning back in my chair. "Something feels—strange."

"Go ahead. Kooper trusts her with everything."

"Good." I sent the manifest to Quin right away.

I see the words on the screen, she sent mindspeech back. *But it feels as if they're empty, too.*

What about this? I sent the vid-images of the disguised Lorvis and Akrinn to her.

I get the same feeling from them, Quin reported. *The outside is empty.*

Then that leads me to believe that there were spells on whatever the ship carried, too, I replied. *The list of parts and supplies is legitimate. What they actually loaded onto the ship probably isn't. I think Lorvis and Akrinn may have had collaborators and masterminds all along. They'd have to, in order to get Sabrina's design data off the planet to begin with.*

Yes. Transmitting data would leave a trail. Carrying a spelled comp-vid or something else that contained the information could be gotten away easily. Whoever is casting these spells is very strong and talented, I think.

What if Lorvis and Akrinn were recruited by the ones they escaped with? I asked. *I worry that the idea to take Sabrina's technology may not have been their idea at the beginning.*

Very possible, she agreed. *In fact, I think it likely. They may have been behind the idea to kill Fergue if any of their subterfuge was discovered. Killing Sabrina would only be secondary to getting away with their misdeeds.*

Since Sabrina's technology was used to destroy the ship heading toward Pyrik, then these have to be connected to that in some way. I wish I could have seen them myself, to determine whether any carry the affliction.

Chapter 9

Lissa says Karzac is examining the bodies remotely, in an attempt to isolate the disease—if that's what it is. So far, I haven't heard any results.

Please let me know if you hear something, I begged. *This is far too confusing.*

I agree. I've never encountered anything so puzzling in my life. Usually I can detect diseases easily. Not this, and I fail to understand that.

Thank you for your help, I said. *You've confirmed my thoughts on this, and I am grateful.*

Then don't hesitate to ask again, she replied. *Send mindspeech anytime. I think this is too important to employ proper etiquette in requesting assistance.*

As you say, I agreed. *Please feel free to do the same.*

"How long will it take before our ships catch up to *Strafer*?" I turned to Travis.

"A day—two at the most. We'll be underway and traveling in that direction before nightfall."

I sagged in my chair. I wanted it done now—and I didn't. The thought of what we could find aboard that ship troubled me.

* * *

Mer'bali, Pyrik

Lissa

"I have the how, but not the what. That is still being processed."

I'd never seen Karzac looking so tired or stressed. He leaned back on the easy chair inside my suite, closed his eyes and pinched the bridge of his nose.

"The how?" I poured a cup of tea for him inside my suite.

"A small disc inserted in the body, just outside the liver," Karzac said. "The disc is designed to expand and puncture the liver if it is exposed to air. It then sprays a bit of bile outward. I imagine that whatever is affecting these people will infect anyone who breathes it in or has contact through exposed skin. The clear hoods worn by the physicians in this case would not be enough, I think, to keep it away."

"What is it?" I asked.

"I don't know, yet. What I know is this—I've never seen anything like it. I'd like to speak with Randl—he was the first to notice it."

"Feel up to hopping onto BlackWing X?" I asked.

"In the morning. The lab-bots are still testing the tissue samples, and I hope to know more by then."

"I can order dinner in, if you'd like."

"I would prefer that."

"Then it's done," I replied.

* * *

BlackWing X

Randl

"We have information from Uncle Karzac," Trent set his breakfast tray opposite mine and pulled out a chair in the galley.

"What information?" I looked up from my egg and ham scramble.

"There was a small device inserted into the bodies, right outside the liver. Mom says it's an old technology, that was used at one time to help diabetics by pumping an emergency ration of insulin into the body. This time, it was used for something else. Karzac thinks it was to spray a micro-mist of bile into the air, so it would either be inhaled or touch exposed skin. Those physicians weren't wearing biohazard suits when they examined the bodies."

"So they were hit with whatever came out in the spray?"

"Looks that way. Karzac is still trying to figure out what that could be. If Uncle Karzac hasn't seen it before, then it didn't exist before."

Trent wore a frown as he snapped a piece of crisp bacon in half and stuffed it in his mouth.

"Uncle Karzac wants to talk to you, too," Trent went on after chewing and swallowing. "Since you're the first one to notice that something was wrong with those people."

"I can't answer much, because I don't know either," I pointed out.

"He knows that. Don't worry, Karzac's more bark than bite."

"Did you intend to make it worse?" I blinked at Trent.

"He and his brother have a penchant for making things worse," Karzac himself pulled out a chair for Queen Lissa, then seated himself at the table after she was comfortable. He had light-brown hair, green-gold eyes that could measure anyone in a matter of moments and a no-nonsense approach to everything, including taking a seat at the breakfast table.

"Hey, Mom," Travis leaned toward Lissa and gave her a peck on the cheek.

"Good to see you again," Karzac gave me a nod and a half smile while extending his hand politely.

"Pleased to have you aboard," I shook with him. To everyone else, Karzac appeared to be a gruff physician, who wasn't accustomed to being questioned or gainsaid. I saw past that, to the caring soul behind the exterior.

"Did young Trent inform you of our findings?" Karzac asked immediately.

"He told me about the device, which appears to spray a micro-mist of bile into the air," I said. "Has it been redesigned to react to oxygen or something?"

"I believe so." Karzac nodded his thanks as Susan set plates of food down for him and the Queen. "I also believe that the cells contained in the livers of the affected ones are mutated—likely from the leaking radiation from the waste dumps we've discovered on Pyrik. What the affliction is, however, continues to elude me."

"Quin and I are baffled as to how an obsession, such as the one affecting the four physicians, can be passed from one to another."

"I've never heard of anything like that," Lissa said. "Obsessions always had to be placed directly by a Sirenali—until now."

"Do you think the mutation and whatever it is that causes the affliction to be passed from one to another is concentrated in the victim's liver?"

"Radiation poisoning and any subsequent mutation can take many forms," Karzac sighed. "You could be correct, however, since the devices were placed in the same location on all three bodies. I hesitate to make an examination on the four physicians, but it will have to be done."

"They won't have the devices," I said.

"Yes, but a biopsy of their liver will have to be handled carefully. I don't want an epidemic of obsession burning through Pyrik."

"What about the original prisoner?" I asked. "Will he have a device?"

"Possibly," Karzac appeared thoughtful. "My dearest, shall we travel to Le-Ath Veronis from here?" He turned his gaze on Lissa.

"That's fine with me," she shrugged.

"They've found the *Strafer*," Trent interrupted. "No signs of life aboard."

"We'll stay for this," Lissa said and rose from the table with a nod. I scrambled to my feet to bow to her.

Chapter 9

"Honey, that's not necessary," she placed a hand on my shoulder. "Let's go see what Travis found for us."

* * *

Sabrina

I couldn't hide in my cabin feeling sorry for myself any longer—an alert sounded for the crew to assemble near the bridge. We were closing in on the *Strafer*, if my guess were correct.

Time to see what sort of mess Lorvis and Akrinn left behind. If I said I didn't feel the hottest kind of fury for Lorvis and her betrayal, then I'd be lying.

When I joined the crowd in the assembly room, I found two new passengers. Queen Lissa and one of her mates had joined us. I'd been wallowing in anger and self-pity and hadn't known of their arrival.

This is Travis and Trent's mother, I reminded myself.

The *Queen* of Le-Ath Veronis.

A *vampire*.

Holy, fucking hells.

"We found the *Strafer*," Randl said quietly when I stopped beside him and attempted to tighten the tie holding my hair back. Against the wall, a vid-screen showed an image of the ship, transferred from the bridge.

The ship floated before us, while two other ships lay at intervals around her. I realized that those two ships and the Raptor II formed a triangle surrounding the targeted vessel.

No ship was in a direct line of fire from its allies, either—by design.

"There are no signs of life," Jayna joined Randl and me. She held a cup of tea in her hands as she gazed at the vid-screen.

"Empty of life," Randl breathed beside me. "I sense bodies," he added. I stiffened at his words.

"How many?" Jayna asked. "Can you sense that, too?"

"Two," Randl replied. "Lorvis and Akrinn."

* * *

Travis

"Akrinn and Lorvis performed their duty, and then were destroyed because they weren't needed any longer. The ASD was on their tail, and they'd become a liability," Kooper Griff paced inside the Captain's cubby. "I figure the ship is set for destruction if anybody sets foot on it. Your mother has offered to *Pull* the bodies away, but the only ship that has a shielded containment compartment is the Melody IV."

"In case the bodies explode?" I asked.

"Or worse," Kooper said. "The containment compartment is set to hold a violent explosion, and Karzac has offered to shield it further, so nothing will be damaged. He's already working on scanning the bodies for any devices, and Ilya Ironsmith is on the way to check for spells of any kind."

"This thing is getting worse by the second, isn't it?" I asked. If Kooper called for a Fifth-level warlock, who many suspected could be a Sixth-level, then he was very worried.

"We've already started moving people farther away from those dump sites, but somebody is using the damage already done to their advantage. What I want to know is this—how the fuck did they know to focus on the mutation to begin with?"

"No idea," I said. "But we'll keep looking for answers, you can count on that."

"What if we're running out of time?" Kooper stopped pacing and frowned at me. "We may have to postpone the Conclave again; it's targeted in some way; you can count on that."

"They tipped their hand when they tried to kill Riffler," I said.

Chapter 9

"They would have killed Riffler and Sabrina, if Sabrina hadn't carried a ranos pistol and if Randl hadn't warned us in time. With Riffler dead and his attackers on the loose, we'd be worse off than we are now, because we wouldn't know anything. Hell, we almost don't know anything, now."

"With Sabrina gone before she could examine those images, we wouldn't know it was her stolen technology," I nodded. "Akrinn and Lorvis would probably still be alive and operating on Jaledis. We've put a crimp in the enemy's plan, Director."

"At what cost? They have a powerful wizard or warlock at their command, and a disease or whatever this is, to pass an obsession from one person to the next. That's more than frightening, Captain Tetsuya."

"I understand that," I said. "I worry about how many of them are out there, and whether they intend to make more. Was industrial espionage the only thing Lorvis and Akrinn were doing, or were they into other things?"

"The local office is going through all their activities—the ones we can track, anyway," Kooper said. "Chief Markus is scheduled to keep us updated. I'd like dates and times when those two were pulled into this, too."

"Shields up, with extras," Trent poked his head in the door. "Mom's about to make the move."

"You think the *Strafer* will explode the minute those bodies disappear?" I asked Kooper.

"I'd say there's more than a ninety percent chance of it," he replied.

* * *

Sabrina

I have no idea why I'd been allowed to witness this, but I stood on the back of the bridge with Randl and Jayna, while Queen Lissa raised a hand and employed power I hadn't known existed.

No wonder Travis and Trent were so talented. Their mother was extremely powerful, if she could do something like this.

Her physician mate, Karzac, was already on the Melody IV, waiting for the bodies to be deposited inside a containment compartment. That ship would be on its way to Le-Ath Veronis shortly after.

We were ready for a resulting blast, once the bodies were removed, too. All ASD ships had moved back and had full shields up, waiting for that explosion.

I wish I could say we were disappointed.

The blast that resulted the moment Lorvis and Akrinn's bodies were moved would have destroyed any ship that hadn't taken extreme precautions.

As it was, the explosion rocked the Raptor II anyway, knocking half of us to the floor.

* * *

Melody IV

Lissa

"The ship was emptied, except for those two bodies and the spell laid on it," I told Kooper. "Either the spell caster was aboard when the *Strafer* left Jaledis, or he's stronger than we think."

"Maybe both," Kooper set his tea on the table inside the *Melody's* galley and took a chair, weariness in his posture as he sat.

"Yeah. I worry about that, too," I said. "He could have been aboard the whole time the ship was docked, wearing a spell that would hide him from anything and anybody."

"I think Randl might have seen him, but he'd have to be close enough to do it," Kooper sipped his tea.

Chapter 9

"Kooper, you need sleep," I told him. "If you refuse, Karzac may have something to say about that."

"How long until we reach Le-Ath Veronis?"

"Six hours."

"Tell the physician to meet me in my quarters in fifteen," Kooper grimaced. "I'd welcome a healing sleep."

Chapter 10

R*aptor II*

Sabrina

If I were at home, my parents would have called a physician specializing in mental problems by now. My circumstances would be laughable if they weren't so fucking tragic.

I should be mourning a friend's death—the best friend I'd had since primary school. Instead, I vacillated between anger and depression. The conflict made me want to throw things—or cry.

"Come on." Randl's hand gripped my shoulder. "Let's go work out with weights. I always find doing something physical helps with conflicting thoughts."

How had he found me in the supply room?

Never mind.

I didn't want to go with him; I forced myself to stand and follow him anyway. My rising wasn't as graceful as Travis and Trent's; I recalled that I wanted to work on that—before things blew up in my face and friends plotted my murder.

It was after hours and I should have been in my cabin, preparing for bed. Randl padded softly ahead of me, his feet and chest bare, clothed in loose-fitting trousers that many used for training or exercise.

Randl's chest wasn't broad or muscled like the twins, but he was trim enough and had nothing to be embarrassed about.

Racks of weights in the exercise room awaited us as the auto-light blinked on. "Stretch, first," Randl called over his shoulder and bent over to touch his toes. Following his lead, I bent over, too, discovering that I was still sore from the workout two days before.

By the time we were finished stretching, my muscles didn't feel as cramped as they had when we started.

"Now we do the leg press," Randl strode toward two machines on one side. "I hear you should start out light and build up from there."

I ended up flat on my back on the bench, pushing weights up with my legs and then lowering them. Up and back, up and back.

"Don't forget to breath," Travis' face appeared over mine.

"Why are you here?" I blew out a breath.

"This is our time," he grinned at me.

"Huh?"

"Bro and I come in late, before bedtime, and whack each other with practice swords," he said. "If you finish with your weights and don't hurt yourself, you can even watch."

"You have so little faith—ugh," I pushed the weight up again, "In me," I blew out another breath.

"On the contrary," he lifted an eyebrow. "I expect the very best from those who show the most promise."

"Right—ugh."

"Come on, you've done enough of that. Much more and Jayna will kill you in the morning."

Chapter 10

Great. We were back to learning fighting and self-defense.

"We've set a course for Pyrik, if you're curious," he stood aside while I rolled stiffly off the bench. "Bend over and stretch your back and legs again," he added. My hair, which was only tied back with a single band, flopped in my face as I bent over.

How did I think to get through the day without embarrassment, depression and anger?

"Come on, ponytail, sit against the wall with Randl. We'll show you how the Falchani do things."

* * *

"Ponytail?" I mouthed at Randl, hoping he'd see my mouth to decipher my question.

The way you have your hair up, he informed me in mindspeech.

He was still shirtless, and the gold medallion he wore around his neck rose and fell with his breaths.

"Does yours have your name on it, too?" I asked, trying to keep my face from heating again.

"It has my name, and a quote," he said, lifting it and turning it over, so I could see the engraving.

"Touch the stars?" I squinted at the small words.

"It's a book title—a classical piece and required reading in some classrooms," he said.

"Hmmph. I didn't read it. What's it about?"

"About a young man who wants adventure, so he joins the ASD in its infancy, to explore other worlds. He doesn't really find himself until he goes home and examines his familial roots."

"Sounds enlightening."

"You know I can sense sarcasm from several clicks away."

"Right." To hide my embarrassment, I turned toward Travis and Trent, then, who appeared to be done with their stretching routine. A large, metal chest shoved against a wall was then opened and Trent drew out four dull, polished blades.

Shortly after, their shirts came off and I blinked at the dragon tattoos running up and down their arms. Travis' dragons gleamed like deep blue sapphires on his skin, while Trent's shone like emeralds.

Until then, I hadn't considered that they'd fight with more than one sword apiece. After only a few moments of the brothers going after each other with a blade in each hand, my mouth dropped open.

They were experts at this, and I never thought to see anything like it—unless I wished to visit Falchan.

I hear you have to start training in this very young, Randl's mindspeech held a hint of wistfulness.

"How long have they had training?" I asked, raising my voice as the clanging of blades grew louder and the movement faster between the brothers.

Since they were seven, came the answer.

It made me wonder how old they were.

In their fifties, but they're immortal so age means nothing, Randl answered my unspoken question. *Their tattoos have to be earned—each one of them, so you can see how many times they've been rewarded for valor.*

I closed my eyes as any hope I had for a relationship with either fled. I was nearly thirty, mortal and had barely done anything valorous. Why would those two want me in three years—or thirty or three hundred, for that matter?

It was the worst ending to one of the worst days of my life. If I could have left the room without anyone noticing, I would have. As it was, the sparring took up the entire floor—what wasn't covered by exercise equipment, anyway.

Chapter 10

I don't think it matters one damn bit to them, Randl's voice floated into my mind. *They're interested, it's just not allowed, according to ASD regulations.*

With my eyes still closed, I blew out a sigh and struggled not to weep.

* * *

After the twins were finished, Randl and I left the exercise room. By that time, I was exhausted and hoped I'd be able to sleep. I didn't see the enormous bouquet of flowers on my tiny bedside table until I'd shut my cabin door.

A small, paper note was nestled among beautiful rose buds and lilies. *A loss, whether by betrayal, death or both, is still a loss*, it read. *Condolences—Queen Lissa.*

I wiped tears away before touching fragile petals with trembling fingers.

* * *

Randl

"Grip the pistol in your dominant hand first, then place your other hand on the opposite side, covering your dominant fingers with the others," Travis instructed. "Hold tightly with the non-dominant hand to reinforce your dominant hand, because you want a firm grip on the weapon. My teachers always said to hold it so hard your hands shake, and then loosen your grip just until the shaking stops. That will give you enough control. Touch here for single fire, here for rapid fire."

I held a replica of a laser pistol in my hands while Travis showed me how to fire the thing after breakfast. We had nearly two full day's journey to Pyrik, and the crew took advantage of the time to teach Sabrina and me.

Somewhere else, Jayna worked with Sabrina on similar lessons while Trent captained BlackWing X. Sabrina and I stretched, did weight training and ran on treadmills together before breakfast, while Jayna supervised.

I looked forward to running outside sometime soon, so I could see and experience new things.

Sabrina didn't talk much during our combined training, but I noticed a new determination in her—to put recent deaths behind her and move forward. She also had a new goal, and that was to find whomever had orchestrated the theft of her design and have them arrested.

I wondered if our opposition realized how angry she'd be, or that a brilliant mind was now focused on finding them.

"Now," Travis instructed, "while holding the weapon firmly with both hands, point it at the target in front of you."

A three-dimensional image roughly resembling a humanoid was directly before me. "Lock your elbows in place," he pushed my arms into the proper position. "Use the sight image the pistol displays above the barrel, to aim at the target. Now, fire once," he added.

The replica jerked in my hand, just as the actual weapon would, surprising me. A harmless laser image was sent out, which the target recorded as the place I'd hit.

"Hmmm, lower abdomen," Travis said with a frown. "You wounded him—not fatal, but bloody. This is why it's important to lock your elbows and keep arm movement at a minimum. Do all that and you'll hit your targets accurately. Don't worry, nobody's perfect when they start out. Practice will make you better. Have you read the information regarding safety standards for carrying a weapon?"

"Twice," I said.

"Good. Lift your weapon, sight your target, lock your elbows and hold your breath before firing this time."

* * *

Chapter 10

Sabrina

"Not bad." Jayna walked around the three-dimensional target, examining it where my shots had hit. I'd hit it three times in the chest, twice slightly lower. "Get your arm movement under control and I'll have you certified in no time."

The fake laser pistol I held had much more kick than the ranos pistol I'd designed. If I'd had my own weapon, all five shots would have been in the proper area.

"Does a standard issue ranos pistol have the same kick?" I asked Jayna.

"Almost the same—slightly less, I think."

"My design has practically no kick," I said. "If Director Griff has taken the time to fire it, he should know that by now."

"I think he's been more fascinated by the shield you incorporated," Jayna said, turning to frown at me. "I'll pass the information to Captain Trent, though. Director Griff needs to know that."

"If I were in my lab, I could make enough of the new design for the crew," I said.

"I'll share that with Captain Trent, too. How long would it take?" she thought to ask.

"I could have them in a day, but the calibration would take longer."

"I'll let the Captain know. Why don't you use the time before lunch to watch training vids and study?"

"I'll do that," I agreed, handing the weapon back to her. "Is it possible to get tea from the galley before I do that?"

"Of course. Just ask Susan or Bekzi. They'll have a snack for you, too, if you want it. By the way, both are fully-trained as backups for us, and neither misses when they shoot."

"So everybody aboard the Raptor," I began.

"It's time you knew," Jayna interrupted, holding up a hand. "You're actually aboard BlackWing X. The entire BlackWing Pirate fleet is run by the ASD."

"Fucking hells," I breathed as Jayna grinned at me. "I guess this is something I can't tell anybody, including my father?"

"Got it in one," Jayna laughed. "Get a snack and tea, then contemplate your new life as a pirate."

* * *

I'm sure they expected me to research the BlackWing Pirates, once I learned I was a member of that elite and nefarious crew. So many sites claimed they were the worst of the worst, and had shot down or taken many ships since their origin roughly fifteen years earlier.

How many of those things were true, and which were planted by the ASD to provide cover?

Rampant speculation ran through the same sites, as to which criminal faction or legally-operating conglomerate actually backed the BlackWing bunch.

None were even close to the truth.

I wondered if the CSD was aware. Perhaps I'd ask Travis or Trent. Another thought hit me—had Randl known all along? He knew everything else. He must be a treasury of hidden secrets, because I'd had no clue.

Randl was the perfect ASD operative, in my opinion. His blindness labeled him as non-threatening. Travis and Trent were teaching him how to protect himself, and how to shoot—I'd gotten that information from Jayna.

Perhaps I appeared to be much the same. Those who'd attempted to kill Jett Riffler could attest to that. They hadn't expected me to have a weapon. If I hadn't broken the law and carried one, Riffler and I would be dead while Akrinn and Lorvis would still be alive.

Honestly, I was glad to be the one who lived.

"Lorvis, what did you do?" I spoke softly before powering on my vid-screen. I had plenty to learn before I took the ASD exams to become a full-fledged agent.

* * *

Mer'bali, Pyrik
Winkler

"That woman is more of a genius than I originally thought," Kooper dumped salt and pepper on his steak before cutting into it.

I'd been invited to have lunch with him, while Lukas met with Rodrik and several others to discuss the drawbacks of the logging industry.

"How's that?" I asked before stuffing a chunk of rare prime rib in my mouth.

"Not only did she design an effective shield for her ranos pistol, but the kick a pistol normally has is practically eliminated."

"Sounds like an excellent design," I said after a moment.

"I've had some of my weapons experts working with it all morning. They can't stop raving about it," Kooper said. "I heard from Trent that Sabrina can provide those pistols for the ship's crew in a day's time, with a bit of calibration afterward. She can probably have them armed successfully in two or three days, if they'll take her back to her lab."

"That's when Conclave is set to start again, or close enough," I pointed out. "Have there been any updates on the presidency?"

"They're still fighting each other, and the vote could be days if not weeks away. I'd like to reschedule the Conclave. It would give us time to investigate everything that's going on without endangering more people, but that could cause the enemy to withdraw into whatever hole they crawled out of to cause trouble."

"Is there a way to postpone it for a month or two, then? Send the attendees home and bring them back? It would be safer for them, no doubt, and the hole crawlers would still be plotting, you can count on it."

"I'll talk to Ildevar and Teeg. They'll have the final say on this."

"I'd say get to talking, then. You need room to maneuver—don't tell me that's not true."

"You're right. They'll complain about the expense, but then nobody expected the president to go nuts, hide nuclear waste dumps and try to kill the Director of the CSD over it."

"Maybe you can fudge a little, and say you're securing the dump sites because there are noticeable irregularities in some residents."

"Well, that's a thought," Kooper considered my words. "I'll suggest that to Teeg and Ildevar when we talk. Maybe they'll see the sense in it and send everybody home with a legitimate excuse."

"It's not an excuse," I pointed out. "Something's going on, and it's worse than just a few irregularities. That's to make sure everybody isn't scared witless over this."

"True enough. When we're done here, I'll see about a word from our sponsors."

"That's funnier than you think," I pointed my fork at him.

* * *

Randl

"The official word has been given—Conclave is postponed for two months, so authorities can research irregularities caused by the waste dumps, and give Pyrik time to elect a new president."

Chapter 10

Trent had called us together to make the announcement. "That means," he added, "that we'll be heading back to Jaledis, so Sabrina can ply her trade and get us equipped with the latest and greatest."

"Will we stay with your uncles again?" Jayna asked.

"That's the plan," Trent grinned. "We'll be safe there, and there's plenty of room for exercise and fresh air. It'll also give us the chance to work with the locals in their search for Akrinn's and Lorvis' contacts."

"At least Lorvis won't know where I am, anymore," Sabrina mumbled beside me.

"She only knew where your comp-vid was, not you," I whispered back.

"Yeah."

Neither of us pointed out that Lorvis was beyond knowing anything, any longer. Her contacts wouldn't have any knowledge of Sabrina's whereabouts, at least. Lorvis' comp-vid, which hadn't been with Lorvis' body, was no longer of any use to them.

"We're putting a new logo on the ship—we're now officially *Gloria I*," Trent grinned. "Just in case anybody asks."

* * *

Sabrina

"How many disguises does the ship have?" I asked at dinner. Jayna, Randl and Travis sat at the table with me while we discussed the new ranos designs, among other things.

"We have six disguises, all with proper identification, issued by both Alliances," Travis said. "Jayna told you about BlackWing X, that's our seventh identity. There's one more thing, too," he added.

"What's that?"

"It'll be a full moon when we land in Jaledis," Travis said.

"So?" I had no idea where he was going with this.

"That means David and Susan will change. Bekzi could change too, but he doesn't have to."

"Change clothes?" I still didn't get it.

"No, they're shapeshifters. David is an owl; Susan is a hen. Bekzi—you don't want to know."

"You're joking? A hen? I've never heard of anyone becoming a hen. Predatory animals, yes, but a hen?"

"I'm a Buff Orpington," Susan walked up to our table wearing a deep frown.

"I'm sorry. A what?"

"Buff Orpington. They're not native to either Alliance."

I'd offended her, clearly. "My apologies," I stood and dipped my head to her. "I'm just—uneducated, it appears."

By that time the heat in my face had become furnace-worthy and I almost tripped over my own feet stepping away. "I'm going to—ah—bed," I turned and walked quickly out of the galley before I made things worse.

* * *

Trent

"Susan thinks she upset Sabrina." David set a comp-vid in front of me, with the latest hyperdrive specs. So far, the systems were functioning normally.

"About what?" I looked up from David's report.

"Travis told her that Susan and I would be changing when we reached Jaledis, because of the full moon. Sabrina's never heard of a shapeshifting hen. To be fair, Sabrina sort of started it, but Susan couldn't help but pretend to be offended that she'd never heard of a Buff Orpington, before."

"Can you take the bridge while I go talk to her?"

"Sure. All I have to do is steer, right?"

"Don't touch the steering wheel," I teased.

Chapter 10

"I would if it had one," David called after me as I walked away.

* * *

Sabrina

I considered ignoring the knock on my cabin door, but thought better of it. Crawling off my bunk, I walked the few steps to answer it.

Travis and Trent stood outside.

"We thought a short debriefing on the crew might be in order," Trent cleared his throat.

"We'll leave the door open," Travis shouldered his way into my narrow room. Both leaned against the opposite wall while I sat on my bunk, waiting to be enlightened.

"Everybody aboard ship—except you—has mindspeech," Travis began. "As you've already been told, David, Bekzi and Susan are shapeshifters. Terrett is Sirenali. We'll discuss his special talents later."

"Everybody has mindspeech? Including the chicken?" I squeaked. *I* wanted mindspeech. *I* wanted to fold space, too.

"Can Susan fold space?" I demanded.

"No, but Terrett can," Trent answered.

"Of course he can," I tossed up a hand in resignation. "Does the hen lay eggs, too?"

"Never," Trent shook his head in an exaggerated manner.

"Almost never," Travis shook his head.

They were teasing me. I bit back a laugh.

"Susan isn't just a cook," Travis became serious. "She fought in the battle for Kifirin a decade ago. When you can say something similar, then you can make fun of the chicken."

"I didn't mean to. It's—I feel so left out," I mumbled, dropping my eyes.

"We know. But don't let your feelings of inadequacy harm another," Trent said. "Susan would die to protect your life—that's how brave and committed she is. She also likes to cook, so she serves double duty aboard ship, as does Bekzi."

"Sorry. I should have realized that an ASD ship would have a fully-trained crew aboard."

"Look, we know you've been through a lot, lately, so we can excuse some of your behavior. Just don't let it happen again," Travis said, pulling away from the wall.

"Yeah. I'm sorry. Tell Susan I didn't mean to upset her."

"She knows."

My face burned as the brothers walked out of my cabin and shut the door behind them. It was their job to maintain order on the ship. I had a lot to learn and a long, long way to go.

* * *

Even Randl wasn't speaking to me when we disembarked from the ship early that morning. If I'd had mindspeech, I'd apologize to him, too. After lying awake most of the night, I realized that I'd treated Susan's shapeshifting ability as a disability, and her job on the ship as a reason to think less of her.

Randl could easily take my words to heart, too, because his eyes didn't work.

He saw with his mental vision, which was his way of compensating for his blindness. I felt like the worst asshole in both Alliances after coming to that conclusion.

As we'd already gone through our exercises and had a rather subdued breakfast aboard ship, my lab was our first destination after landing on Jaledis.

I'd led the way toward the door to my lab, ready to submit to hand and eye scans when Randl shouted mentally for me to back away.

Chapter 10

We're being watched, he informed us. *Like someone was watching the building in Mer'bali.*

"Well, I think we ought to go visit the uncles," Trent declared, and just like that, we all turned away from my lab door and walked out of the facility.

* * *

Randl

Ilya Ironsmith arrived shortly after we'd settled in at Turtle and Flyer's compound. "You're sure it feels the same?" Ilya asked. "Since I wasn't the one to check the other building, I really need as much information as you can give me."

"It feels exactly the same," I said. "I could feel the prickle of unseen eyes all over me."

"This puts a crimp in our plans to make additional weapons," Travis pointed out. "We need Sabrina's design and her machinery to do that."

Ilya looked thoughtful for a moment. "How difficult would it be to confiscate the contents of her lab—by the local ASD office? Say it's evidence in an industrial espionage case—because it is."

"Randl?" Trent looked in my direction. "Do you think it's only the lab, or the space it occupies that we need to worry about?"

"I think it may be just the space, but if everything inside it is crated up and hauled away to a secure location, I can get a feel for the crates and let you know if anything from the lab is affected."

"That sounds like an excellent idea," Travis said. "And, if I put in a request now, I can have a High Demon crew come in to pack everything up. If a spell is responsible for this, they'll nullify it."

"High Demons nullify spells?" Sabrina whispered.

"When they're within a certain range," Trent explained, "and it's usually temporary. When they leave, the spell is the same as before, unless the one placing it removes it, as they did in Mer'bali."

175

"Do you think they didn't want a closer examination of the spell used?" Terrett asked. He didn't speak often, but when he did, everyone listened.

"That's what Wellend said," Travis agreed. "The type of spell could leave a signature of some sort, leading them to the spell caster. When Wellend showed up, the spell disappeared."

"You don't think the caster will know the High Demons are nullifying it?" Susan asked.

"I doubt it—usually they only notice if the wizard or warlock can't fold space or make an adverse spell work in the presence of a High Demon," Ilya replied. "I've seen it happen," he added.

"How many do you think it will take to crate everything and move it?" Travis asked Sabrina.

"Half a dozen or more," she sighed. "Please tell them to be careful."

"I'll make sure of it," Travis nodded. "Ilya, would you like to travel with me to Kifirin?"

"I'll drive," he laughed and both disappeared.

* * *

Veshtul, Kifirin
Travis

"Kory, we need at least six High Demons to pack up lab equipment on Jaledis," I told Kordevik Weth, Crown Prince of Kifirin.

"That tells me there's a spell involved somewhere," Kory grinned at me. "Lexsi and Reah got in last night, and they say there's something other than waste dumps involved in all this."

"There is," Ilya said. "We need the equipment away from the building, so I can check the type of spell laid."

"You got it. I've got a few who are careful enough, I think, to pack up sensitive equipment. How soon?"

"Now," I shrugged. "If they're available."

"Have lunch with me, and they'll be ready to go back with you," Kory said.

* * *

Sabrina

"I'm sorry, Randl," I said, touching his arm lightly. "I just wasn't thinking."

"You'd be surprised how often that happens," he said, although he refused to turn and look at me.

"That people inadvertently mistreat others?"

"I was talking about people not thinking, but the other is true, too. I know you've had trauma in your life, and that you saved lives with your abilities in the past. Yet you look down on the woman who feeds you aboard ship, as if she's somehow not as important."

"I wish I had some of your talent for seeing things about people," I sighed, dropping my face in my hands. "I'm confined within my own brain matter, though. I hope you can look past that, sometime soon. I miss having a friend and ally."

"I can understand that. You've recently experienced loss and betrayal. Try not to pass that along, all right?"

"Yeah." I dropped my hands and stared at his ear, because he still had his face turned away. "Will you look at me, at least?"

"I can't," he admitted.

I gasped at his bluntness.

"Not for the reasons you might think," he held up a hand. "It's just difficult for me to see you in so much pain."

I sobbed before I could stop myself.

Chapter 11

urbak, Jaledis

Trent

"Everything is out of Sabrina's lab and on its way to a local ASD warehouse," Travis dropped onto the floor cushions next to mine. "The High Demons are already back on Kifirin."

"Are we saving the trek to the warehouse until after dinner?"

"Yes. No sense in trailing the hover-vans now—they'll have to unload everything first, before we can have Randl take a look. Besides, if anything is affected, it will have to be separated from the rest and locked away. Ilya will visit the lab in the morning, to see if the spell is still in place."

"You think it will be?"

"No idea. In Mer'bali, it's as if the spell could sense another spell caster and expired immediately."

"Is that common?" I asked. I wasn't an expert on anything to do with a wizard's or warlock's spells. Our older brother, on the other hand, *was* an expert, as was our older sister.

"You think Ry and Nissa would have dinner with us?" I sat up straighter and turned toward Travis.

"Maybe," Travis shrugged. "I'll send mindspeech and find out."

* * *

Sabrina

"We're going to Karathia for dinner," Travis announced after I answered his knock on the door. "Wear something suitable for dinner with the King."

"You know the King of Karathia?" I asked.

Travis grinned. "Ry's my older brother."

"Are there any other important family members you haven't mentioned?" I asked.

"Sure. Be ready in an hour."

I watched him saunter away, wondering why he hadn't informed me in mindspeech that we were going to dinner.

Randl's words came back to me then; *they're interested*, he'd said. I sighed and closed my cabin door.

* * *

Randl

Morrett was more than happy to see me when we landed in King Rylend's palace vestibule. He was happy to see his brother Terrett, too. Another guest arrived that I knew; Master Morwin had come with Chloe, his wife.

I understood then that Morwin was related to David by marriage.

"Young one," Morwin came to shake my hand. "How are you getting along?"

"You were taught by Morwin?" Travis and Trent now flanked me.

"Yes."

*T*urbak, Jaledis
Trent

Chapter 11

"You must be special," Trent slapped my back. "Morwin taught us and our brothers and sister, plus he's teaching Quin's daughter now."

"I owed a debt," Morwin's lengthy, red eyebrows wiggled as he drew himself up and glared sternly at the twins. "The payment was teaching this one, which turned into a decided pleasure."

"You owed somebody?" Travis teased. "I've never heard of such."

"I owed Zaria. I still do."

Zaria. My hand immediately went to my chest, where the medallion she'd given me lay beneath my shirt. Travis and Trent had gone silent while watching my swift reaction to Zaria's name.

"What did you owe Zaria for?" Travis turned back to Morwin.

"I will not say; it is a private matter." Morwin's tone informed all of us that this path of conversation was now closed.

"It's good to see you," I said. "And your wife, too." I'd only seen Chloe a time or two, but Morwin clearly loved her more than anything.

"Please, come in." King Rylend himself had come to welcome us. Beckoning with a hand, he invited us inside his palace.

Queen Lissa arrived at that moment.

"Ry, we have a problem," she announced. I drew in a breath at the worried look on her face. Something terrible had just happened, and it worried me more than it did her.

* * *

Travis

Only a few Alliance worlds still buried their dead. Most opted for cremation or another, more practical form of disposing of remains. Growing a tree from them, or creating jewelry from their carbon was popular in some places.

Not all the graves had been opened in this cemetery on Cle-Morness. At this location, it was very early in the morning and the sun was barely above the horizon. Fingers of light filtered past high gravestones, revealing many empty graves.

Shadows created by the gravestones lent a terror-inducing pall to what should have been a peaceful graveyard. Piles of freshly-turned earth littered the ground around each opened grave. I glanced in Ry's direction as he frowned in concentration.

Mom, Bel Erland and Ilya had come, too, to survey the damage, if you could call it that. Randl, too, had been brought, to employ his particular talents.

"The stink of power is all over this, but it's not a wizard or warlock's power." Ry lifted his head and grimaced. "Look here—you can see the footprints walking away from the graves. All the burial boxes are opened, too, and they're usually so tightly sealed it would take a grenade to open them."

"Are you saying we have zombies to worry about, now?" Mom asked. Her hands were on her hips, too, and that was never a good sign.

"I don't know. No wizard or warlock has this kind of power."

"I can confirm that," Ilya spoke for the first time. "This puzzles me greatly."

I stood close to one of the emptied graves; it was neatly excavated, as if it had been done by a hover-digger. There were no vehicle tracks in the freshly-dumped dirt, however, so a machine of any kind wasn't involved.

It had been done with power.

"How many?" Dad's arm dropped over my shoulder as he appeared. Uncle Drew did the same for Trent, who stood across the cemetery, examining another empty grave.

Chapter 11

"Twenty-seven," Mom replied. "The most recent burials. I sent mindspeech to Kooper—he's putting all the worlds on alert that still bury their dead."

"What about the non-Alliance worlds that do it?" Randl spoke for the first time.

"We don't have many ways to police those," Dad said, turning his gaze on Mom.

"This feels familiar," Randl said. "The power that lingers—it feels similar to what I felt when the three walked past me at the restaurant in Mer'bali, although that was much, much weaker than this. This," he swept out a hand, "is terrifying in its strength."

"That could mean the spell placed on those three was only a tracking spell of some sort," Ry suggested. "You say they disappeared off the street after a while?" I nodded at his question. "That makes sense for it to be only a tracking spell," he said.

"You mean to tell me that those fuckers disappeared off the *Strafer* after leaving the two from Jaledis dead behind them, and then, to cap things off, came to a cemetery and raised the dead?"

"Queen Lissa?" Randl's voice had gone quiet.

"What is it, Randl?"

"Has Karzac examined the bodies of Lorvis and Akrinn, yet?"

"Not yet; he's still studying ways to proceed, to keep any implanted devices intact," Mom said.

"You may want to make sure they can't get out of wherever they are."

"Holy, fucking hell," Mom snapped and disappeared.

* * *

Randl

I was grateful that stasis spells could be placed on food; we didn't eat until long past midnight, Jaledis time.

By that late hour, at least six graveyards had been visited, and more than two hundred bodies removed—all of them dead within the past three years.

So many possibilities revolved in my brain, and none were pleasant to dwell upon. Whatever—or whomever—was responsible held a power I'd never experienced, and was able to hide behind it in ways I'd never encountered.

Morrett and his brothers had a way of concealing themselves, and this, I felt could be similar, but different at the same time.

How could that be?

Two words kept repeating in all my wild theories, however, and I wondered if anyone else had turned in that direction.

They were supposed to be myths, after all.

"Bro, you need to tell us what's going on in that head of yours," Travis sat down next to me.

I'd chosen a bench in his uncles' courtyard to think before going to bed.

Somewhere within the compound, David and Susan, owl and hen, had turned and then flew or wandered within the safe enclosure.

"I'm afraid to say it," I confessed.

"Say it anyway. It can't be any worse than the nightmares I've had after watching horror vids when I was young."

"They're just tales," I said.

"Then put it out there and we'll poke holes in the theory."

"Necromancy—by a sorcerer," I winced as I said the last word. As I'd said, both those things were myths and open to ridicule.

"Well, that's different," Travis sighed. "I was worried you were going to say zombies for real—you know the brain-eating, virus-toting kind."

"You've already seen a stasis spell placed on your food tonight," I sighed. "What if the one who pulled them from their graves has employed something similar, to keep them whole and functioning?"

"That makes terrifying sense," Travis admitted. "Anything else?"

"If he can hide from us while doing this—and while invading Sabrina's lab, he—or she—could have been under our noses on Pyrik and we'd never know."

"You had to make it worse, didn't you? I need to get with Kooper. Go to bed, you look worn out. No early call tomorrow—sleep as long as you can while we get the wheels turning on this."

Both of us turned our heads as Susan the hen wandered past, singing a hen's song as she stepped daintily along. My smile was a tired one, but it came anyway.

* * *

Travis

That's what he said—that the one behind this could have been under our noses on Pyrik, and we wouldn't have guessed, I sent to Kooper.

He really said necromancy and sorcery?

He did. He wasn't comfortable doing it, but I doubt he'd have said either of those things if he didn't have strong suspicions.

Then let's hope there's a more mundane explanation. A rogue wizard or warlock would be bad enough. Bringing something out of the realm of myth to trouble us—we may not have an answer for this, because we've never dealt with it before.

Ry says that no wizard or warlock has been able to reanimate the dead like that—they might manipulate a body, but it would take careful concentration to do just one. This was done on a large scale.

What the hell do you suppose anybody would want with reanimated bodies, anyway?

No idea. I doubt it was done for fun, though.

MindSighted

All right—I'll tighten security on Pyrik. Let me know if you find anything in the equipment from Sabrina's lab, Kooper said.

Will do. I'm letting the troops sleep in—we've had a rough day.

Good. Have a report to me by tomorrow afternoon, at the latest.

Yes, Director.

* * *

Sabrina

If I'd still been my own boss, I'd have called in sick. I doubted anyone in our party felt like rolling out of bed at ten bells the following morning. Nevertheless, we shuffled into the courtyard, where breakfast was being served.

David looked as if he were asleep sitting up, and had barely touched his food. Susan was nearly the same at a table farther down.

The difference was this; David had nobody to prop him up. Susan was being propped up by Uncle Flyer, who wore a grin as she slept on his shoulder.

David has a wife, but she's an owl, too, so the best they could do is lean into one another, Randl informed me while shoving a mug of tea in my direction. I frowned at him, hoping he'd tell me the story of how Susan and Flyer had come to be together.

Mutual attraction, he informed me without hesitation.

I wanted mindspeech. How did one go about getting it? Was it even possible? *If it were, everybody would have it*, I told myself sternly.

"Kooper wants a report on the lab equipment by this afternoon," Travis announced at the head of the table. "Eat and be ready in an hour."

I slurped tea, hoping it would wake me enough to do a proper inventory later. If I were to fabricate ranos pistols for the ship's crew, I needed everything there and in working order to accomplish that.

Chapter 11

I'd have to unpack and set it up, too. I hoped I'd have help for that part.

* * *

Randl

Uniforms weren't advised for this or any mission on Jaledis, so we dressed casually. We'd be unpacking and examining lab equipment, which would require comfort and ease of movement. Sabrina was in charge of inventory; I was in charge of reporting any abnormalities about it.

"Ready?" Trent asked as I joined him and Travis in the courtyard.

"Yes."

"I'm here," Sabrina walked up while pulling her hair into the usual ponytail she preferred when she worked or exercised.

"Good. I'm taking you two in first, to check things over," Travis said. "Trent will bring the others when we know it's safe."

I nodded my agreement—that was safest, in my opinion. No need to expose the others if danger waited.

Without a word, Travis folded space with Sabrina and me, landing us in a cavernous warehouse, where Sabrina's equipment was dwarfed by the empty space around it.

High, overhead lamps brightly illuminated the space, as if it had been used before to closely examine evidence and other confiscated items. The lamps hung from the ceiling on extended rods, which were roughly the height of a tall man. Still, they were elevated far above anything placed on the floor, so even a tall vehicle could be set there and not disturb them.

"This much space makes it look pitiful," Sabrina sighed as she studied the boxes and crates at the center of the concrete floor.

"Will you do your thing, Randl?" Travis asked.

"Yes." I walked toward the boxes and crates, reaching the first one. I felt nothing from it, even when I placed a hand on the outside.

"Nothing," I turned toward Travis.

"That looks like my parts printer," Sabrina said and walked forward to lift the lid.

At that moment, a metallic ping brought our heads up—as if something had bounced off one of the metal lampshades hanging over our heads.

The mental buzz filled my head the moment something dropped near Sabrina's feet. "No," I shouted as she bent to pick it up.

Her scream was cut off as she disappeared, but the ringing of the object she'd lifted as it hit the floor a second time will haunt my dreams forever.

* * *

Mer'bali, Pyrik

Kooper Griff

"What is this?" I fingered the coin after we'd determined it was no longer dangerous—to us, anyway.

Randl and Travis sat in my makeshift office at the hotel. Travis' gaze was on me; Randl's head was bowed and he looked ready to crumble.

Travis wasn't happy—I could see that. He and Trent apparently had a m'fiyah with Sabrina, and Lissa had muted it until Sabrina's three years were done with the ASD.

As for Randl and his feelings for her, I had no idea whether there was any affection for him from Sabrina.

It made the circumstances that much worse.

"It's a coin. An old one, from long before the fall of Vogeffa II," Randl whispered. My fingers stilled on the coin in question.

Why had they chosen what was surely a valuable object? It was gold; I knew that much, and the design was still visible—it hadn't worn away from age, as many coins did. It didn't escape me that Randl was born on Vogeffa II, just as his parents were. *At least his father was*, I amended my assumption. Few knew anything of his mother, but she was long dead.

"What does this mean?" I asked. Did the enemy know we had a clairvoyant working for us, from Vogeffa II? Was this their way of taunting us? Of showing us that they could take what they wanted with impunity?

They'd certainly taken Sabrina, and nobody could get a hint of her location, not even Randl and Quin.

I worried that she'd been killed outright, but she was valuable as a brilliant scientist, and I hoped that would keep her alive long enough for us to find her.

That was before I considered that they'd wanted her to die along with Fergue. I wasn't about to say that to the two men who sat before me. Sabrina's death could destroy both of them.

"Randl, do you have any idea of a connection?" I asked the obvious question.

"I don't know," he half-sobbed. "I can't see it, if there is."

"Travis, bring your ship here. We have to start somewhere, and this is as good a place as any."

"Right away," Travis stood and nodded to me. Randl was slower to rise. "Come on, bro," Travis draped an arm over Randl's shoulders. "We'll figure this out."

* * *

Sabrina

I landed hard, wherever I was, and it took several seconds for my eyes to adjust to the dim light.

A stone wall was behind me, a cold, stone floor beneath my body. Close, stone walls lay to the left and right of me, but bars lined the space in front of me.

Bars and a man outside them, I realized. I scrabbled backward and pushed myself against the wall as hard as I could, once he became visible to me.

"It won't do any good to attempt an escape." His voice was rough, as if he weren't used to speaking. "You belong to us, now, and you'll do whatever we want."

"Fuck you," I hissed, desperately attempting to get my feet under me so I could stand and defend myself if necessary.

"Oh, we'll get to that," he laughed.

* * *

Queen's Palace, Le-Ath Veronis
Lissa

"Now what?"

Karzac and I had stood outside the glass-walled, sealed room and watched the reanimated bodies of Akrinn and Lorvis stumble about the enclosure for several minutes before I could bring myself to form a sentence.

"Do you suppose the spell will wear out eventually?" Karzac's train of thought was certainly different from mine.

"Why would you want to know that?"

"There has to be a purpose behind the reanimation—otherwise, why expend the effort?" Karzac's mouth was set in a grim line after he spoke, and his brows were knit in concentration.

"True," I acknowledged.

"If these wear down, it will give us an idea of the timeframe for their use or purpose, wouldn't you say?"

"Yes, unless the one responsible keeps topping off the spell," I replied.

"Also a concern. Still, I wish to know the extent of the spell and how long it lasts. That will give us some information. After all, it isn't as if they can speak—and won't require feeding. We merely have to keep an eye on them."

"Also true. I'd like Quin and Randl to take a look, though," I said.

"Then arrange to bring them here," Karzac nodded.

"Lissa?" Drake and Drew appeared at my side; they'd folded in from somewhere. Drake was the one to speak, though, and I knew immediately that something was wrong.

"What is it?" I turned to my Falchani mates.

"The enemy has taken Sabrina," Drew said. "Our boys are devastated, even with the mute in place."

"Holy, fucking, butt-busting hell," I snapped. "Come on, let's get started on finding her. Karzac, will you ask Kooper to bring Randl and Quin? If there are any answers in those two," I jerked my head toward Lorvis and Akrinn, "Then we need to know what they are."

* * *

BlackWing X, Orbiting Pyrik
Randl

Travis and Trent had employed power to move the ship into an orbit around Pyrik. Kooper didn't want us to dock—the twins could take us to the surface if it were necessary.

Kooper appeared after our midday meal, saying that Queen Lissa wanted Quin and me to examine the reanimated bodies of Lorvis and Akrinn, to see if we could tell her anything regarding Sabrina's whereabouts.

I was ready to go in an instant. I had no other options at the moment; Sabrina's kidnapping and my imagination had begun to play tricks on me. Truthfully, I was very close to black depression, as she was all I could think about.

"Take them to Mom," Travis told Trent, meaning Quin and me. "See if there's any information they can get from those two traitors."

"I'm ready now," Trent said, lifting a jacket from his chair in the lounge. "What about Quin?" he asked Kooper.

"I'll bring her. Go ahead and take Randl now."

With a nod to Kooper, Trent folded space with me, and we landed in his mother's private study, where she waited for us.

* * *

Queen's Palace, Le-Ath Veronis

Lissa

Trent arrived with Randl first. I went to my son and pulled him into a hug. *I'm sorry, honey*, I sent to him.

We have to find her, her replied before pulling away.

That's when I really noticed Randl. Pale and drawn, his face was like a mask. He, like my twins, was terrified for Sabrina.

Kooper arrived at that moment with Quin and Justis. Both looked as if they'd dressed hurriedly. "Bel and a few others are on their way," Kooper informed me.

"Good. I know it's late, Pyrik time. If anybody wants a bed for the night, I'll arrange it."

Healing sleep? Trent asked. *For Randl and me?*

I'll see to it, I replied.

* * *

Randl

"We can see in, they can't see out—just in case," Queen Lissa said as Lorvis and Akrinn shuffled about inside their cage.

"This is frightening," Quin whispered. King Justis, who stood behind her, gripped her shoulders as red wings tightened against her back. His red wings rustled, indicating his displeasure at what we were seeing.

Chapter 11

At least Sabrina hadn't seen this, which brought me back to the reason I was here. "I get nothing about Sabrina from these." I shivered, which embarrassed me. "I think they were used and then discarded. Whether their knowledge of Sabrina was utilized in her capture, I have no idea. I can't see through them to the one who did this."

"What about the coin?" Bel Erland asked.

"Ilya believes it to be a focused spell, meant for Sabrina only," Kooper replied. "Geared to her fingerprints or DNA or whatever. It didn't escape any of us that it fell near her, either."

"My warning came too late—she'd already touched it." I admitted my guilt in the matter. "The fact that it's an ancient coin from Vogeffa II hasn't escaped me, either."

"You think they're taunting you personally, or sending a challenge?" Lissa asked.

"No idea. It could just be coincidence."

"What does your gut say?" she asked.

"My gut says Vogeffa II is involved somehow."

"We know that V'ili and Cayetes were taking locals from Gungl, and planned to take those from outlying villages to supply Cayetes' nccd for bodies," Kooper said. "That's why Randl and his people were moved to Harifa Edus. How difficult would it be for V'ili to place obsessions on some of the population there?"

"Easy enough," Lissa snorted softly. "I have to say, though, that this," she pointed at the bodies inside their glass cage, "is a new twist, don't you think? If V'ili could place an obsession on somebody able to do this, then we could be in bigger trouble than we think."

"There were plenty of mutants living on Vogeffa II," Trent said, dropping a hand on my shoulder. "No offense, bro," he added.

"None taken," I replied. I knew as well as anyone that those from Gungl were exceedingly strange at times. Had that world spawned a sorcerer? Was that why he'd used an old coin from Vogeffa II's past?

"I'd like to talk to Pap," I said.

"He's on the light half of the planet—I can bring him in the morning for breakfast," Lissa offered.

"That would be fine," I sighed. Pap had plenty of experience with those from Gungl—he'd bartered with many of them, trading meat and vegetables from our village in exchange for other goods and coins from the capital city. Maybe he'd heard rumors of a power wielder among them.

In my mind, I'd skirted the issue of my mother coming from there—she'd died shortly after I was born, and Pap was reluctant to talk about her. I saw very little of her in him, too, and that left a blank spot in the record of my existence.

I knew she hadn't been the power wielder, though, because others in my old village never said anything, other than she was kind and a welcome member of the community. If she'd had power, she wouldn't be dead. Instead, someone else with power was alive and causing trouble.

I wanted Sabrina back. Therefore, I'd be forced to hunt him or her—more diligently than I already was.

How to do that plagued my mind. I'd already exhausted all my resources, and nothing had come. Perhaps my mind was frozen because Sabrina had been taken. No new ideas on how to find and rescue her would come from a frozen mind—of that I was sure.

"Young one?" Karzac the physician stood before me. I blinked, bringing myself away from my thoughts to focus on him.

"Sir?" I croaked as green-gold eyes gazed into mine. I blinked again while he studied me curiously, like a bird who'd found an unlikely creature in its nest. Then, he tapped a finger to my forehead and that's the last I recalled until the following morning.

Chapter 11

* * *

Trent

Rigo carried Randl to bed; Mom called him to the dungeon just before Karzac placed the healing sleep. It wasn't difficult to see the toll this had taken on Randl, and, according to Karzac, his mind was in turmoil over it.

"That will affect the body, too," Karzac said, his voice gruff as we left the dungeon behind by folding space.

He'd said that to me once I was in bed. I felt like a child again, as Karzac placed a finger against my forehead so I could sleep.

Morning had arrived, and although the fear and worry came rushing back, at least my body was rested enough to deal with another onslaught.

I wanted to see Randl's father, too. If he had information regarding the coin or anything else, I wished to hear it myself. Therefore, when Mom's mindspeech woke me for breakfast, I was out of bed, showered and dressed in no time.

"Pap, this is Captain Trent," Randl introduced us as I sat down at the table placed in the arboretum. Only a few would come to this private meeting, after all. Kooper had also come; he was just as curious as I was regarding Vogeffa II's involvement.

"Captain Trent," Brandl Gage held out a hand and we shook.

"He knows you're my son," Mom said, causing me to release a pent-up sigh. Brandl was her employee, now, so I wasn't surprised that she'd confided in him.

"What can you tell us about this coin?" Kooper leaned in and set the old coin from Vogeffa II in front of Brandl while Randl watched.

"I have one like it, but it's not nearly as well-preserved," Brandl stood to reach in his pocket. "My late wife gave it to me, and as you will see—it's had a much harder life than the one you have."

He drew a gold coin from his trousers and set it beside the other. He was correct—his showed signs of much use combined with age. "You have to understand, however, that these coins floated about Gungl regularly. We were seldom paid with them, because they were more valuable than most of our vegetables and meats. They weren't common, but not too uncommon, either."

"So it could have come from anyone." Kooper lifted the one he'd brought and slipped it in a jacket pocket, while Brandl reclaimed his.

"Yes. As for power wielders, I have no information. I'd never heard of such until Randl mentioned it this morning. You understand, however, that we only took our goods to sell and trade twice per month. That wouldn't give us too much gossip, as you well know."

"I know this is a delicate subject, but did your wife ever talk about Gungl?" Mom asked Brandl.

"She hated it," Brandl said. "We met in the marketplace one day—she was looking to buy any fruit we had. She came back every time afterward, and we'd talk. After nearly a year passed, I asked her to marry me. At the time, I worried that she wouldn't want to leave Gungl. I was wrong."

"She never said anything about anyone unusual in the city, Pap?" Randl asked.

"Son, she didn't want to talk about it, and if she were here, she'd just tell you that everyone in Gungl was unusual in some way. If a power wielder existed, he didn't expose himself as such."

"Or she," Mom suggested.

"Yes. Or she, as the case may be," Brandl shook his head. "I wish I could help you more, but that's all I know."

"It's all right, Pap. Anything might help. You never know."

"What do we do now?" I asked.

Chapter 11

"I think it's time we took Randl to Gungl, so he can look around," Kooper said.

Chapter 12

G"Did you ever come here with your father?" Kooper asked as we walked along a brick-lined street with many of the bricks missing from it. The remaining bricks were slowly disintegrating from the passage of time and lack of maintenance. From what I could see, the city was mostly deserted, now.

"No—I was kept at home. Pap said this was no place for a son whose lack of sight could work against him in a city of thieves and cutthroats. Did Cayetes kill the inhabitants after we left?" I asked.

"Most," Kooper agreed. "Many fled into the outlying countryside. Some of those survived. When Cayetes abandoned the planet, it was almost empty of life. You know how the outlying villages were rescued."

"Yes." I recalled it very well. Quin had sent mindspeech, and Queen Lissa and others had come to our rescue. It also infuriated Cayetes, who attempted to exact vengeance for that rescue.

He and V'ili were now dead, and I was even more grateful for that. "How did Cayetes and V'ili die?" I asked. I'd never heard the how or who, just that it was.

"Zaria," Kooper said. "Took down both at the same time, as I understand it."

"If I'd known that, I would have kissed her feet when I met her," I breathed.

"She'd probably tell you it wasn't necessary," Kooper chuckled.

My hand went to my chest, to touch the medallion beneath my shirt. Sabrina had a medallion like mine—from Zaria. *Keep her safe*, I sent to Zaria. I had no idea whether that was possible, or what the medallion was for, even. It couldn't hurt though, could it?

"Randl, are you getting anything?" Kooper's voice interrupted my thoughts.

All about us, crumbling buildings stood on either side of the broken street. Most of the structures were uninhabited. A few birds, nesting in empty spaces between bricks, called out in the hush our arrival precipitated. I felt eyes upon us, however, and soon enough, two faces appeared at broken windows.

They were starving; that was easy for me to understand.

"If you'll talk to us, I'll make sure you get food and supplies," Kooper called out. He understood their hunger, too.

Slowly, those two disappeared from their windows. Moments later, they tentatively stepped outside their separate buildings.

"Shall we sit?" Kooper indicated a rough curb that was still intact. "We're not here to hurt anyone, we just have some questions."

"Here," Trent held out a bag. I could smell the food inside it, as could they, no doubt. I wanted to ask where it came from, but that could wait. Someone had sent it to him in response to mindspeech.

"Set the bag down and back away," one of the men croaked. He walked with a pronounced limp; I knew it was from an old injury and not misshapen from birth. I sent that information to Trent, who'd already set the bag on the street in front of him.

He, Kooper and I backed up until we were several yards away.

The second man didn't limp. He bore a terrible scar, which ran down his face and neck before disappearing below a ragged collar. He approached and cautiously lifted the bag, as if afraid it would explode in his face. With shaking hands, he opened it and, after glancing inside, turned to his companion and nodded.

The other limped forward and they divided the food and containers of water between them.

Kooper waited patiently until they'd finished everything inside the bag, down to the last crumb of the thick sandwiches provided.

"What do you want?" the man with a limp asked.

"We'd like to ask you about the times before and during Cayetes' Storm," Kooper said.

"That filth." The scarred man spat on the bricks at his feet. "He promised us everything. You see what's left, now." He flung out a hand.

"Actually, Cayetes is dead now, and no longer our concern," Kooper admitted. "What we really want to know is this—was there ever anyone here that held power—like a wizard or warlock might have?"

Both men looked at one another. I understood then that they had no knowledge of such. "If we had, you think we'd be living in crumbling ruin?" the scarred one asked. "If he had such talent, he'd have left this place long ago. Why stay to squabble and fight for food and clothing? That's all I've known since I've been alive. We know of no such person."

"Thank you," Kooper sighed. "Are there any others here who would know anything?"

"There are few of us, and most are worse off than we are," the limping man confessed. "They know nothing more than we do—we are the oldest of the survivors and more used to living without."

"Randl?" Kooper turned to me. He wanted to know if they were being truthful.

"It's the truth," I blew out a breath. "I feel nothing here," I added. If there were spells and such, I'd likely feel the buzzing in my brain. Gungl, in my estimation, was dead or dying, and nothing had impeded its fate.

If someone were here with the power to reanimate the dead and create the other spells I'd seen, they'd left long ago, as the scarred man said.

"Thank you," Kooper nodded to the two men. Trent and I were folded back to Queen Lissa's palace moments later.

* * *

Sabrina

I'd fallen asleep after being left alone for hours. Keys rattling woke me. The same man I'd seen before was unlocking my cell.

How did this add up? They had spells to pull me away from Jaledis, and then employed old-fashioned locks and keys to imprison me?

That didn't make sense.

Whatever it meant, I didn't want him in my cell or anywhere near me. I wished Director Griff hadn't confiscated my ranos pistol; I'd be out of here already if I still had it.

"What do you want?" I scrambled to my feet and glared at the man, who now stood inside my cage.

"Just a little fun. You'll get food afterward, and we'll let you know what we want from you."

"You get nothing from me," I hissed at him, and went into the stance Jayna taught me to defend myself.

"Think that'll work against this?" He pulled a laser pistol from his waistband. He'd hidden it behind his back so I wouldn't know. His wide grin told me he'd meant to intimidate me all along.

"Then kill me. I'd rather die than have your hands on me, anyway."

"That's not what the boss wants, now," he said. "Since you're still alive, anyway. Things will go a lot easier if you cooperate."

"No, thank you." At least my voice was steady enough; I was quaking on the inside, though, and had no idea whether I'd be raped or killed in the next few seconds. Blood pounded in my ears and my heart wanted to beat its way out of my chest as I held my stance, waiting for him to make a move.

Had I been this frightened when I was fourteen? Then, I'd been one of many. This time, I was singled out and alone. My assailant was too far away to land an effective kick, and the pistol in his hand was steady and pointed at my chest. A shot from that close meant I'd die quickly.

I opted for that—a swift death.

I leapt at him, hoping to land a blow before he fired, aiming to do some damage before he killed me. Whether intentional or not, his pistol fired just as my clenched fist landed against his face.

I felt nothing—no pain as expected, except for that in my bruised knuckles as light bloomed all about us and we were knocked away from each other. I hit the floor with a muffled grunt and when my vision cleared, the laser pistol lay at my feet. My unconscious assailant, however, had been thrown against the wall opposite my cell.

The cell door creaked on rusty hinges as it swayed back and forth, still, after he'd been blown past it.

What the bloody, fucking blazes had happened?

Gathering my scattered wits, I snatched the pistol off the floor and left my cell behind. I had no idea where I was or how to get away without being seen, but I was now armed. That in itself was a welcome turn of events.

* * *

Quin

I'd been sitting on the balcony outside Justis' and my shared suite at Avii Castle, having tea with Bel Erland, Lafe, Justis and several others. Dena stood at the door, watchful as always.

I leapt to my feet, my teacup crashing onto the glass stones of the terrace as the information hit me like a storm. Until then, my attempts to find Sabrina had been futile.

Whatever had blocked her from me had disappeared, somehow. "She's on Cord'ilus," I shouted.

* * *

Winkler

When the mindspeech came, I was ready, as were several others, including Drake, Drew, Rigo and Gavin. Kooper had gotten word from Quin and he'd taken her, Randl, Travis and Trent with him, to narrow the search.

Cord'ilus was an empty world, devoured by Ra'Ak long ago. Jungle had taken over much of it; the rest lay in decaying ruin. Word of illegal animal hunts reached the ASD from time to time, but as it wasn't in either Alliance, there wasn't much done to prevent it from happening.

I'd followed Kooper's mental sending, landing my party outside what was once a large city.

Kooper, Quin and the others waited there for us. "She's in there?" Rigo asked, indicating the massive ruin ahead of us.

Chapter 12

"I can get us closer, as long as whatever hid her before doesn't do it again," Quin breathed hard, as if she were terrified for the kidnapped woman.

"We'll shield you," Wellend and Warlend appeared as if called. "Fly, Quin. Find Sabrina, so the others may get her away."

"I've got a call in for ASD troops, but the ships won't arrive until late tonight," Kooper said. "Let's go. She may be in terrible danger."

* * *

Randl

Remember your lessons? Travis placed a laser pistol in my hand. I worried that I'd impede the rescue, rather than helping, but for whatever reason, Kooper wanted me to go in with them and I was grateful.

Sabrina was in that jungle-covered city, and I wanted her away from it.

What do you sense? Kooper sent as I checked my weapon as Travis taught me.

Animals. Some humanoids—going in and out of my perception, which puzzles me.

Snakes? Kooper returned.

Yes.

I watched as Quin flew away with her two red-winged protectors. We'd know soon enough if they could spot Sabrina from the air.

Do you sense Sabrina? Kooper asked.

I turned toward Kooper then, prepared to shake my head in denial. Unintentionally, I touched my chest where my medallion rested.

Like a bolt of energy, her image ran through my mind. She was in a vine-choked alley, where several men were converging upon her.

"They've found her," I hissed. At that moment, Kooper slapped his hand on my head, the vision was pulled away from me with power and he folded all of us into the ancient city.

* * *

Winkler

None of us were prepared for a battle, but it was unleashed on us anyway. Whatever the hidden army had employed to protect themselves had worked for the most part.

Was it a trap to lure us in? I had no idea, but I sent mindspeech to Lissa the moment we landed, because we were under attack from that point forward.

* * *

Sabrina

An ancient, brick chimney jutted out from the building beside me. I hid behind it, desperately shooting at anything that approached. I'd killed three already, but there were more waiting behind them.

With no idea how long the charge would last on the laser pistol I held, I ducked behind crumbling brick every time one of the kidnappers fired at me.

That's not what the boss wants filtered into my brain as I ducked behind the chimney again. What *did* the boss want?

We're here and trying to get to you, Travis' mental voice informed me. I wanted to weep with joy and scream in terror at the same time, because an explosion rocked the ground beneath my feet.

Another shot from the approaching enemy broke concrete near my head, forcing me to make myself a smaller target. Kneeling, I hoped the grass and broken blocks of brick from crumbling buildings

Chapter 12

would hide me well enough so I could shoot from a lower vantage point.

Touch your medallion, Randl's voice came. *Try to send mindspeech when you do*, he added.

My medallion? I'd forgotten it. Slapping my hand against my chest, I told Randl he was crazy to think that would work.

It's working—I heard you, he returned.

Holy bleeding hells, I'd had mindspeech all along if I needed it. With my hand still over the medallion beneath my shirt, I tentatively sent mindspeech again. *I'm stuck in an alley, and they keep coming and firing at me*, I struggled to keep my mental voice calm.

We're having some trouble, too—somebody put an army here, and we're doing our best to keep them away from you, he informed me.

I hadn't realized my terror could ramp up several more notches, but it did. Too afraid to ask whether the explosion had hurt or killed any of ours, I struggled to keep my hand steady as I fired at another attacker who'd leapt over a large pile of fallen bricks to level a shot in my direction.

* * *

Travis

Keep your shields up, Kooper shouted into all our minds. This was after the first hundred or so of the dead troops leapt up from high grass and weeds, only to explode together, nearly knocking us off our feet and rocking the ground beneath us.

Randl said we were getting close to Sabrina's hiding place—somehow, he was using the medallion Zaria gave him to make that determination.

Our shields had been up from the moment Kooper folded us into the city, too. Those of us who had them, anyway. Someone, likely Winkler, had included Randl inside his. I was grateful, because a green mist blew away from the place where the bodies exploded, and I was beginning to believe this was a carefully laid trap to lure in ASD troops or others who had no way to protect themselves against it.

I had several guesses as to what the green mist was, but each was too terrifying to contemplate, so I shoved them out of my mind.

Sabrina was out there and vulnerable, as far as I knew. My heart squeezed at the thought of it, and understood that Trent was just as fearful as I was.

Brace yourselves, Kooper shouted as more of the dead popped up ahead of us and exploded in unison, causing most of us to fall as the terrible sound raced through the city and the ground bucked and rolled more violently beneath our feet.

* * *

Quin

Randl had sent information to me regarding Sabrina's hiding place. Below Wellend, Warlend and me, the ancient city was smothered in creepers, grass, trees and collapsing bricks, making it more than difficult to locate the alley where she was hiding.

At times, we saw grasses move as the enemy army swarmed toward Kooper and the others, and twice we heard explosions, so we knew this had to be a planned attack.

Someone had laid a trap, hoping to take or kill those who had no power to overcome what was aimed in their direction.

There, Wellend's voice invaded my mind. He pointed below, toward a narrow alley cluttered with plant growth and debris. Sabrina fired at enemy invaders coming from one end of the alley.

They're sneaking in behind her and she doesn't see it, Warlend snapped.

Chapter 12

We dived, just as Justis and Ardis had taught us. Wellend, however, folded space, appearing a moment later at Sabrina's back to protect her.

Warlend and I heard her shriek of surprise, but she got herself in hand quickly to fire at two more who'd entered the alley to shoot at her. It was a distraction—the real attack was advancing from behind—until Wellend leveled a blast at the encroaching robotic device, picking its way along the back entrance like a spider making its way over a web.

Wellend's power blast knocked the robot against a wall, crushing half of it immediately. The rest of it disappeared beneath a rain of bricks from overhead—revealing another worry.

The ancient city was a weapon in itself, and unstable structures were ready to collapse after two explosions had already rocked it.

Get her out of there, Warlend sent a shout to Wellend, who pulled Sabrina against him and folded space.

Warlend and I watched as the walls on both sides of the alley collapsed in slow motion, beginning at the back, where the robot had crashed against the wall, initially bringing part of it down.

Several attackers then aimed indiscriminately into the air, shooting wildly at something they couldn't scc while the wall collapsed back to front, like a giant row of gaming tiles.

* * *

Winkler

We have Sabrina, Wellend informed us. At least that worry was resolved, but we now had more to deal with.

Hundreds of dead troops were now marching toward our small company, shielding living troops who stalked behind them. It didn't matter if the live ones hit a dead one in front of them with their laser pistols—the dead were already dead and kept walking.

Every time we destroyed a dead one, an explosion came, followed by a release of green mist. *We need to blow the hell out of this place*, I hissed in mindspeech at Kooper.

Gavin, who'd rushed a few of the dead to decapitate them, discovered that even headless, the bodies still moved forward. Several were now sliced to ribbons, thanks to his swift claws, but the flesh continued to wriggle in a horrifically fascinating way, as if it were still attempting to accomplish the mission.

Agreed, Kooper's mindspeech answered mine. *Frankly*, he added, *we need to destroy the entire planet. The whole thing could be hiding more of these abominations*.

I'm here, Lissa sent as she dropped at my side. *Kooper, get the others off this planet. I'll take care of this.*

I'm staying with you, I insisted. Maybe she hadn't noticed the new development in her normal condition, but I had. We'd discuss that later, after this world was less than space dust.

Fine, she turned blue eyes on me and frowned. *Kooper, make sure everybody is disinfected and cleaned with power. We don't need this shit landing anywhere else.*

On it, Kooper agreed and folded the others away.

"Just you and me, baby," I grinned at Lissa, who wrinkled her nose at me before lifting a hand and gathering power.

* * *

BlackWing X

Sabrina

I have no idea what the red-winged men were doing, but power shone brightly about them as they moved in tandem around me.

"They're clearing away any contamination you may have picked up from Cord'ilus," Quin, the red-winged Avii Queen, informed me.

Chapter 12

"Contamination?" I squeaked. I didn't want contamination. I wanted out of my clothes and boots immediately, because my skin suddenly felt as if it were crawling with some infestation.

"Relax, I think the medallion protected you, but we have to make sure," one of the red-winged males reassured me.

My shoulders sagged in relief. "I think that was a trap," I managed to mumble as they continued their trip around me.

"We're pretty sure you're right," one of them agreed. "That green mist—whatever it was inside the dead ones—that's a new twist and would have infected those without power and shields in place."

"Cord'ilus has been destroyed," Kooper said as he and the others arrived and surrounded me.

"Is she clean?" Travis demanded, jerking his head in my direction.

"We can't find any contamination," the red-winged men stood back.

"Good." Travis strode forward. What happened next I'd never have guessed. I was in his arms, my legs wrapped around his waist as he held me and kissed me repeatedly, while Trent stood behind me, rubbing my back and neck.

"Well, this calls for a bit of shuffling in the rankings," Kooper spoke dryly. I ignored him. Finally—*fucking finally*—I was where I wanted to be.

* * *

Randl

I could only watch Travis, Trent and Sabrina for a short time before slipping away to my quarters.

I wanted what they were getting, and it would never come to me. Pulling my comp-vid from my pocket with a sigh, I began writing my report. Director Griff would want one from all of us; I'd learned that from my vid studies.

Every ASD agent filed a report after every incident. It was a standard rule and better not left until later, when details could be lost or confused with the passage of time.

Regarding Cord'illus' destruction, Kooper's mindspeech came, *We have vid images and an official, logical explanation for its destruction, which will be transferred to your comp-vid. Please include that in your reports*, he added.

I set a reminder on my comp-vid to notify me when the information and images were transferred, then forced my mind back to writing the report.

* * *

Lee'Qee, Pyrik
Varok

The Prophet was angry. More than angry. I was grateful he wasn't destructive toward us in his anger. We'd obeyed his commands and everything had been set up according to his wishes.

We hadn't expected what happened.

Neither had he, and that was far from the fault of the Ke'Leru pirates under my command.

The trap was laid as instructed. The first thing to go wrong was the escape of the woman. The Prophet had a new purpose for her after using her as bait to lure in unsuspecting ASD troops. Initially he'd wanted her dead, but after two failed attempts, he revised his plan.

The ASD troops who'd arrived on Cord'ilus should be under our control, now, and their weapons, codes and ships in our possession. The woman would have been forced to work for us, designing weapons to protect us and further our cause.

Never forget, we have other abandoned worlds, ripe for implementation of the same plan, we merely have to construct

Chapter 12

another trap, the Prophet informed me earlier. He was quite well-spoken when angry, unlike most others around me.

I knew better than to tell the Prophet that he'd misread this, somehow. His talent was too reliable, otherwise. Besides, saying anything of the sort could result in a very nasty death for me, as he was also quite powerful. I wished to avoid that at all cost.

* * *

BlackWing X

Randl

Sabrina had been reclassified before Kooper ever left the ship. She was now employed as a Special Liaison and not subject to the rules of relationships with superior officers.

The knot between my shoulders tightened as Travis and Trent joined her for breakfast in the galley the following morning.

"Feeling left out?" David set his tray on the other side of my table.

"And how are you, this fine day?" I snapped at him. "Sorry. I'm just," I didn't finish the sentence.

"Feeling left out," David reiterated. "Look, be patient. Nobody knows how this will turn out."

"Remember who you're talking to?" I frowned at him.

"Oh. Sure. That. Sorry."

"Right."

"Did you shoot anybody yesterday?"

"Some. A few were dead already, so that was a waste of time. One of Queen Lissa's vampire mates sliced some of the dead into tiny pieces. Those pieces still tried to move."

"That's unnerving," David swiped butter across his toast and crunched into it.

"I don't understand how it was accomplished," I admitted. "Not that I truly want to, but we need the information in order to combat the anomaly."

"You're calling it an anomaly? I consider it a fucked-up evil, myself." David finished his toast and turned to the scrambled eggs on his plate.

"You, sir, are a distinguished and well-spoken diplomat of the highest order," I lifted my teacup in a salute to him.

"It's about time somebody recognized my importance," David grinned and waved his fork in a regal gesture.

* * *

Queen's Palace, Le-Ath Veronis
Lissa

Winkler stood behind me, Karzac at my side as we studied the strips of flesh I'd removed from Cord'ilus before destroying the planet.

"They're moving like caterpillars," Winkler breathed against my ear as his arms went around me.

"It's gross," I pointed out.

"Feeling queasy?" Winkler rubbed my belly with his left hand while holding onto me with his right.

"How did you know?" I asked. I wanted to snort, too, but I didn't.

"I know I'm being selfish, but I hope this one's mine," he kissed my temple.

"Another month along and I'd have locked her inside her suite and sent someone else to handle that mess," Karzac snapped.

"Geez, does everybody know?" I tried to move away from Winkler, who wasn't having any of it. He just pulled me tighter against him, instead.

Chapter 12

"Everybody knows—in your Inner Circle," Karzac informed me. "When did you know?"

"When I almost lost my lunch after seeing that shit," I jerked my head toward the small, shielded cage that held crawling strips of human flesh. I knew Karzac would want to observe how long the spell lasted, because we knew when the bodies had been taken to produce the grisliest army I'd ever encountered. Therefore, I'd shipped some back and placed them in the shielded clear cage Karzac had hurriedly constructed for me.

At least these dead hadn't appeared hungry in any way, likely due to the stasis spell we'd discussed before. That was a definite plus, because the word zombies pissed me off in ways I couldn't describe.

"Necromancy." Karzac voiced the term Randl had employed first.

"We've never had anything like that, in the whole history of the Alliances," he added. "This falls outside all parameters."

"Just what we need—a new kind of enemy, who can do that to unsuspecting dead people," I pointed at the crawling bits inside the clear cage.

"Are dead people capable of being unsuspecting?" Winkler asked.

"Stop splitting hairs," I grumped.

"Come on, let's go to the kitchen," Winkler said. "This is making me hungry."

"Oh, my God," I breathed before finally losing my lunch. I didn't care that some of it spattered his boots, either.

Chapter 13

B*lackWing X, Orbiting Pyrik*
Sabrina
"We have to assume that there may be more crumbling cities on other uninhabited worlds that are filling up with the enemy," Travis said during our after-breakfast staff meeting.

"Kooper is in the process of compiling a list of likely candidates, most of them outside the Alliances. A few inside one or the other," Trent took up the topic. "Regular troops will be forbidden from checking those worlds, which leaves the BlackWing fleet in charge of that."

"As of now, no demands have been received, no taunts or factions claiming responsibility for any of this. We're fighting a phantom, in other words, and he could take any form and attack in any way, and we'd be none the wiser," Travis said.

Trent nodded at his brother's words before saying, "By not declaring themselves, they can take any form and strike anywhere. Yes, we still expect a strike on Pyrik when the Conclave resumes, but if they intend to bring in an army from elsewhere, half or more of which could be dead already, then we could be in deep excrement."

"How will they arrive?" David asked. "Will they be transported by ship or with power?"

"No idea," Travis said. "They flew a ship away from Jaledis, and then were taken off it with power later, to leave a trap for us. Kooper has already pulled in scout ships and has most of the sat-bots in the area tuned to tracking ships traveling in or out of Pyrik's orbit. All manifests, crew and passengers are being scrutinized."

"You know it will be a mess when the world leaders begin to arrive for the Conclave again," Jayna pointed out.

"Kooper is working on that. He'd like to assign arrival times for all of them, but that will only make them more suspicious than they already are."

"Are any of them refusing to come back—for safety reasons?" Randl asked.

"A few are grumbling, but so far, nobody has filed a petition to stay at home," Trent shook his head. "Looks like they still want to party."

"They already have the outfit—what else should they do?" David asked. "Voting from home is just boring."

"Will Director Griff let us know if any of those abandoned worlds need investigating?" Randl asked.

"That's what he wants. I have a preliminary list; we're just waiting on better drone scouting before going in," Travis said. "All the BlackWing ships have been redirected for this task."

"And if we find anything?" Terrett spoke, this time.

"Then we get the hell out and call for assistance," Travis said. "Like last time. I think we have a few volunteers to handle the destruction."

Chapter 13

"I worry that the enemy may spread his resources," Randl sighed. "After all, how many of the enemy present on a world will warrant the destruction of the planet?"

Travis frowned for a moment as if considering that. "Good point," he said after a moment's consideration. "I'll send your observations to Kooper."

* * *

Queen's Palace, Le-Ath Veronis
Winkler

"He has a point," I said. "We could end up with a lot of obliterated planets, if he's right. What will you do when they invade an inhabited one? You can't go around destroying everything and you know it."

Kooper paced inside my suite, fairly bristling with contained anger. Occasionally, Kooper's face bore a momentary resemblance to the scales of his lion snake. Randl had pointed out the flaw in Kooper's plan, and Kooper was now looking for a solution to that problem. It didn't mean he couldn't be pissed at the same time.

"I'll have Quin and Randl look at the drone images collected, then proceed." Kooper's shoulders sagged and much of the anger drained out of him. "Maybe they can tell me something the drones can't."

"You understand that we didn't get advance notice that anyone was there on Cord'ilus, until Quin sensed Sabrina there," I said.

"I know. Do you have a better idea?" Kooper turned slitted eyes in my direction. The snake still threatened to make an appearance, looked like.

"Not at the moment," I held up both hands. "Reel in the snake, man. Let's go find Teeg, Ildevar and Jett Riffler, so we can sort this thing out."

* * *

Founder's Palace, Campiaa City
Garwin Wyatt San Gerxon

"The Campiaan Alliance doesn't have High Demons. You do," I told Kooper Griff. "In my estimation, I'd add at least two to each ship you send out."

Dad was content to sit back in his desk chair and let me handle the meeting between him, Ildevar Wyyld, both Directors for the respective Alliance Security Details and a few extras, including Winkler, Dragon and Edward.

"I'll add my ships to yours, but I don't have access to as many power wielders as you do," Jett nodded in Kooper's direction.

"Send what you have, then," Kooper said. "Don't send regular troops—they'll be in too much danger. Besides, we don't need them added to the enemy's numbers, and that's what will happen if they're exposed to this virus or whatever it is they've concocted."

"Here's my thought on that matter," I said. "Why haven't they sent those infected with that filth running through the streets of major cities to affect anyone and everyone? Why target ASD and CSD troops and leaders? Don't tell me they haven't targeted you," I frowned at Jett. "Because they have."

Kooper and Jett exchanged glances for a moment before turning back to me. "What do you think?" Kooper asked.

"I think they want ships, supplies, weapons and equipment," I said. "What better way to get the best both Alliances have to offer, and infect troops to fight for them at the same time?"

"That's a frightening concept," Jett rumbled.

"What do they intend to do with all that?" Kooper whispered.

"You have to ask yourself who'd want it and why," I went on. "Who'd benefit from adding ships to their fleet?"

"You're assuming they have a fleet to start with," Kooper's voice trailed off.

"They have to have pilots and captains ready to go—there's no way they'll leave those positions to newly-infected agents. They already have those things, in my estimation. You know as well as I do that there are dozens of small-time pirating factions that strike only now and then, before disappearing for an extended period. We know about the larger pirate fleets—they have ships all over the place. Those are the ones the BlackWing ships usually investigate. The smaller operations are like ghosts—you can't track what doesn't show up on a regular basis."

"They're so small and the attacks are infrequent," Kooper began before pinching the bridge of his nose between a thumb and forefinger. "Fuck," he breathed. "BlackWing has instructions to ignore those most of the time."

"If they're behind this, then we know much less than we should," I said. "Because we've never actively investigated their crimes. Add some kind of powerful entity to their operation, and you have the makings of an epidemic and a takeover."

"I was much happier when I walked into this meeting," Jett observed dryly. "I wasn't particularly happy then."

"I'll present this to Quin and Randl," Kooper said. "Is there anything else before I switch ASD gears and get the ball rolling on a new investigation?"

"No, that's what I have for now, and trust me, I've given this a lot of thought," I told him.

"How would you like to travel with the crew of BlackWing X?" Kooper lifted an eyebrow.

"That's fine with me. I've enjoyed working with Travis and Trent in the past."

"Good. I'll send two High Demons, too. You may have to squeeze in, but I'd like you to help with this. Run your theory past

Randl, too, if you wouldn't mind. He has a way of poking holes in the best of plans."

"When do you want me to join the crew?" I asked.

"Yesterday," Kooper said and disappeared.

* * *

BlackWing X, Orbiting Pyrik
Travis

I'm on my way, Wyatt informed me. *Has Kooper told you about the High Demons, yet?*

We have two on the way, I returned. *I think I can give them the larger cabin so they'll room together. You'll have the smaller, private one.*

Thanks, man.

Wyatt appeared in front of me, but I was expecting him. He held a bulging duffle in each hand and had a shoulder bag hanging at his side. He'd brought his own comp-vid and equipment, it appeared.

"Where's my bunk?" he grinned at me.

"Nice to have you aboard, Ambassador," I slapped him on his free shoulder. It didn't make him move an inch. He had too much of his vampire father and grandfather in him to do otherwise.

"When I'm settled in, I need to talk to Randl," he said. "Kooper's orders. You and Trent can be there if you want."

"Probably so. I'll set it up an hour from now. Come on, you'll be down the same passage, near Sabrina and Jayna. The High Demons will be next to Randl; those were the two cabins I had left."

"Good enough."

I led the way, he followed.

* * *

Wyatt

I hadn't been in so small a room since I'd hidden in a broom closet at home when I was younger. The bed took up most of the

space, with a tiny, bedside table at one end and a chest at the other. Between that and the door was a closet, which no self-respecting skeleton would inhabit.

See this? I recorded an image of the narrow closet and sent it to my brother Bel Erland.

Is that where you keep your sword?

Funny, bro.

I heard Lexsi and Kory are heading your way.

They're coming? Wait, you're teasing me, aren't you?

No, man. Serious as a coronary.

That would be outstanding. I hardly ever get to see baby sis for longer than ten minutes.

If you need a warlock, you know who to call.

Ilya Ironsmith?

Funny, bro, he replied.

That's for the sword remark. That was my closet and you know it.

Mom says she's letting Lexsi go on this little outing in case you need a controlled burn.

That—makes sense, I conceded. *Randl says burning can get rid of the anomalies.*

That's what Mom suggested, too. It's much better than destroying the entire—you know.

I do. Thanks for the heads up. Things could get interesting from here on out.

Keep me posted. You know I love a good story.

Will do. Gotta go so I can unpack and fill my empty closet.

That'll take two seconds, dude.

Where will I ever put my winter wardrobe? I teased.

Maybe you can convince Travis to get a trailer for number X to haul your extras.

That's almost funny. See ya, bro.
Yeah.

* * *

Randl

"The Crown Prince and Princess of the High Demons are here to help?" If I hadn't seen Travis' serious expression, I'd have thought he was teasing me.

"Just got here, actually. Wyatt's here, too, and he wants to meet with you. Trent, Lexsi, Kory and I will probably sit in."

"All right. Where will we meet?"

"In the Captain's cubby—I think there's enough room there for all of us. Bring something to drink—this could take a while."

* * *

A few minutes later, with a mug of tea in my hand, I joined Travis, Trent, Wyatt and two others in the Captain's cubby near the bridge.

"Director Griff wants me to tell you my theory of who may be behind all this," Wyatt began.

"You have a theory?" Lexsi, Crown Princess of Kifirin, was suddenly sitting up straighter in her seat. I could see that she clearly trusted Wyatt. Shoving long, white-blonde hair over a shoulder, she gazed at Wyatt expectantly.

Wyatt was her older brother. He was also slightly older than Travis and Trent, who were his uncles. I turned back to Wyatt, although his idea was already forming in my mind.

The terrifying part was that he could be right.

* * *

Travis

"So those two-bit pirates we haven't bothered with could have joined forces with a sorcerer or some other powerful being, and hatched this plot?" Trent didn't sound happy. Hell, I wasn't happy, either.

All along, we'd been instructed to ignore small-time piracy in favor of the bigger boys in the shipping lanes. It was similar to ignoring the occasional pickpocket in favor of chasing the bank robbers.

"Do we have incident reports on any of those smaller pirate attacks?" Randl asked quietly. He was thinking hard about this, I could tell.

"I'll see if there are any to pass along," I offered. He dipped his head in a nod. "I'll do research on Cord'ilus, too. I know it's destroyed, but there had to be a reason they chose it, don't you think?"

"That makes sense," Wyatt said. "Let me know if you find anything."

"I will."

"Dinner is waiting, according to Bekzi," I announced. "Is there anything else before we haul ass to the galley?"

"Not from me," Kory grinned and held up a hand.

We ended up shoving three tables together, so Sabrina, Jayna, David and Terrett could join us. I told them Wyatt's theory, and that we'd be ready to go whenever Kooper sent the word.

That word wouldn't come until likely signs were recorded by micro-drones. "I'd like everyone to meet in the exercise room for a bit of meditation an hour after dinner," Trent said. "We need to get rid of some stress, I think, or this could keep most of us awake, worrying about it."

* * *

Randl

Sabrina hung back when the rest of us left the table to head for our cabins. I wanted to dress more comfortably before sitting cross-legged on the floor for meditation.

Travis and Trent stayed behind, too.

They wanted time together with Sabrina, and I understood that—because I wanted time with her, too.

Time to tell her how grateful I was that she was alive.

Shoving that aside, I focused on walking toward my cabin, and ended up behind Lexsi and Kory, whose shared cabin was right next to mine.

He smiled down at her and leaned in for a kiss just as they reached their cabin door. Nearly tumbling inside after Lexsi turned the handle, the door was shut quickly behind them.

With a heavy sigh, I opened my door and walked inside, where only things that didn't really matter waited for me.

* * *

Later, I sat cross-legged between David and Bekzi in the exercise room, while Sabrina's familiar ponytail taunted me two rows up.

Her eyes would be locked on Travis and Trent at the front, who'd be guiding our meditation.

Closing my eyes to shut out what I couldn't have and therefore shouldn't want, I began early, searching for the peace that meditation could provide.

Like in my occasional dreams, the stars in the darkness appeared after a while, sending a shiver of wonder through me.

They were there, as always, like they were waiting for me to touch them.

Zaria's inscription floated through my mind.

Touch the stars.

What would it hurt?

Chapter 13

Reaching out mentally, I attempted to connect with one or two of those shining lights.

* * *

"Randl?"

I woke with a gasp to find David's face in front of mine. He was smiling. "Somebody always falls asleep," he teased. "Come on, man, let's go sneak a beer from the galley before bed."

"I'm right behind you," I said, rubbing sleep from my eyes. "Damn, I didn't realize how tired I was."

"Stress can do that," David said. I rose and followed him out of the exercise room, turning left to navigate the corridors back to the galley.

"Cheers," David clinked his bottle against mine before drinking.

I turned away from the dimly lit galley to stare at the stars surrounding Pyrik. From our orbiting position, they weren't streaks of light, although they did move out of my window's range rather quickly.

It didn't matter; there were always more stars to see as we continued our circular path around the planet.

"You're having a beer and didn't invite me?" Wyatt appeared at our table and pretended offense.

"Sit down, I'll get one for you," David said and slid off his chair.

"Thanks, man," Wyatt nodded.

"How soon do you think we'll be called away?" I asked Wyatt.

"It'll take a day or two before we get reliable reports from the drones," Wyatt said. "After that, it's anybody's guess."

"I looked up information on Cord'ilus," I said. "Other than it being abandoned for nearly a thousand years, it was on a list for the logging industry to study for potential logging. Doesn't matter now, because the planet and all its trees are now space dust." I took another swig from my beer.

"We know they're not really interested in any of those worlds that don't have the technology and population to support their logging crews," Wyatt sighed. "That's why the question is on the ballot for Conclave."

"I understand that," I agreed. What I didn't understand was why it troubled me. Cord'ilus was gone and a moot point. Still, I intended to dig deeper into its history, to learn all I could about it.

David came back at that moment with Wyatt's beer. "Down the hatch," Wyatt grinned and held up his bottle.

"Here, here," David said and we drank.

* * *

Lee'Qee, Pyrik
Varok

"The troops are ready to go," Perill informed me. "Will others be waiting on the designated planets when their transport arrives to take them?"

"All is set, according to the Prophet," I turned toward Perill after finishing the last of my star charts for the various journeys. "We have trained ours well; they will take command upon arrival."

"Will they be shielded well enough? We do not need discovery by either Alliance until all is ready," Perill pointed out.

Perill's whining made me want to lash out at him. He'd lost trainees in the attack on Cord'ilus, so his questions were justified. I merely didn't want to hear them. Perhaps it was fortuitous that the Prophet had canceled his journey to Pyrik after Cord'ilus was destroyed; Perill would surely have embarrassed himself and warranted a death sentence. The Prophet would make sure I'd be responsible for performing the execution. Perill and I had already lost our father, Vrak. I didn't want to destroy my only remaining kin.

Chapter 13

It was now known that the Reth Alliance had a ranos cannon at their disposal; how else could they have destroyed Cord'ilus? I imagined that the Prophet was focusing his abilities on obtaining such a powerful weapon, as it would ensure our victory in the end.

"Brother, I know Cord'ilus' destruction troubles you," I told Perill. "Focus on the plan. Make those deaths count. They gave us information we didn't have before, and perhaps a link to a weapon we will seize."

"I hope that is the case," Perill grumbled and turned away. I watched him walk out of my command center, his back stiff and his gait stilted. Eventually, he would get over this—he had to or the Prophet would watch him die.

* * *

Randl

Perhaps I should meditate then have a beer every night, I mused as I received my shooting lessons the following morning. All night, I'd dreamed I could fly, and so I'd flown over multitudes of forests, watching the green of tree tops blur past me, I was moving so swiftly.

I'd never had such dreams before—until then, the stars in my dreams had been the best ones I could recall. As a result, I had to force myself to focus on shooting at the target with my practice laser pistol, while Travis stood beside me, grinning whenever I hit the target at the center of its holographic chest.

I was hitting it more times than missing it, too, and he was quite happy with the results. "I can have you certified in no time," Travis' grin widened as I hit the target dead center. "How are your other studies coming along?"

"More than half done," I said before sighting the target, gripping the pistol firmly and holding my breath before releasing the single laser shot.

"Good. Does that mean you could pass the exams now on that material?"

"Probably—I have a good memory."

"You can designate which exams you want to take," he said. "When you pass them, you can move on to the next. Once you pass all of them, your records will be updated and your status and pay elevated."

"Is it possible to start training at hand-to-hand combat?" I asked. "Breaking out of holds is one thing, but I'd also like to defend myself if necessary."

"I can ask if Bekzi wants to train a beginner," Travis said. "He's actually good at that."

"I'd be happy to train with him," I agreed and fired another shot at the target. I didn't want to train with Sabrina—for obvious reasons. She was far ahead of me in self-defense, and it would be better for both of us if we weren't in close quarters.

I'd want to touch her instead of spar with her, and that would never do.

"You did pretty well with a pistol on Cord'ilus," Travis went on. "Kooper was very happy about that."

"It all happened so fast, I didn't think he'd have time to notice," I said. "I only hit three with any accuracy—not counting the dead ones, of course."

"Hmmph. Being in close quarters and having the enemy rush you like that—that's actually a pretty good result," Travis replied. "That's enough for now—clean your pistol and put it away. Lunch is almost ready."

"Good. I'm starved," I said and lowered my weapon. I'd eaten a huge breakfast, too, so it was a surprise to be as hungry as I was.

"Come on, then, get your stuff done and get to the galley." Travis gave me a grin before stalking toward the shooting range door.

* * *

"I heard you may have a real weapon soon," David set his lunch tray next to mine at the table I'd chosen.

"I have one," Wyatt grinned and joined us. "I take it everywhere."

"Yes, but you have diplomatic immunity," David said, pointing his fork at Wyatt.

"I know. I'll never catch diplomacy because I'm immune," Wyatt teased.

"Hey, nobody else is allowed a sense of humor at this table," David grumped. "Besides, it's meatloaf day. Stop ruining it for me."

"It is good meatloaf," I agreed and stuffed a chunk in my mouth to chew. *Susan, Bekzi—amazing meatloaf,* I sent to them.

We thank, Bekzi's shortened speech floated back. *We train tomorrow.*

Thank you, I returned. *I'm grateful you're willing to do this for me.*

Not worry, I teach. Tell David we have more meatloaf if he want.

"Bekzi says they have extra meatloaf if you want it," I informed David, who nodded because his mouth was full.

"We have a target," Travis appeared at our table. "Finish your food, we'll be on our way in half an hour."

Chapter 14

A*SD Headquarters, Le-Ath Veronis*
Kooper Griff
"It hasn't escaped me that Bornelus is less than a day's travel from Veechee," I told Lissa. Veechee was a concern, as it was the planet where Vrak had apparently hidden himself for at least two decades. The possibility of a connection between Veechee and Bornelus, the latter of which mirrored Cord'ilus' evenvironment, had certainly piqued my interest.

Lissa, Winkler, Drake and Drew had come when I sent a message to the palace. I'd already given orders for BlackWing X to head in Bornelus' direction, and they were on their way to that deserted world.

"And because there's an obsession on Vrak, we can't get anything from the bastard," Lissa grumbled. "He eats, sleeps and paces inside his cell. That's it."

"Do you think he has thoughts of his own?" I asked.

"He hasn't talked, so no idea," Lissa shrugged.

"He ought to be destroyed," Gavin rumbled. That verdict came as no surprise to me, since Gavin was vampire and more than two thousand years old.

"Honey, we'll get to that," Lissa rubbed his back. "He still may be of use to us. After all, he was important enough for somebody to destroy a ship because he wasn't on it."

"That's very true," I said. I hadn't considered how important that key to the puzzle might be. A part of me wanted to set Vrak down on Pyrik and follow wherever he went, but I considered that Opal and Kell had followed three others as mist and those three had disappeared beneath their noses.

So far, those same three hadn't appeared again, and that led me to believe they knew they were followed out of the restaurant. That didn't make me comfortable at all. Usually, nobody knew or suspected we were tailing them when Kell was mist.

"I'll keep you in the loop when BlackWing X begins its orbit around Bornelus."

"I have a lot of kin on that ship," Lissa reminded me.

"Don't I know it," I said.

* * *

BlackWing X
Randl

Bornelus. That was our destination. My research on that abandoned world hadn't provided much in the way of useful information. War and disease had killed it long ago, and nobody thought to repopulate for fear of the disease spreading. Currently, it was covered in trees, plants, animals—and nothing else, according to official reports.

ASD micro-bots had detected life forms which couldn't be attributed to normal wildlife; therefore, we were on our way.

Chapter 14

The images included in the research materials were out of date, having been taken years earlier. Those only showed crumbling buildings and infrastructure, overcome by unchecked plant growth and the passage of time.

What I had found, however, was that Bornelus, like Cord'ilus, was on the list to be considered by the logging industry. Their scheduled date for visiting the planet was less than a month away.

Cord'ilus' scheduled date was in six months. I hoped the industry received information so they wouldn't arrive in Cord'ilus' air space, only to find the planet missing.

Veechee, where Vrak had boarded a pirate ship bound for Pyrik, was only a day's travel from Bornelus. That fact hadn't escaped Travis and Trent—they'd likely gotten the information from Kooper.

The knock on my cabin door interrupted my research. Setting my comp-vid aside, I rose to answer it. Wyatt and David were outside. "Dude, come on or we'll be late for dinner," David said. "Jayna and Terrett are joining us tonight."

"Let me grab my jacket," I said.

* * *

Can you see through Jayna's disguise? I sent to Wyatt as we sat around the table, talking and laughing while we ate.

I can. She just doesn't know it.

It was something I'd already known—that Wyatt was interested in Jayna, but I hadn't said anything to anyone about it. Jayna wore a plain disguise for a reason—not only was she strikingly lovely beneath that disguise, but she was afraid of becoming close to most men.

Someone had frightened her when she was young, and she didn't trust many men as a result. Hiding behind her warlock-created disguise made her more comfortable, because most men wouldn't

235

approach her due to her appearance—or what they perceived as her appearance.

Shallow, bumbling fools that they were.

"What will we do once we get to Bornelus?" Wyatt asked, pushing the salt toward Jayna's end of the table before she had to ask for it.

"Send out sensors to check for anything harmful before setting down on the planet," David said. "We'll know pretty fast whether we can go down or not. This time, we'll choose a clearing outside the largest city—we set down in the city on Cord'ilus and that's where we found the enemy last time."

"I didn't see any Sirenali with those we fought on Cord'ilus," Terrett commented. The moment he spoke he had everyone's attention, because he seldom said anything. It came from years of being unable to speak. "It makes me wonder how so many were hidden, so none could sense their presence."

"Did you miss us?" Travis asked. He, Trent and Sabrina arrived and pulled chairs up to our table.

"We were just discussing the absence of Sirenali on Cord'ilus, and the inability to sense most of the enemy anyway," Wyatt gave Travis a nod.

"Sirenali bones?" Trent asked.

"Did anybody take the time to find out?" Wyatt countered.

"No time, man," Travis said. "Maybe we can do a more thorough search if we find somebody on Bornelus."

"Did you see anything out of the ordinary?" Travis turned to Sabrina. "Bones, maybe?"

"I didn't see any bones," she shook her head. "I did run out of that building as fast as I could, though, so I wasn't really looking for anything other than somebody who wanted to kill me or keep me from getting away."

Chapter 14

"Bones can be hidden in walls and still be effective," Terrett pushed potatoes around his plate. I knew this information upset him—that his bones could be taken and used to hide anyone from the powerful. His life meant nothing to those who were so minded to use him for that purpose.

"That information stays on this ship," Travis warned.

"Of course," Wyatt agreed.

"I saw very little in those who attacked us," I confessed. "In the dead, I found nothing. The living were following instructions, as you might imagine, but there was an encroaching obsession similar to that of Pyrik's President."

"With no way to tell what that could be," Trent frowned.

"It's confusing," I admitted. "I wish I knew more or could have seen more."

"Stop worrying about it—you did what you could in a limited amount of time," Trent said. "You'll end up second-guessing yourself to death."

"What he said," Wyatt lifted an eyebrow and nodded toward Trent.

I didn't tell them that I'd had disturbing dreams about Pyrik the night before—I'd dreamed that the dead we'd found on Cord'ilus were walking the streets of Pyrik instead, specifically, the streets of Mer'bali.

It was shiver-inducing, and in my dream, I'd shouted and screamed for the dead-walkers to stop or they'd infect the living.

It had been a frustrating experience, and one in which I'd felt particularly helpless, thinking all the while that I should be able to do something more to stop them.

An overwhelming urge had come over me to burn them, but the practical side of my brain informed me of the impossibility of that act.

Yes, I had lucid dreams at times—since I was quite young. Always, my rational self pulled my dreaming self away from such foolish notions and efforts.

I'd already known that those affected by the anomaly could be destroyed by burning, and that had carried over into my dream.

Burning was also the reason we had two High Demons with us. Both could make fire in their demon form, but Lexsi far outshone her husband Kory in that respect. Lexsi was Wyatt's sister, and the youngest of his siblings. I knew they were having silent conversations now and then, because I caught them smiling, then attempting to hide their smiles.

"We'll reach orbit range of Bornelus tomorrow afternoon, so be ready to go if we get an all-clear from our sensors," Travis said. "We'll go down heavily armed, just in case."

I wasn't looking forward to a repeat of what happened on Cord'ilus—I'd been on the verge of panic when the dead popped out of tall grass to attack us.

The whole, grisly experience was difficult to eradicate from my waking thoughts, too, as I could easily recall my visions of bodies nearly blasted to pieces still coming toward us, following the instructions of who knew what—or who.

I was beginning to consciously call whomever it was the necro-sorcerer, as I had no other functional explanation for his or her talents.

"Who could spawn such?" I blurted aloud, stopping all other conversation at the table.

"Spawn what?" Travis asked.

"A necro-sorcerer."

"Now there's a new term," Trent sighed. "But it fits."

"It troubles me," I admitted. "It doesn't fit within the universes. To me, it feels as if it doesn't belong, somehow. A mistake, perhaps, or the worst sort of aberration."

"You think Mother Nature was misbehaving, in this case?" Kory asked.

"I can't give credit for this to Mother Nature, and, if she exists, I'm sure she wouldn't accept credit," I shook my head at the High Demon Prince. "If this wasn't a design from what we consider normal, thinking creatures, then it is perhaps the strangest of accidents. However it happened, it has the stink of interference all over it."

"I get that idea, too. Mom and Gran worry that V'ili may have had a hand in all this, but even he couldn't command the dead. He had obsession, yes, but not this. Nothing even close to this," Lexsi shivered. Kory placed an arm about her shoulders to ward off the sudden chill enveloping his mate.

"I'm sure he never placed any obsession that could grow until it consumed the victim, either," Terrett grumbled. "No Sirenali could do that. V'ili never demonstrated those talents during his long life, and he would have if he could do so."

Yes, I knew the one called V'ili was Terrett's father. Terrett wanted nothing to do with his murderous, criminally-inclined paternal figure, whom he'd never actually met. I wasn't about to upset Terrett with the information I knew. He didn't deserve it and Quin loved him, so I understood there was nothing but good in Terrett's intentions.

In fact, he'd have gladly killed V'ili if he could. I was grateful Zaria had done it, however, as that removed an additional burden from Terrett's and others' shoulders.

"At least we know V'ili's dead," Wyatt said, echoing my thoughts.

"I'll drink to that," David raised his glass.

* * *

I was invited to the bridge after breakfast and training with Bekzi the following morning. Bornelus had come into view and became larger as we neared orbiting distance.

"Three very active volcanoes," I reported what I knew at Travis' request. "My guess is that nobody will want to be within range of those—the living won't like breathing ash, I think."

"That's what we think, too, which eliminates six large cities," Travis concurred.

"Kooper had someone go through all the flight plans from Veechee for the past several years, and nothing was recorded," Trent added. "This shores up Wyatt's theory that small-time pirates are involved, because they'd have no need of arranging flight plans. Do you suppose their base could be on one of these abandoned worlds?"

"That's possible," Travis agreed. "I'd hole up somewhere like that—a place where nobody wanted to go or thought to look."

"Is it possible to get all the locations where the logging industry has gone—all the deserted worlds they've visited in their search for suitable trees to make wood products?" I asked.

"I don't see why not," Travis said. "How far back do you want to go?"

"Several years," I said.

"I'll ask Kooper to find out when they started looking into this sort of thing, and work their way forward," Trent offered.

"Thank you."

"You got a hunch, bro?" Travis asked.

"My ASD instructors say to check every lead. Perhaps those who've visited these worlds looking for suitable forests stumbled across something and thought it wasn't important enough to report. We may need that information."

"Bro, you're a genius," Trent said and pulled his comp-vid from a pocket. A message was composed and sent to Director Griff in short order.

"We should have an answer before long," Trent said and pocketed his comp-vid.

"If we find nothing here, I'd like to dock on Veechee and check Vrak's former address," Travis said. "I'll send that message to Kooper after we've searched the planet."

"You think he may have hired somebody to kill the one who arranged his travel with those pirates?" Trent asked.

"Anything's possible. I'm hoping bro here can tell us something from his former neighbors."

"That's a thought," I agreed with Travis' assessment. "We'll check on that, if Kooper allows it."

"Here's my thought," Travis said after a moment. "If small-time pirates are involved, why would they hire another faction to haul an important cog in their wheel to Pyrik?"

"To keep attention away from them, in case they were caught—which they were," Trent suggested.

"Besides, Terrett was with you the whole time, wasn't he?" I asked.

"Yes," Travis admitted.

"What if our enemy can't see that, like most others can't? Can Sirenali detect one another, or is that impossible for them, too?"

"Let's ask Terrett," Travis suddenly looked grim. He sent mindspeech, because Terrett folded onto the bridge in moments.

"Can Sirenali detect other Sirenali, or are they just as hidden from each other as they are from most people?"

"Ah. I wondered when you'd ask that," Terrett replied. "If Sirenali could detect one another, do you think V'ili would have survived as long as he did? V'ili and others of his ilk were undetectable to anyone, including other Sirenali."

"That's sort of fucked up," Trent breathed.

"You wonder why Cayetes and V'ili were so interested in creating young Sirenali, before cutting their tongues out so they couldn't place obsession? That is part of the reason. I and my brothers hadn't a vision of V'ili or others like him."

"That's messed up, bro," Trent shook his head.

I'm sorry this upsets you so much, I silently sent to Terrett.

So many younglings died, and their bones were sold to criminals, to hide them from others with power.

He didn't say everything he knew, either—that some of those young ones had been thrown to flesh-eating worms while still alive, to fill the orders coming in from the criminal factions clamoring for more Sirenali bones.

Sirenali bones worked, and never had to be fed like the live ones did. The thought of such horrible deaths made me ill, just as it did Terrett.

"How close do you have to be before feeling the buzz from a spell?" Travis switched to a safer topic.

"I had to be at the building in Mer'bali before I felt it," I admitted. "I suppose that means I have to be practically on top of it."

"When did you feel it in the coin that dropped next to Sabrina?" Trent asked.

"Just before it dropped beside her. The buzzing became overwhelming, almost, as if the spell had been timed for release."

"There's a thought," Travis frowned at his brother. "I'll ask Bel if that sort of thing can be arranged."

"I've never heard of such, but warlocks and wizards do have their secrets," Terrett observed.

"That's for damn sure," Travis chuckled.

Chapter 14

* * *

Sabrina

So far, Travis and Trent hadn't made a move, other than to have meals with me and kiss me before I went to my cabin to sleep.

I'd be lying if I said I didn't want more, because I did.

A part of me understood that they had to remain loyal to the ASD and wanted to prevent any ideas of favoritism from invading the crew. My body, on the other hand, was screaming for them to ignore everything and take the advantage when it was offered—and it was certainly offered.

Fuck protocol, I growled mentally.

Baby, don't be like that, Trent teased. I hadn't meant for that to be heard—*how* had it been heard?

Removing my hand from my chest where the medallion rested, I considered how lucky I was that they'd only received two words from me. It could have applied to almost anything upon examination, and I examined it from every angle, torturing myself with the idea that I'd come across as a wanton if I weren't careful.

For a moment I contemplated taking the medallion off before reconsidering such a rash decision—it had saved my life and kept me from getting raped on Cord'ilus. Nobody should argue with those kinds of results.

The other thing I considered was that Randl had almost stopped speaking to me. That I couldn't explain. I went out of my way to be nice to him, but still he felt distant, as if I'd offended him somehow.

There were no more confidences from him; no explanations when I failed to understand something. Our training had gone in different directions, too, and I missed having him in the same sessions.

He was a good friend—perhaps the best of friends, now that the others had betrayed me as they had. I considered that I had no

243

friends, now, only potential lovers, and I had nobody to tell my troubles to about the lack of an intimate relationship.

Before Lorvis' treachery, I'd have been in constant communication with her regarding my relationship—or lack of one—with the twins.

Perhaps it was better this way. My instructional vids from the ASD said to keep personal secrets personal and secret, or they could be used against you or those you cared about.

Damn.

Why couldn't I be more like Randl in that respect? I figured there was a mountain-sized pile of information inside him—information that would never see the light of day so as to keep others protected and safe.

I guess he'd had to learn that from an early age, being what he was. After all, if you found out your cook was having sex with the next door neighbor, both of whom were married to others, it might have been better to keep that to yourself rather than announcing it at the dinner table as I'd done when I was twelve.

The ensuing battle between families resulted in the loss of our cook, a refusal by my father to give a reference and at great cost to the neighbor, who ended up never speaking to us again, even when my father supported him during a legal battle over property after his two wives left him.

That's how I knew to always be honest and transparent in every relationship I'd had. Too bad Fergue hadn't learned that lesson.

"He's dead now," I whispered, as if reminding myself of that fact. "Lorvis, too."

"We're moving into orbit around Bornelus," James, our pilot, announced throughout the ship. "Sensors will begin a sweep shortly."

* * *

Chapter 14

Randl

"Something here," Travis indicated the spot on a three-dimensional map created by the on-board mapping system. "Sensors suggest it isn't native to the planet and appears newer. It's what Kooper's drones pointed out, too."

"No humanoid life forms detected," Nathan, the navigator, read the console in front of him.

"No surprise—especially if they're dead," Trent responded. "Well, we haven't found anything else. Let's go down and take a look."

"It feels empty to me, but that doesn't mean we won't find something or learn something," I said.

"You'll be issued a weapon before we go down," Travis clapped a hand on my shoulder. "Get dressed for jungle conditions, bro, and meet us in the galley."

Half an hour later I walked into the galley where the others were gathering. Everyone was dressed similarly, in high boots to our knees, variegated green fatigues, helmets and an equipment belt.

Weapons were being issued by Terrett, who handed a pistol to me when I walked in. As my equipment belt also had a holster, I checked the gun as I'd been instructed before placing it in the holster and snapping the strap over it.

"We're ready," David came in last. James and Nathan would stay on the ship, but they'd been issued weapons, too, in case someone attempted to board the ship in our absence.

They'd also been instructed to get the ship away if everyone in our landing party were killed. It would be their duty to report everything they knew to Director Griff afterward.

I saw the determination in Travis and Trent's eyes—they intended to get us in and out safely, even if it cost them their lives.

I sincerely hoped it would never come to that.

"Ready?" Travis asked.

"Ready," we said in unison. He folded space with all of us in tow.

* * *

Spread out, Trent's mental voice advised after we landed on the planet's surface. He and Travis, armed with ranos rifles, held them at the ready as they stepped forward, walking through vine-and-grass-covered terrain that appeared even on the surface. Beneath that plant-covered surface it was anything but even.

I stepped carefully as a result, my pistol gripped tightly as I searched with mindsight and senses for anything that didn't belong. In the distance, perhaps a mile or more, lay the outlying buildings of a large city.

We were walking through the remains of the city's suburbs—the homes of which had been built of less permanent materials and had long since decomposed or sunk into the ground.

That's why I was careful where I stepped. Vines could conceal anything beneath their surface, as their roots could be far away from the leaves I stepped through.

On foot, it would take a while to reach the location Travis marked on the holo-map. I worried that tension would only ramp up the closer we came to that epicenter.

I noticed that Terrett and Bekzi were at the back of our group, constantly watching behind them while Travis and Trent led the way. If anything came at us from either direction, the most seasoned would handle the initial attack.

In the middle, keeping all of us within their nullifying range, stalked Prince Kory and Princess Lexsi. If any spells were thrown at us, they'd be nullified quickly by our High Demons.

Wyatt walked near the back, close to Terrett and Bekzi. We were guarded well enough for most emergencies. I hoped it would be enough, as visions of Sabrina's disappearance from the ASD warehouse kept playing through my mind.

None of us were expecting that, and Sabrina had reached out for the gold coin as anyone might do in similar circumstances. I had no desire to see that happen again. Perhaps that was why Travis and Trent saw to it that she walked near Kory and Lexsi.

Susan and Jayna guarded the sides—I walked ahead of Jayna while David walked ahead of Susan opposite us.

All of us froze when the snapping sound came—as if a twig had broken underfoot. I'd gone still, and once I knew we were temporarily unharmed, I closed my eyes to reach out with my mental sight, as if worried that what I'd registered with them open had to be wrong.

We'd triggered a trap.

Not a spelled trap; a more mundane variety of a trap. *Nobody move*, I cautioned in mindspeech.

We have to all disappear at once, I informed Travis. *It's coming.*

It? He sounded incredulous for a moment, until the ground rumbled beneath our feet.

Something was burrowing toward us.

Something very large.

"Get ready," Kory gritted between clenched teeth. "Trav, get the others out of here."

I felt my body jerk away as Travis and Trent did as Kory asked, leaving him behind. We landed quite a distance from our original location. Kory changed quickly. I'd never seen a High Demon in Full Thifilathi before.

I also had never seen what erupted from the ground to attack his Full Thifilathi before.

We'd been dropped far back along the path we'd taken while Kory, seventeen feet of black-scaled, fiery High Demon took on the most terrifying creature I'd ever seen.

Like a giant ground worm, it erupted from the ground at Kory's feet, tearing through the grass and plant life with a terrible roar, its huge maw filled with wicked, sharp teeth. It snapped at Kory's Thifilathi, which swung at and missed hitting the creature.

"Holy fucking hell, it's a hybrid Ra'Ak," Trent shouted over the noise of battle ahead of us.

Kory's answering roar of frustration shook the ground, and a subsequent bellow from the creature followed, before it leaped forward to snap at Kory's leg. Lexsi's nearby shout as the creature bit Kory's thigh almost deafened me.

She turned Thifilatha, then, and rushed the creature, while it was attempting to score another hit against a wounded High Demon. Once she arrived at the battle site, another creature tore through the ground to distract her from helping Kory.

"Fuck that," Wyatt snapped and became vampire mist.

I'd seen it in his eyes, however—what he planned to do.

His grandmother had taught him that trick, after all. Mist inside their head and blast the mist outward, making their heads explode.

That thought had bare seconds to form in my head before the ground rumbled again and more creatures exploded from the ground.

If anyone thought to have a more effective security system for Bornelus than this, I had no idea what it could be.

"Wait here," Travis turned to shout at us before he and Trent became what their fathers and grandfather were—dragons.

Travis was deep-blue sapphire, Trent was emerald, their scales gleaming in the light of Bornelus' sun as they leapt toward the fight.

"I get us away if necessary," Bekzi informed me. He could fold space and take us with him.

Chapter 14

I wanted him to take Sabrina and the others out of here. Instead, I ran toward Travis and Trent's last spot before becoming dragons, and lifted Travis' ranos rifle in my hands.

No, I hadn't trained with one, but things were about to get much, much worse.

"Get back," I shouted to the others and raised the rifle.

"No!" David yelled. "You could kill Wyatt!"

"You think I can't find Wyatt?" I leveled the gun, closed my eyes and waited for my mindsight to kick in. I'd know moments ahead of time where each creature would be by the time I fired my weapon.

If I didn't act now, the entire space around us would be boiling with these creatures, and I wasn't about to leave Wyatt, Travis, Trent, Kory and Lexsi behind to die.

Time to let them know how tough we could be.

I fired.

Chapter 15

B*lackWing X*

Travis

"Randl's exhausted. There isn't a scratch on him otherwise," Karzac informed me. I wasn't in the greatest shape, either, but at least Karzac left me awake. The others bore wounds of some sort, and were placed in a healing sleep.

"The poison in these Ra'Ak hybrids isn't as potent as that of a normal Ra'Ak," Karzac added.

"A normal Ra'Ak doesn't live underground and burrow through it like a giant earthworm," I responded before lifting my glass of bourbon and draining it.

"Enough of that," Karzac removed the glass from my hand. "You only had a few scratches, and somebody has to captain the ship," he reminded me.

"How the hell did Randl know where to shoot?" I asked my next question.

"Hmmph," Karzac snorted. "I believe it involves the prescience he has. Susan said he was shooting with his eyes closed."

"Damn," I sighed. "Thanks for coming and bringing Quin with you."

"She was needed to heal the High Demons," Karzac said. "They were impervious to the poison but had deep bites and gouges. Quin healed that while I tended to the poisoning of the others."

"What do you think Kooper will do when he gets here?" I asked.

"No idea, although I worry about the planet's fate after the discovery of these hybrid creatures."

"That makes two of us, and we still haven't had time to examine what we went down to see."

"I'd suggest going straight to it next time," Karzac said. "You can't be any worse off than you were before."

"True."

"I'm bringing in BlackWing VII and IX," Kooper appeared in the Captain's cubby, where Karzac and I sat. I wished for another glass of bourbon, but knew better than to suggest that to Karzac.

"I want to go back down there after the other ships arrive," I said.

"I'll let you. Take Randl with you, too."

"Are you kidding? You think I'd go without him?" I asked. "He told us something was coming for us. Turns out, he was not only right, he was really right."

"We don't have micro-drones that can see very far beneath the surface," Kooper sighed and walked to the hidden liquor cabinet behind the desk. He grabbed two glasses and the bottle of bourbon, poured one for himself, handed a second one to Karzac, then refilled mine.

Karzac lifted an eyebrow but drank anyway.

"There was no indication of any of this—it was all hidden, just as it was on Cord'ilus," Kooper went on. He poured himself another glass of alcohol after draining the first. "Could be Sirenali bones or a steep spell we haven't encountered before."

"Randl said something similar—he called the enemy a necro-sorcerer and said he'd never seen anything like it before."

"That title gives me the shivers, but I can't say it's inaccurate," Kooper grumped. "For now, we'll use it until something better comes along."

"Let's hope it's resolved before we have to rename it," Karzac huffed and emptied his glass.

* * *

Randl

I was asleep for nearly a day after the attack. I knew the creatures—what remained of them, anyway—had retreated deep into the ground before I stopped shooting.

It felt like hours, although it had probably been more like minutes while I fired Travis' weapon at the giant, worm-like creatures. I hadn't kept track of time—I'd been more focused on keeping track of the creatures and where their wriggling bodies and heads would go next so I could aim ahead of time and shoot when the right moment came.

After a shower, I dressed comfortably and made my way toward the galley, hoping something would be available to eat. I was famished and hoping for good food at the end of my search.

I found Travis, Trent, David and Terrett sitting around a table, eating and talking when I arrived in the galley.

"Have a seat, bro," Travis indicated a chair across from his.

"How are the others?" I asked as Susan set a plate of food in front of me. Bekzi showed up with a glass of fruit juice shortly after.

"Everyone's fine. Quin and Karzac patched everybody up—Kory's leg is healed, but he's still in a grumpy mood, according to Lexsi. VII and IX are on their way to help out, if necessary."

"Are we going straight in, next time?" I asked before lifting food to my mouth.

"That's the plan," Trent said.

"This is delicious," I said after chewing and swallowing.

"Boeuf Bourguignon," Trent said. "It's a favorite, but takes a while to cook. Susan made it for us."

"We're hungry, too." Wyatt and Jayna walked into the galley together. Wyatt held a solicitous hand at her back.

She didn't blush like Sabrina would have, but she was happier than I'd ever seen her, and it was due to spending time with Wyatt after the attack. It's strange—and wonderful—how dire circumstances can force people to acknowledge feelings they'd kept hidden before.

Sabrina had confessed no such feelings for me after her kidnapping. She'd been swept into Travis' arms and allowed her desires free rein by kissing him repeatedly.

People suffer through unrequited love every day, I reminded myself. *It's only the worst ever if your heart is the one involved.*

"I'll bring plates," Trent offered and rose from the table. He winked slyly at Wyatt, too. At least Jayna didn't see the wink; she was trying to hide the fact that Wyatt had linked his fingers with hers beneath the table.

"When will we go back down?" I asked. "To the planet?"

"Tomorrow, after the others get here. It doesn't look like these creatures can fold space like regular Ra'Ak, and that's a real plus," Travis said. "How the hell they got there to begin with is anybody's guess—this wasn't a world destroyed by the Ra'Ak. Bornelus killed itself with nuclear warfare long ago."

I mentally added that fact to the information I'd accumulated on the planets affected so far. Pyrik was afflicted in some way by nuclear waste dumps. Here, a hybrid race existed that had never been seen before, and could also have been greatly affected by nuclear poisoning.

Perhaps when we returned to examine the anomaly inside the city, I could get a better idea of what went wrong with this world.

"What did the micro-drones get, image-wise?" Wyatt asked.

"It looks like a concrete block—a big square with no doors, windows or anything else. The sensors couldn't penetrate any part of it, but the ground around it emitted a high level of radiation. Nothing else on the planet was affected like that," Travis explained.

"That would be an anomaly, all right," Wyatt agreed.

"The radiation shield provided by our utility belts will protect us well enough, but some of us can put up extra shielding if it's necessary," Trent said.

I had a feeling that the medallion I wore could protect me against that sort of thing, too, but I didn't say it. I'd already determined that whatever the concrete block's purpose was, it and the surrounding area was now empty.

Like the ship carrying the bodies of Lorvis and Akrinn was empty.

Would we discover bodies or bones? I wondered. Perhaps the creatures had devoured everything and we'd find nothing.

I suppose we'd learn what we could the following day. Too bad Quin had gone back to Le-Ath Veronis with Karzac the physician. I'd discuss this with her if she were still here.

"I sincerely hope those creatures don't come anywhere near that anomaly," Jayna sighed. "I have no desire to see those things again."

"We'll just hand the ranos rifle to Randl to begin with," Travis grinned at me.

There was something about the experience of shooting those creatures that I hadn't told anyone. At the time, I wasn't thinking about it—my goal was to kill as many of those beasts as I could.

Reflecting on the incident later, I felt as if I'd willed my shots not to miss. Travis, while teaching me to shoot a pistol, always said that during a stressful encounter, some shots always missed their mark.

This time, mine hadn't missed. I had no idea whether I could repeat my performance a second time, and felt concerned as a result. My accuracy the first time was extreme good luck, perhaps, and I was grateful for it.

"May we have a safer journey and a better day tomorrow," David lifted his glass. I lifted mine in return and nodded at the stoic dwarf.

* * *

Queen's Palace, Le-Ath Veronis
Winkler

"Is it my imagination, or has Amlis actually become more reasonable?" Lukas asked. I'd invited the Grand Master of Harifa Edus to dinner after he'd contacted me, asking for a meeting.

"Quin may have had something to do with that," I speculated after clearing my throat.

"The Avii Queen?"

"Yes. She's a powerful healer," I said. "That's privileged information, by the way," I added.

"I'll keep that to myself, then," Lukas agreed. His dark eyes narrowed for a moment as he considered everything I'd said. "You think she may have corrected his, ah, mental instability?"

"It's happened before."

"Is it something you can expand on?"

"Not really, no." I didn't want to get into the whole story of the previous King of the Avii, or how he'd become more rational after a healing from Quin. I also didn't want to explain how Justis had gained the throne; his brother, King Jurris, was murdered by an obsessed journalist who'd asked for an interview.

"Sounds like a long story," Lukas sighed. "No," he held up a hand, "Maybe another time; I don't need to hear it now. What I wanted to talk to you about is the number of letters Amlis and I are getting from the logging interests, asking to scout our forests. My replies have always been a polite *hells no*, but Amlis had already said yes months earlier while still suffering from his affliction, shall we say. One of those scouting parties is scheduled to arrive next week. Amlis contacted me three days ago in a panic, because he doesn't want them on Harifa Edus now."

"Fuck." I couldn't help cursing.

"My thoughts, exactly. Amlis wants me there when they arrive, to make sure they don't get away with anything. I'm asking you to come with me, to doubly ensure they don't get away with anything."

"I'll go. Perhaps I'll ask Lissa to come with me, in case they get unruly. Compulsion isn't off the list for her, at least."

"I wish we could bring in Randl," Lukas chewed his lower lip for a moment.

"Maybe we can," I said. "I'll ask Kooper if we can borrow him. He may not want to see Amlis, but we need his talent—or, we could ask Quin. She can see what's in that scouting party and keep us informed of their true intentions."

"After what she did to Rodrik, she may not want to see Amlis, either," Lukas pointed out.

"I'll ask for one or the other. Surely we can bring in one of them to help us sort this out. Look at it this way," I pointed my fork at Lukas. I think the logging industry was jumping the gun somewhat on this. If the Conclave hadn't been postponed, then the vote would already be taken. They were counting on it passing, don't you think?"

"That would make sense, since they were asking for permission to allow scouting parties long before the Conclave was scheduled."

"Yeah. Makes me wonder how many other worlds got messages, and how many of those said yes."

"You think they were gauging the vote by the number of acceptances?" Lukas lifted an eyebrow in speculation.

"Possibly. Damn, why didn't we see this before? Did Amlis get the names of the scouting party?"

"Just the supervisor's name," Lukas shrugged. "I can give you a copy of the message—it's on my comp-vid." He pulled the device from a pocket and tapped it a few times.

"I'll have somebody look at it," I responded as he pocketed his comp-vid. I intended to send it to Kooper, who'd forward it to Quin, no doubt. Something about all this was making my wolf's fur itch, as my father used to say.

"How many big logging concerns are involved?" I asked. "How many letters from different companies did you get?"

"The big six," Lukas said, giving me the nickname for all the major logging concerns combined. There were many subsidiaries of each of those six, but nearly all of them were connected to one or the other in some way.

"You think they're getting together on this?"

"With the vote in the offing, it wouldn't surprise me at all."

"Just what I was thinking," I confirmed. "Maybe I'll do some digging myself, or ask Rigo's network to look into it."

"Rigo's network?"

"Vampires." That one-word answer was all I needed to give Lukas. If a vampire couldn't get to the bottom of this, especially a vampire *spy*, then not many could.

"How soon?"

"Yesterday soon enough?"

"Thank you. The time of the scheduled meeting is on the communication I sent you. Bring anyone who can help—that will agree to come," Lukas said. "I worry they'll roll over Amlis like a bump in the road."

* * *

BlackWing X, Bornelus Orbit
Randl

"How do you suppose the presidential election is going on Pyrik?" David asked as he and I worked out with weights after our meal. I needed physical activity of some sort to clear my mind before going back to my research.

"I hear it's down to a run-off, as there was no clear winner in the first election," I grunted and pushed weights up with my legs.

"So, another election between the two with the most votes?"

"Looks that way, although I don't think either remaining candidate has stellar qualifications. I think they were elected because they had good hair and teeth." I'd quoted my father, who often said that of elected officials.

David chuckled and agreed with me.

"It may take another month to set up the subsequent vote, to give those two blusterers a chance to further their cause with the people of Pyrik. That means they won't have much time to settle into the office before the Conclave reconvenes."

"I hope we have this mess sorted out by then, or we may be in horrible trouble," David grunted as he lifted the weights above his head.

"I agree," I said and shoved my leg weights up again.

"We have a new twist, and it's not a good one," Travis folded into the weight room.

"Now what?" David dropped the weights at his feet and frowned at Travis.

"The concrete block we were going to examine?"

"Yeah, what about it?" David asked.

"It's gone. Disappeared right under our noses."

"Holy, fucking, bloody hell," David cursed.

* * *

"Micro-drones show a deep hole there, now," Trent leaned back in his chair. We'd gathered in the Captain's cubby to discuss the disappearance of the anomaly. "They've gone down into the hole for at least twenty feet, and there's nothing except the roots of trees and vines smashed against the dirt that surrounded the concrete block. Down there, the radiation is stronger, too, and I've sent the specs to Kooper's science team to see whether they can figure out why."

Like the vanishing of three people on Pyrik, the disappearance of a seemingly innocuous block of concrete made little sense as to how and why it was accomplished.

"We should have gone directly to it," Sabrina tossed up a hand.

"Yes, but we found ourselves in a war the last time we set down near our quarry," Travis pointed out. He didn't add that Sabrina's rescue had been our objective on that mission, and we'd set down as close as we could to the spot Quin indicated.

We'd been surrounded then by tall, crumbling walls and debris of a disintegrating city that required careful maneuvering to locate Sabrina. With Quin and two others flying above us, we'd been better equipped to find Sabrina—even though we were involved in a battle almost immediately.

Cord'ilus was now just a memory, because it had been crawling with the enemy, most of whom were affected by the strange, growing obsession we'd discovered on Pyrik. The rest had been literally raised from the dead and rigged to explode, spreading green mist and the encroaching tendrils of an obsession to anyone who physically came in contact with it. We'd been shielded against it, or we'd be in even more trouble.

I couldn't shake the feeling that someone, somewhere, had a terrible motive in all this, and that we'd barely touched on any part of it—as if creeping obsession wasn't bad enough.

"Are we still going down there tomorrow?" Jayna asked.

"I want to," I spoke immediately.

"We'll take Randl down. Anyone else who wants to go will be allowed. We won't stay long, bro," Travis nodded in my direction. "Get what you want and get out, all right?"

"I'll be done quickly, I think."

"Good. Anything else, send mindspeech or comp-vid messages. Dismissed."

* * *

Once inside my cabin, I pulled out my comp-vid to do more research. Specifically, I wanted to know which logging concerns had marked Cord'ilus and Bornelus as possible locations for their logging efforts.

I found what I wanted after employing the ASD key, as it was called. It could get past security walls to enable agents to cull certain information from a company's main comp without detection.

Bornelus was chosen by Burche Industries, Cord'ilus by WildTree Industries. In all, there were six major logging concerns, with many smaller ones connected to those six. Like the previous information I'd found, Cord'ilus was scheduled for a visit in a month, Bornelus in six months.

Neither of those things should happen, now—Cord'ilus because it was impossible, and Bornelus due to the creatures inhabiting the underground. A scouting party sent there would be destroyed quickly by those enormous worms.

I was now back to the concrete behemoth and what it actually was. It had a purpose—likely a sinister one, because it disappeared after our arrival. Somehow, I was convinced that the same person—or someone similarly talented on Pyrik, had removed the block before we could examine it closely.

That sent me back to the information gathered by Kooper's micro-drones. Those tiny bots were limited in the type of information they could gather, so a sample of the concrete block wasn't a possibility. A scan of its makeup revealed nothing out of the ordinary—the bots had been more interested in the amount of radiation surrounding the block.

Darkness covered the location of the hole on Bornelus, or I may have asked Travis to take me immediately. Something troubled me greatly about this, and I wondered why someone had removed the block now, instead of doing it before we arrived.

Something precipitated its removal immediately—of that much I was certain. The why of it kept digging its way to the surface of my thinking, much like the creatures on Bornelus had dug their way to the surface of the planet to attack us.

Tomorrow morning, I reminded myself. It was past time for sleep, so I switched off my comp-vid and pulled covers back on my bed. I doubted sleep would come easy, but I had to make the attempt anyway or I'd be fog-brained when I woke.

* * *

Avii Castle, Le-Ath Veronis
Quin

"What can you tell me about this person?" Kooper arrived to have breakfast with Justis and me. He handed me a comp-vid with a man's image displayed.

Chapter 15

"Phorde Gaster," I said immediately. "Works for WildTree Industries. Kooper, there's something odd about him. I think I need to see him in person," I said, handing the comp-vid back.

"You can do that very thing next week, because he's the supervisor of a scouting party sent by WildTree to Harifa Edus. Amlis, in his previously impaired condition, invited WildTree in to evaluate New Fyris' forests."

"Oh, no," I closed my eyes with a sigh. This meant I'd be forced to deal with Amlis and Rodrik again. "I'll go," I said. "Although I'd prefer not to speak with Amlis or Rodrik, if that's possible."

"I'll do what I can, but I can't promise anything. Lukas and Winkler will be there, as will Halimel."

I knew Halimel—he was a vampire spy in Rigo's network of vampire spies. He could also become mist, walk in daylight and consume normal food, to hide what he was and what he was capable of doing.

Zaria knew him better than I—she'd worked with him before. "All right," I agreed. "Let's have breakfast, shall we?" It was the polite thing to say, although my appetite had deserted me the moment Amlis' and Rodrik's names had come up.

"Dearest, I believe you should consider a disguise—we wouldn't want them to see the Queen of the Avii on Harifa Edus, I think," Daragar appeared, made himself smaller and pulled out a chair at the breakfast table.

"Good idea," Kooper agreed. "Can you get Bel Erland to do it for you? If not, I can find someone."

"No, Bel Erland will do it, I'm sure," I said. "How early next week?"

"Third day, and be ready at dawn. I'll have Winkler transport you in."

"All right. Dena, will you put that on my private calendar?" I turned to Dena, who nodded and pulled a comp-vid from her pocket.

* * *

BlackWing X, Bornelus Orbit

Travis

Bro, the hole is gone, Trent informed me.

I'd just gotten out of the shower when Trent's mindspeech came, and I froze for a moment.

What do you mean, it's gone?

Like it was never there gone. Grass and vines growing over it gone.

Fucking, mind-blasting, bloody hell, I cursed. *Where's Randl?*

Staring at the new bot images from the bridge, Trent replied. *Get your clothes on. He still wants to go down there.*

So do I, I snapped and grabbed my uniform.

* * *

Randl

My dreams from the night before had connected eerily with my reality as I studied the micro-drone images sent live from the planet's surface.

At first, I'd considered how much I'd wanted to visit the site before going to sleep the night before, and I'd had strange dreams about being there as a result.

I'd stood on one side of the square hole left from the absence of the concrete block. It was dark in my dream, as it should have been in reality. A sliver of moon played hide-and-seek with clouds sliding across the sky, although I didn't need the light to see.

My mindsight had supplied the images for me.

Terror had gripped me early on in the dream, when a robed and hooded figure appeared on the opposite side of the hole. For whatever reason, I was afraid he'd see me or sense my presence.

Chapter 15

He acted as if I weren't there, raising his arms while red light bloomed about him. In horrified fascination, I'd watched the hole fill quickly with dirt and detritus, pulled from elsewhere, I suppose.

Then, when the ground was even with its surroundings, a layer of grass and creepers appeared, as if they belonged there.

The figure disappeared and I'd awakened with a start—only to learn the reality of my dream in images from the micro-drone Trent sent to the surface.

Had I seen the truth in my dreams, or was it merely the imaginings of my mind as it played its dream tricks?

It worried me now, as I'd never seen the face of the man in my dreams. In fact, I wasn't sure it was a man, although that felt right to me, somehow.

Had the necro-sorcerer visited us twice, and we'd been unaware both times?

"What's going on in that mind of yours, bro?" Trent's hand dropped on my shoulder, startling me.

"Just—trying to reconcile this in my mind," I said after regaining my composure.

"Trav says we're still going down to get a look, but I've already advised Kooper and sent him the first micro-drone images. He's not happy, as you've probably guessed."

I considered telling Trent about my dream, but decided that could wait. What credence could I give it, other than the end result being the same? I saw no reliable image of the perpetrator in my dream, which was a significant drawback.

Nevertheless, I resolved to record my dream later in a personal journal, in case something similar happened again.

"I'm ready," Travis appeared on the bridge while straightening the collar of his uniform and tossing his long, black braid over a shoulder once the collar was in place.

"I'm ready, too," I said, although I felt nervous about going, now that the time was at hand. Would I find anything helpful, or was this a useless trip to satisfy my curiosity?

With a nod, Travis folded me to the planet's surface.

* * *

Travis

"The grass and creeping vines are wilting," Randl pointed out as we walked the perimeter of the space. So far, Randl hadn't ventured onto the soil covering the filled-in hole. He'd reported early on that he didn't feel the creatures near us, as he had before.

"What's your initial assessment?" I asked.

"That the grass and vines were removed from another spot and dropped on top of the covered hole," Randl replied. "The roots were disconnected at their original place, without being reconnected here."

I ran my recorder while Randl and I observed the site, for Kooper's benefit and for later study. "What else can you tell me?" I asked.

"Let me see," Randl said and knelt on the perimeter to place his hand on the edge of the covered spot. His body stiffened. I called out before jerking my ranos pistol from its holster, but Randl held up his hand to stop me.

"It's nothing you can shoot," he croaked. "Not now. Perhaps never."

"What the hell is that supposed to mean?" I demanded.

"Give me a few moments, Captain Travis. I'll tell you what I can afterward."

I watched as he placed his hand on the freshly-covered space, as if it were a grave. I almost spoke again, before determining that Randl needed my silence. I jerked too, the moment Randl connected with me mentally.

Chapter 15

Few could send images to another, with or without mindspeech. This wasn't just images.

Randl sent me visions.

I think I forgot to breathe for a while.

* * *

"Where is Randl now? I'd like to speak with him," Kooper said. I couldn't get the images Randl sent out of my head, and I'd gotten a filtered version of them.

"In his cabin, meditating with Trent," I confessed. "We don't have the talent to lay a healing sleep, so that's the best we could do on short notice."

Kooper had come the moment I sent mindspeech after bringing Randl back to BlackWing X. The ASD Director and I sat in the Captain's cubby, drinking tea and likely wishing for something stronger.

I knew *I* wanted something stronger.

"You'd better tell me what you know, then, so I can ask proper questions," Kooper gruffed.

"I saw a crowd of people around the site. It felt like years ago, although I can't explain why I thought that," I began. "In the hole was freshly-poured concrete, more liquid than usual—enough to drown in if you walked into it," I added. "One side of the squared site remained open. I didn't know why that was until a new crowd of people—men, women and children, were herded toward that clear space."

I forced nausea away before describing what came next. "What happened?" Kooper prompted.

"The new arrivals reached the edge of the concrete and stopped. That turned out to be a mistake, as those people standing on the other sides crowded them, knocking the first few into the hole."

I sipped tea and considered my next words.

"They ah, sunk into the liquid immediately, while some of their companions screamed. As if that weren't horrible enough, the original crowd began shoving the prisoners—that's how I saw them—as prisoners, into the hole while they screamed and begged for their lives. Children were tossed in with their parents, and the crowd cheered as they all sank below the surface, choking on liquid concrete until they were asphyxiated."

"How many?" Kooper whispered into my prolonged silence.

"Hundreds," I shuddered. "They weren't even granted a merciful death before they were shoved into that muck."

"That may explain why the fucking block disappeared, then," Kooper growled. "They were worried we'd discover it was a mass grave."

"This wasn't from when the planet originally died, I swear it," I said. "Perhaps Randl can pinpoint a better time, but in my estimation, and from the way the victims were dressed, I'd say it was during the last twenty-five to thirty-five years."

"There are no records of this planet being inhabited for centuries, and with the creatures you found the first time you went to the surface, I can't see that anyone could survive here for long," Kooper mused.

"Unless someone can control those creatures," I said.

"True enough," Kooper rumbled. "True enough."

Chapter 16

BlackWing X, Bornelus Orbit
Randl

BlackWing X, Bornelus Orbit, Randl. I wanted to apologize to Travis, for putting him through the horror of what I was seeing when I touched the filled-in pit, but I desperately needed someone to be with me as the dreadfulness of it washed through my mind.

Therefore, he'd witnessed it, too. It made us both ill. The why of it kept my mind confused and continuously working—those people were being sacrificed, although I couldn't imagine what their sacrifice would accomplish.

That concrete block had held the bodies of hundreds, who'd decomposed inside their concrete prison until bones were all that was left.

Kooper was aboard BlackWing X and wished to speak to me when I was able. Until then, he debated whether to send a digging bot to the site to collect data from the original space.

Why was it important that the block be removed? We had no idea who'd placed it there—none of the people I'd seen drew my attention in any way, and no names surfaced in my mind.

Were they being hidden, somehow? Were those perpetrators still alive? That thought troubled me more than many others. Had the same scenario happened before or since, in other places?

Kooper would probably begin a search for evidence soon.

The other question that plagued my mind was this—where had those perpetrators gone? I had the impression that the sacrifice had taken place in the past twenty-five years or so, as time was measured on Bornelus.

Had they been devoured by the giant, worm-like creatures that threatened us? I'd found no evidence that anyone had lived on Bornelus for centuries, and Kooper's micro-drones confirmed that.

My dream worried me, too. Everything I'd seen in it had been verified, except for the hooded figure. I hadn't found him anywhere in the crowd during the sacrifice.

Why would someone with so much power involve himself now? Where was the concrete block after he took it—if he did take it?

Why hadn't he filled in the hole right after taking the block?

I had far too many questions and no answers.

"Feel like talking?" Kooper walked into my cabin without knocking. Travis was at his heels, with Trent close behind his brother.

"I suppose. It won't get any easier the longer I wait, so we may as well discuss it now," I agreed.

* * *

Sabrina

Trent wouldn't tell me anything, and that frustrated me. Travis and Randl had seen something horrible on the surface, and nobody was saying anything. Director Griff arrived, too, but that only tightened the secrecy surrounding the visit to the planet's surface.

What I knew was this—somehow, the concrete block had disappeared, leaving a hole behind. Then, the following day, the hole was magically filled in, leaving little evidence behind.

Randl's gift had enabled him to see something connected to all that, and Travis had somehow connected to Randl and saw it, too.

Curiosity plagued my mind while everyone else went about their usual business, as if nothing had happened.

I wanted to scream at them.

"Screaming not help," Bekzi the cook warned and placed a cup of tea in my hands.

Was everybody a fucking mind reader now?

"Not," Bekzi turned slitted eyes on me. I blinked—I'd never seen that from him before.

"Hmmph. You not see a lot," he commented and left me standing at a galley window, gazing at the stars surrounding Bornelus as the ship orbited the planet.

"Suddenly I feel like the most useless person on BlackWing X," I mumbled and sipped my tea.

Bekzi had put plenty of honey in the cup, just the way I liked it. That made me feel like a spoiled brat on top of everything else. So far, I hadn't contributed one useful thing to the ship's crew, and that left me feeling anxious and superfluous.

Maybe I ought to learn to cook and help out in the kitchen, I mused, before realizing I'd probably poison the crew accidentally, the way my luck was running.

I still hadn't done what I'd said and produced weapons for the crew. Perhaps I should concentrate on that, rather than feeling sorry for myself for being left out of the secret stuff.

"Back to the drawing board," I sighed and headed for the galley door. I had a comp-vid and draw-pad in my cabin, and could work out plans and schematics well enough with those. *Go to work. Take your mind off this shit*, I chastised myself.

* * *

Travis

Has Kooper given the word to get away from that place, yet? Mom's mindspeech came while I worked on reports to clear my head of what I'd seen. Randl and I had given our report directly to Kooper, who'd recorded audio of our briefing on his comp-vid. We'd get a printed version on our comp-vids later, so we could revise if we wanted.

We're leaving in a few, I answered Mom's question. *Kooper says to go back to Pyrik, although I don't know what good that will do. He's sending digging bots and bigger drones to the surface to collect soil and plant samples; the science ship is scheduled to arrive in the next two hours. Number Nine will stay here with it, in case anything weird happens.*

I think he wants Randl on Pyrik, Mom pointed out. *The presidential race has turned nasty there, and Kooper wants Randl's take on both candidates.*

Yeah. I can understand that, all right, I agreed and tossed my comp-vid onto the desk in my cabin. Trent was taking care of Captain's duties today, so I wouldn't have to.

Honey, I'm not going to ask you what you saw—I'll get a filtered version from Kooper, I think. Don't let it consume you. It happened in the past. Those people are long gone and feel no pain, now.

How can people do that to other people? I asked. *I've seen plenty of awful shit before, but this may be the worst yet.*

I know. Where did those people come from? she asked.

I still can't figure that out. They had to be shipped in from somewhere else—all of them. I don't believe the concrete block had been there more than thirty years at the most.

I think you're right, and that's a huge puzzle to solve. I wonder if Randl got anything more from all that?

I don't know. All I saw were the images he sent me—as if he wanted a witness to the horror so people would believe him or something.

I realize that, Mom agreed. *We may not have believed him, or completely believed him. After all, the block is gone and we have no remaining evidence, except what Randl saw and passed to you.*

Yeah.

Look, I'll come to Pyrik when you get there and we'll have a family dinner. Invite Sabrina, too, if you want. We can talk more about this then.

Mom, I can't tell her about this, I said. *It's too awful.*

Perhaps you should tell her eventually, when talking about it doesn't upset you so much.

I'll consider it. Thanks, Mom. I feel better, now.

Good. Send mindspeech anytime. I'll be here.

I know.

* * *

Randl

I was supposed to be resting.

Instead, I was on the bridge, going over the recorded images of the location—where Travis and I had witnessed past events surrounding the massive, concrete block.

It had been placed on the outskirts of a large city, with crumbling buildings acting as a backdrop on one side, while an encroaching forest lay on the other three sides of the block.

Those trees had to be a century old or older, and were quite tall. Many were evergreens, and could live thousands of years, perhaps.

They'd witnessed the horror, as had Travis, by a connection I'd forged between us. I imagined trees had no care for humanoids, who were a fleeting thing as they counted time—*if* they counted time.

Were they aware enough that humanoids often cut them down and destroyed them? I had no idea.

I figured these trees would be safe enough, since Kooper had quarantined the planet after the discovery of the massive, worm-like creatures living beneath the soil.

I sighed and my shoulders sagged. Weariness was taking a toll, but I knew I couldn't sleep if I wanted to; the same, horrific images invaded my mind if I tried.

Perhaps meditation would work.

"I think I'll go to my cabin and meditate, if that's all right," I rose and turned toward Trent.

"I'd recommend it," he agreed. "We'll be underway in two hours or less to Pyrik, Kooper's orders," he added.

"All right." I walked toward the doorway and off the bridge, heading toward the ship's sleeping quarters. Travis hadn't felt the fear beating with the victim's hearts like I had. There wasn't any way to convey that, and I'd have stopped it if there had been. He was traumatized enough by what we'd seen. No need to add to the horror of it by feeling the terror, sadness and overall hopelessness of the victims as they were forced into liquid concrete.

As for the final, terrifying moments while they struggled for breath and inhaled concrete in their mouths and noses—I felt ill just recalling a portion of that.

Whoever was responsible for that—and for whatever reason, I promised myself I'd hunt them down if it took the rest of my life to do it.

Chapter 16

For that horror, they needed to pay. As an agent for the ASD, I'd work diligently toward that goal.

More than diligently—it would become my own obsession.

Just got a message from Kooper, Trent's voice filtered into my mind as I reached out to open my cabin door. *He says we're stopping at Le-Ath Veronis before going on to Pyrik. He wants you to go with Winkler, Lukas and Quin to New Fyris in a few days. WildTree is sending a scouting party to New Fyris, and we need your help with that. When we get there, you can talk to Winkler and Lukas ahead of time about the scheduled visit. Quin says there's something odd about the supervisor WildTree is sending.*

I know about the scouting trip—Amlis told me to make the reply to WildTree months ago, I responded. *I knew it was a mistake when he ordered me to do it.*

Kooper says we can have shore leave while we're docked, Trent said after considering my reply. *I just talked to Mom; she's providing space for us at the palace.*

Thank you—that sounds good, I said, although my response was parroted. A day earlier, perhaps, the promise of shore leave would be welcomed. Now, it felt just as empty as I did.

* * *

Lee'Qee, Pyrik
Varok

The command compound looked as though it were inhabited by swarming ants. I'd received information moments earlier that the Prophet was coming to visit shortly.

I'd put everyone on alert; none of us wished to be found not working when he arrived—that could lead to terrible things best left to the imagination.

I'd just finished the reports on the presidential election—the latest information I had was that the election would be held in three eight-days.

"You will not have an election." The Prophet appeared as he often did, unannounced and unaccompanied.

He needed no guards—his power was enough protection. With the hood traditionally falling over his face, he saw everything anyway, and I wondered at that before going to a knee and bowing before him.

The others in the command center had done what I did, kneeling, bowing and remaining on our knees until he ordered us to rise.

"Rise," he tossed out a hand. "You will not have an election," he continued his announcement. "I have seen the death of one of the candidates. The other will take the President's position. The Conclave will convene after that."

"As you say, Mighty Prophet," I dipped my head to him.

"I charge you with ensuring his death," the Prophet went on. "I care not how it is accomplished, only that it is. Kill Lebbon, as he will be the least cooperative with our wishes. O'Tunne is more to our liking."

"Of course. It will be done," I bowed again.

"Do it in five days."

"I will see to it."

"Good. Very good. Keep me informed."

He disappeared as quickly as he'd appeared, and a collective sigh of relief went through my underlings. No sacrifice had been demanded this time, and I was grateful.

* * *

Sabrina

Chapter 16

"Will Queen Lissa have access to a manufacturing facility?" I asked at dinner. We'd been on our way to Pyrik, until Director Griff changed plans and sent us to Le-Ath Veronis for a few days' shore leave.

David, Terrett, Jayna and I sat together at a galley table, eating and discussing shore leave. At least *they* were discussing shore leave. I wanted to manufacture weapons for the crew so I'd feel less of a burden.

Travis and Trent were noticeably absent at dinner, and I hadn't gotten mindspeech from either of them.

Randl, too, wasn't there.

"You can ask," David said, lifting his beer bottle to drink. "Lissa has access to just about anything, if it's for a worthy cause."

Inwardly, I was quaking over asking Queen Lissa for anything. *Suck it up*, I reminded myself. I'd had a new idea for creating a temporary version of a ranos pistol, made from hardened plastics which would carry the shielding device and could easily be set to destroy itself by melting into a pile of unrecognizable junk.

Therefore, if you were about to be searched by the authorities, you could effectively get rid of any evidence that you'd carried a weapon.

My fingers itched to hold a prototype in my hands and fire it before setting it to self-destruct. It was a portable, undetectable, disposable weapon, and I wanted it to be as amazing in reality as it was in my head and my drawings.

If I'd only had one before Kooper confiscated my previous shielded version, I'd be back on Jaledis and—*dead*. As sobering as that thought was, I still wanted this idea to become reality. It would greatly enhance the ASD's abilities in undercover operations.

I had to think about that for a few moments. *Make it operable only by the assigned agent*, I mentally added another feature to the list. If it melted when anyone else touched it, all the better. They couldn't take it apart to see how it was made, and that would protect the ASD and my creation.

"You look like you're a thousand light years away," Trent set his tray next to mine at the table.

"I'm glad to see you," I whispered, staring at my plate.

"Stop worrying about stuff you can't fix," he said and scooted a chair out so he could sit beside me. "Trav is asleep. Randl is still fretting, so I had a tray sent to his cabin. We'll be at Le-Ath Veronis' space station late tomorrow morning. We're staying with Mom, of course. I'll take you to Niff's in Casino City while we're there."

"I have a new design I'd like to have manufactured—it shouldn't take long if the right equipment can be found," I blurted.

"Mom can point you in the right direction." Trent lifted his roll and bit into it. "Besides, you have to eat and have a little fun, you know. That's what shore leave is."

"All right."

"I can see those little wheels turning in your mind," he teased. "When I look in your ear, all those little people in your head are just bustling around."

"I don't have little people in my head," I made a face at him.

"Have you ever looked into your own ear?"

"That's practically impossible," I began.

"Then how do you know you don't have little people in your head?" Mirth glinted in his dark eyes.

"When I look in *your* ear," I sassed, "I can see clear through to the other side."

"Oooh—burn," David raised his beer bottle in a salute to me.

"All my little people are on shore leave, just like you will be tomorrow. Tell your little people to knock it off for a while," Trent grinned.

Chapter 16

"After I get my new design manufactured," I countered.

"All right, we have a deal." He lifted his beer bottle and drank.

* * *

Randl

The tray of food was provided by Trent; the four bottles of beer came from David. My attempts at meditation had mixed results at best—if I managed to clear my mind, it didn't last long and I was back to the visions again.

I stared at the food and beer before reaching for a beer first. Maybe alcohol would take the edge off what kept running through my mind. So far, nothing else had worked.

Want company? I received mindspeech from David.

Sure. Bring more beer, I instructed.

On the way, he replied.

Soon enough, David elbowed his way inside my cabin, allowing the door to swing shut behind him. He carried a crate of cold beer in his hands and set it on the floor with a slight thump.

"You're barely started," he complained as I drank from a second bottle. Lifting a beer from the crate first, he climbed onto the end of my bed and settled there to drink it. "Lexsi and Kory skipped back to Kifirin—there wasn't any need for them to stay, but Wyatt's still aboard and plans to stay with us for a while," David reported.

"Wyatt and Jayna," I began.

"We know that. *Now*. It appears they've been pining after one another for a while."

"Will she drop the disguise?" I asked.

"If she attends official functions with Wyatt, I think so," David nodded. "Otherwise, while she's on ASD business, it's the disguise as usual."

"Makes sense," I agreed. "Although the news outlets will all be wondering who the mystery woman is."

"Wyatt's a diplomat and a good one. He'll figure this out."

"Then I'll wait and watch," I shrugged and drank more beer.

"Need to talk about it?" David asked. He meant the visions from Bornelus.

"No."

"Ah."

"Just want to get as drunk as possible, since the meditation didn't really work out."

"I'll drink to that." David lifted his bottle before drinking again. "Will you see your pap while you're on Le-Ath Veronis?"

"I hadn't thought about it, but sure. I'd be happy to visit him. I hear he's staying at Lissa's beachfront palace on the light side most of the time."

"I've only been there once. It's really nice."

"I've never been. It'll be a first for me."

"It took a while for me to get used to all this," David said, waving his free hand. "I'm from Old Earth, but you probably know that already."

"I do. Some of the circumstances that brought you here are a little murky, but that's all right."

"Zaria," David nodded and touched his chest where the medallion lay hidden beneath his shirt.

The medallion—it was something I hadn't considered. I disliked asking for help in this, but gave myself permission to request it from Zaria if the visions didn't disappear after I drank myself into a near-coma. Perhaps she'd consider my request.

"To near-comas from drinking too much," I lifted my bottle.

"I'll second that motion," David affirmed and clinked his bottle against mine.

* * *

Queen's Palace, Le-Ath Veronis

<h1 style="text-align:center">Chapter 16</h1>

Lissa

"So far, it's like a battle of second-level students," Kooper settled onto a chair at the dinner table. He meant the presidential race on Pyrik; everyone at the table understood that. "It goes from *says who* to, *you're guiltier than I am.*"

"Always play the guilt card against your opponent. It gives the journalists exercise running back and forth," I pointed out.

"Hello, dearest," Reemagar and Connegar, my Larentii mates, arrived unexpectedly.

"Hi, honeys. I didn't know you were coming," I said.

"The Wise Ones say it is time to tell you who the father is," Reemagar's grin was so wide and bright you'd have thought the sun shone in the dining hall.

"We only came to deliver the news, then we will go," Connegar's grin mirrored Reemagar's.

"So you're just going to drop that announcement on us and take off before we can ask questions?" Winkler demanded and rose from his seat beside me.

"Ah. The father speaks first. No need to say more," Connegar chuckled and disappeared with Reemagar.

"Wait a fucking minute," Winkler half-shouted at empty air. "Boy or girl?"

"Honey, I think we'll have to wait for that," I pulled on his sleeve to make him sit down again.

Everyone watched while Winkler took his seat—with as much decorum as he could muster under the circumstances.

I figured he'd be cursing under his breath during dinner, but instead, he turned a wide, wolfish grin in my direction. "Fucking finally," he growled a laugh. "We get to be parents together."

* * *

BlackWing X

Randl

My alcohol-induced dreams from the night before now invaded my mind, rather than the visions from Bornelus.

In my dreams, I'd gone looking for the hooded man. Somehow, I knew it to be a man although I couldn't say why, as I'd never seen his face. During my dream, I'd chased him from planet to planet, dimension through dimension, and always he'd sensed me after a while and disappeared again.

At one point, we'd even been on Vogeffa II—I recognized the broken, uneven brick streets as if I'd actually been standing there.

The hooded man had spoken to someone there, whose back was turned toward me. I considered it was all a dream, as I'd been quite drunk when I finally fell asleep.

Dreams are often wish-fulfillment, I reminded myself. That's why, I'm sure, the hooded man had run from me every time. In my dream he'd been afraid of me. A heady satisfaction had come from that, and carried over into my morning, when I woke hungry with almost no hangover.

Grateful for both those things, I showered and dressed before heading toward the galley for breakfast.

"Feel better today?" Bekzi asked when I accepted my tray from him.

"Much better," I agreed. "Food smells wonderful, thank you."

"You eat. Headache leave," he grinned. "David not do so well."

"So my more experienced drinking buddy is feeling the effects?" I asked.

"He feel, all right."

"That's a first," I grinned at Bekzi and turned to locate a table. I found Travis and Trent sitting at a table that could accommodate several more. I walked toward them.

Chapter 16

"Have a seat," Travis kicked a chair out opposite his. I nodded in acceptance and set my tray on the table.

"I hope you're doing better this morning," I said.

"I am. It's not nearly as bad as yesterday."

"Same here." I considered whether I wanted to eat eggs or bacon first.

"Trent says Sabrina wants to do some manufacturing while we're on Le-Ath Veronis. There's a small facility that may work for her on the light half—the comesuli farmers use it to make temporary replacement parts for gardening equipment and such, until something more permanent can be ordered."

"Sounds good," I mumbled around a mouthful of food. "You want me to go with you," I lifted my head as the realization came to me.

"We do. Have a problem with that? We can drop by to see your pap afterward, if you want, or while we're waiting for the machine to produce the parts Sabrina needs, anyway."

"All right." I nodded and went back to my food. I worried that having Sabrina that close would only cause me pain, but I had to work with her whether I liked it or not, or whether I felt the pain of it while she didn't.

"We'll be at the space station in less than three hours, bro," Travis informed me. "Want to shoot targets after breakfast?"

"Sure."

* * *

Avii Castle, Le-Ath Veronis
Quin

"Randl will be there with you," Kooper said. He and I sat on the terrace outside Justis' and my suite, talking and having a mid-morning cup of tea.

"I'm grateful," I said. "He and I—we have our reasons for being uncomfortable with Amlis and Rodrik."

"I know. If I hadn't asked Randl to go, he would have refused. His ah, last meeting with Amlis wasn't a pleasant one, I understand."

"Amlis trying to make him feel guilty for leaving, no doubt," I snorted.

"Most likely," Kooper agreed. "I'm asking you to set your feelings aside in this, and be there with Randl, Winkler, Halimel and Lukas when this landing party arrives. I don't want any shenanigans going on beforehand, as Lissa would say."

"I worry that the unusual feeling I get from Phorde Gaster's image will be much worse in reality," I mused.

"I'm concerned about that, too. I've searched his background, and there's nothing out of the ordinary there. His schooling and work history is on the bland side, and he was married until his wife left him because he worked too much. His evaluations say he's a hard-working asset to the company."

"What about his banking records?" I asked.

"Pay deposits, nothing else. No outrageous expenditures or anything like that."

"So there's nothing to put him on anyone's suspicions list."

"Not until you said there's something unusual about him. That's why I want you and Randl to take a look. I have a hunch currently going, and I've asked a few trusted agents to look into past scouting trips or other travel plans made by Supervisor Gaster."

"Thank you," I said and sipped my tea, which had grown cold while Kooper and I spoke. "If you have more information before the visit, I'd appreciate getting what you have."

"I'll pull you and Randl into the loop," Kooper promised. "Currently, I have research teams putting lists together of what was stolen by the lesser-known pirates in the past ten years or so. I should be getting that information in the next day or two."

"It can't have been anything important, or we'd have heard about it, wouldn't we?" I asked.

"True. It's why I've instructed the BlackWing ships to focus on the big boys who steal what they can sell for the most credits. The smaller concerns often slip through the cracks, because they avoid taking those things."

"How are they equipped, weapons-wise? They have to have something in order to stop and board ships to take their cargo," I pointed out.

"Good question. I'll look into that, too." Kooper rose from the bench he occupied and stretched, rolling his shoulders to work out kinks.

"I can help relieve that, if you want," I offered.

"No, it reminds me to keep my ass moving," Kooper grinned at me. "I only stiffen up when I'm sitting still."

"How is Jett Riffler?" I asked.

"Traveling with Teeg, and I'm grateful for that. Teeg can usually hear a pin drop and feel an attack coming from a mile away. We need Jett—he's the best at his job. I really don't want to work with anyone else in that position."

"Then I hope they stay safe," I said. "Thanks for coming. I was worried about going to Harifa Edus."

"Thank you for agreeing to go," he said. "I'm off." He disappeared while I studied the space he'd occupied moments before.

Chapter 17

*S*pace Station, Le-Ath Veronis
Randl

*S*pace Station, Le-Ath Veronis
Randl

I didn't expect Pap to meet us outside security at the space station, but he was there, waiting with Drake and Drew, Travis and Trent's fathers.

"Pap," I grinned at him and walked into his open arms. He patted me on the back while I hugged him tightly.

"Queen Lissa says you can stay at the beach palace with me while you're here," he said when I let him go.

"That sounds great," I told him, feeling somewhat relieved. Perhaps I could avoid seeing so much of Sabrina that way, as the vision of her could make my heart hurt at times. I knew I'd be going with her, Travis and Trent to the small manufacturing facility on the light side of the planet, but I hoped it wouldn't take long and I could spend time with Pap while they went on to the main Palace in Lissia.

The realist in me was cursing love, while I did my best to shut off that part of my brain.

"I'm going with Randl, if that's all right," David said.

"Mom won't mind, if Randl and Brandl don't," Travis nodded.

"We'd welcome company," Pap chuckled. "Good to meet you, David. Randl says you're a good friend."

"Aww, that's so nice of you," David teased. "Mostly we get together at night and have a beer or six," he told Pap.

"The best kind of friends, then," Pap laughed. "Come on, we'll grab a shuttle to the surface."

"We'll find you in a bit," Travis said. "Go with your pap and we'll show up later."

"All right," I agreed. David and I followed Pap to the shuttle stand, so we'd get transport to Sun City on the light half of Le-Ath Veronis.

* * *

Sabrina

I'd been inside a palace or two in my lifetime, but never inside the Queen's Palace in Lissia. This one made me feel small, it was so massive. The marble on floors and walls alone must have cost a fortune, it was so fine.

Travis and Trent were at my side, walking me through the grand entry to meet their mother in her private study. Jayna and Wyatt, walking together, followed us. It made me wonder if they were holding hands in public, yet.

Bekzi, Susan and the others had gone straight to the palace kitchens, to get something for lunch and plan their day. The rest of us were invited to lunch with Queen Lissa.

"There you are," Queen Lissa and three assistants waited outside her study door. "Lunch is already laid out in the arboretum, if you're hungry."

"Thanks, Mom," Travis stepped forward to hug her first. Trent was next, then came Wyatt.

"Wyatt, honey, you should visit more often," Lissa gave him an extra hug before letting him go.

"Uh, Queen Lissa?" Jayna's voice sounded tentative.

Shy.

"You want the disguise removed while you're here?" Queen Lissa smiled brightly at Jayna.

"Yes, please, if it's not too much trouble."

I turned swiftly and blinked at Jayna. *Disguise?* What disguise?

Lissa motioned her forward, then placed her hands on Jayna's face. The transformation was startling—breathtaking, actually.

Jayna was stunningly lovely. She'd been under my nose the whole time and there I'd thought her plain.

"Thanks, Gran," Wyatt leaned in to peck Lissa on the cheek. "Now everybody will see what I see." He turned a blinding smile on Jayna, who couldn't help but smile back at him.

"All right, then, lunch it is," Lissa clapped her hands. Someone, I have no idea who, transported us to the palace arboretum in a blink.

* * *

Sun City, Le-Ath Veronis

Randl

"You've been here before?" Pap asked David as we hefted duffels over our shoulders and left the train behind.

"Not to the train station, but Sun City, yes," David said. "Even put a few credits in the slot machines at a casino."

"The tourists do love to gamble," Pap laughed. "Not that you're a tourist," he amended.

"Oh, definitely a tourist. Brought the wife and everything. We saw the beach palace because we paid for a tour."

"Then you'll get to see the parts the tourists never see," Pap said. "Come on, we have a hover car waiting to take us in. We can even get a boat to Avii Castle if you want."

"Seriously? I'd love to see Avii Castle."

"Good. I have a suite there, if I ever need it. Quin and Justis say we can visit while you're here."

"Sounds like you're treated like family by both royal houses," I teased Pap.

"I am, actually. It's completely opposite to my treatment in New Fyris."

"Yeah. About that," I sighed.

"I know you're going back there with Mr. Winkler," Pap said. "You'll be fine with him there. Winkler doesn't take well to mistreatment, I've learned. He appreciates a good beer now and then, too."

"You've been out drinking with Winkler?" I asked.

"Don't sound so surprised. That old wolf knows a hell of a lot," Pap couldn't hold back the smile. "He told me Amlis wasn't exactly polite when you saw him last."

"That would be putting it in the mildest terms possible."

"I read in him what he wasn't saying," Pap nodded. "Here's our car." We'd walked toward the entrance of the train station, and waiting in a reserved parking space was a hover-limo.

"Fancy," David grinned as two comesuli climbed out to take our bags and make us comfortable in the back seat.

"Master Dwarf, there are beverages in the cold-keeper inside the vehicle," a comesuli bowed to David. "Lunch is waiting at the palace for all of you."

Will it do any good to ask him to stop bowing? David sent to me.

Probably not, I struggled to smother a laugh. *They were told to treat us with honor and respect, bro.* I borrowed Travis and Trent's nickname—it fit, somehow.

Chapter 17

"Well, I'm hungry," David said aloud and clambered onto the seat facing Pap and me.

"We'll be there momentarily," the comesuli driver replied and shut the door.

"Beer?" David was already digging in the cold-keeper.

"I'll have one," I said.

* * *

Sabrina

From the arboretum at the top of Lissa's palace, I could see the glittering lights of Lissia below. It looked like a fairy city at nightfall—one I'd read about when I was young.

"It's more mundane when you get to it," Lissa smiled. "The boys can take you, if you want. Have they offered a trip to Niff's, yet?"

"That's the first thing they said."

"Good."

The remnants of our lunch were all about us, and we'd talked and laughed about mostly nothing while we ate. If Lissa meant to make us feel comfortable, she'd done a fine job. Jayna had laughed more with Wyatt than I'd ever heard her laugh. I still couldn't imagine why she'd hide her beauty behind a plain façade, but what did I know?

"The manufacturing facility is waiting for you this afternoon," Lissa said. "I've instructed them to leave it in your hands while you're working, so they won't see anything they shouldn't." Her smile let me know she understood my designs were secret.

"Thank you. I appreciate that more than I can say," I acknowledged.

"You can freshen up in your suite first, then go," Lissa suggested.

"I'd like to change clothes," I agreed. "This really isn't the best outfit for working on designs." I'd dressed in a calf-length skirt, boots and a nice blouse to have lunch with the Queen.

"Lissa used to say the same thing before going out to lop heads," a smiling, dark-haired man appeared at Lissa's elbow. His sudden appearance made me smother a gasp. Travis's hand was at my back quickly, soothing away the fright.

"Merrill, stop scaring my guests," Lissa complained. I wanted to ask him about the lopping heads comment, before recalling that I'd seen Travis and Trent do it. Travis' hand went to the back of my neck to massage away the tension forming there.

"I came to issue an invitation to NorthStar," he said. "While your guests are here. They're most welcome to come with you."

"When?" Lissa asked, gazing up at the one she called Merrill.

He leaned down to kiss her. "Tomorrow good enough?" he asked.

"I'll alert the kitchen," she said dryly when he pulled away.

I knew she had many mates—this must be one of them.

"Good. I'll see all of you then." He disappeared as quickly as he'd appeared.

Damn. I wanted to do that.

"Come on, baby," Travis said. "Let's change clothes and go out."

He didn't need to ask twice—I was ready to go.

* * *

Randl

"I don't think I can move," David patted his stomach. We'd had roast chicken, a delicious vegetable casserole, fresh-baked bread and salad before dessert was brought out.

"Are you staying here while I go to the manufacturing facility?" I asked him.

Chapter 17

"Not on your life," David grinned. "I need to walk some of this off."

"There's a walk involved?"

"From the hovercar to the door," Pap grinned.

"Anything will help," David laughed.

"I'll change clothes, first," I said.

"The car is waiting whenever you're ready," Pap said.

"Thanks, Pap."

* * *

"My suite is cavernous," David said while leaning back in his hover-limo seat half an hour later. "I could invite a circus, with elephants and a tent," he added.

"Are those still legal? With the animals?" I asked.

"Not in the Alliances," he shrugged. "Old Earth, remember?" He tapped his chest.

"I remember. Can you actually invite a tent?"

"Poor phrasing," David defended himself.

"Just to be clear," I nodded. "Your owl has plenty of room to fly, though."

"True enough."

I turned toward the window, to see we were passing through farmland. Rows of ripening fruit and vegetables stretched across the landscape.

"This is amazing," I breathed as the farms captivated me.

"Le-Ath Veronis grows most of its own produce," David said. "It only imports a few things from Kifirin and a few other places."

"Harifa Edus, too, although the werewolf farmers have a decided advantage over New Fyris, because Amlis has been backward about importing equipment and supplies."

"Maybe he'll come to his senses someday," David said.

"I'm not holding my breath."

"Wise decision."

The vehicle began to slow, indicating we were nearing our destination. The facility, once it came into view, proved to be a small, cube of a building, with little indication of what it was. Something this small could make replacement parts but little else.

Sabrina's workshop had been larger than this, but it was housed inside a massive manufacturing facility that was many times larger. This—I hoped it was good enough to create Sabrina's designs.

"I hope she's making something cool," David said when the vehicle pulled to a stop. The driver opened his door, allowing him to exit first.

"About time, bro," Trent opened my door with a grin.

"I told you to go on without me," I joked.

"Nah. No fun, dude. Come on, Sabrina's looking the place over. No idea what she's looking for, so any distraction is welcome."

We were worried, Trent sent mindspeech as we walked into the small building. *Sabrina was, too, but it appears to have everything she needs, including the laser trimmers.*

Every bit of space inside the small building was utilized for maximum effect, I discovered as I looked about the building.

"He can see well enough," Trent waved off a concerned comesula, who'd stepped forward to help me if necessary.

"Of course," the comesula dipped his head to Trent and backed away.

Aboard ship, I was a regular member of the crew. Here, and for those who hadn't been informed, I was still a blind man.

"I can do it here," Sabrina called out. The comesula's shoulders sagged in relief.

Has she been terrorizing the staff? I turned to Trent with a smile.

Chapter 17

Maybe a little. They heard her last name and scattered like birds.

"We will leave now, as instructed," the comesula said. "Contact us when you are finished, or if you need help."

I could tell he was worried for his equipment, and worried about having so many unsupervised strangers—one of whom was a Kend—inside his facility.

"Do not worry," I told him. "All will be well."

"As you say," he nodded, although he remained unconvinced.

When the last comesuli employee was out the door, David and I found chairs against a wall while Sabrina connected her comp-vid to the facility's main comp and went to work.

* * *

Winkler

"She has working models?" I asked. Kooper had come for dinner at the palace, asking for a private meeting with me afterward.

"Looks that way. The one she tested blew a stack of bricks apart. Preliminary estimates show a decent range for the weapon, which could last for up to a hundred shots before it needs recharging. The solar battery can only hold so much energy in this case, because of the temporary materials involved."

We were discussing the new ranos pistols Sabrina Kend designed at the facility Lissa commandeered for her. In all, she'd manufactured twenty weapons in the time she'd had.

"We've removed all traces of the design before allowing the regular employees back in there. This means that on one of the larger ships, they could actually manufacture their own weapons if needed."

"That's something to think about," I said.

"For undercover operations, definitely," Kooper confirmed. "Equipment and supplies could be crated up unassembled, in case the ship is boarded by authorities elsewhere. This has potential."

"What are you planning to do with the prototypes?"

"They have the shield she designed built in. I'm allowing her, Travis, Trent, David and Randl to carry one, to make sure the shield holds up. We can control the situation here on Le-Ath Veronis, in case they're discovered. I can identify them as agents, and Lissa can back me up."

"Good idea. You wouldn't consider letting me carry one to the WildTree meet-and-greet in a couple of days, would you?"

"You think you need one?" Kooper eyed me curiously.

"Never know," I grinned. "Better to have a weapon than pull out power and tip your hand that way."

"Agreed," Kooper said. "I'll get one to you."

* * *

Randl

"We're invited to NorthStar tomorrow for dinner," Travis said. He, Sabrina and Trent had come back to the beach palace with David and me for dinner after Sabrina finished her designs and tested the weapons.

"Good. I'll see if the wife can come," David hauled out a comp-vid. We sat around the table after comesuli servants cleared everything away except wine glasses and beer mugs.

I felt left out in the mate department. Sabrina sat between Travis and Trent, happy and half-drunk, after a successful day designing temporary ranos weapons.

I and the others with me carried one hidden on our persons—Kooper allowed it to test the weapon's shields.

I'd also received my certification on ranos pistols and rifles; Kooper grinned when he told me the news earlier.

Chapter 17

Pap had excused himself after dinner—said he had things to do before bed. I felt inclined to do the same, but didn't want to be the first to go after Pap.

"How about a walk on the beach?" David suggested. "We should be safe enough."

"Sounds like an excellent idea," Travis agreed.

"I'm going to bed," I said when I caught the hopeful look in Sabrina's eyes. She was watching Travis as he rose from his seat.

I had no desire to watch those three stroll along the beach while Travis and Trent stole kisses now and then.

"Weenie," David frowned at me.

"I don't under—oh. Never mind," I held up a hand as he started to explain exactly—in Old Earth terms—what weenie meant.

"Still going to bed?" David asked.

"Yes. Feel free to talk amongst yourselves. When I see you in the morning, I'll know exactly how many times you called me weenie in my absence."

"He can do that?" Sabrina asked Travis.

"Probably."

"Look, I'm tired, too. I think I'll take an extra beer to my suite and watch the news vids," David said. "Have fun," he told Trent. "See you at breakfast."

* * *

Stop trying to play matchmaker, I sent to David as he and I walked the hallway leading to our suites. *There isn't a glimmer of hope for me in Sabrina's eyes.*

Unless you put it there. She has no idea what she wants, David snorted. *Sure, Travis and Trent are there, so you have to catch her attention in other ways.*

"What else do I have to do, man?" I said aloud while flinging out a hand in frustration. "I've played all my tricks. You see how unimpressed she is."

"I wouldn't call them tricks," David turned and stopped in front of me, causing me to stop, too. When he put fists on hips, I knew I was in for a lecture. "She's alive because of you. Admit that, at least. Sure, Travis and Trent can draw any woman's eye, but to say she ignores you completely—that's harsh, man. I think she's better than that."

"She's better than me," I sighed and moved around David, who didn't want to budge. "Why would she want anyone who's a half-freak from Vogeffa II?"

"Bro, you just described me on Old Earth," David stomped after me. "Dwarves aren't common there, as you bloody well know already. I outrank you. Stop thinking like that, you fucking sod."

"Right."

"I'm not kidding." He was still castigating me when I shut my suite door in his face. "Bloody bugger," I heard him growl as he strode off.

"Fuck." I sat on the edge of my bed and dropped my face in my hands. "Stop letting your insecurities out after a few beers, Randl," I mumbled. It never did any good and only served to make me feel worse than I did already.

"Learn to live without her," I added. "People do it every day."

* * *

Travis, Trent and Sabrina were gone when I made my way to the kitchen for breakfast the following morning. A hangover pounded in my head, too.

"A few too many last night?" Pap asked while shoving a cup of tea toward me. I landed roughly on a barstool at the kitchen island, grateful my journey was over for the moment.

Chapter 17

"Maybe." I answered his question.

"I'll get you something." He rose, pocketed the comp-vid he'd been working on and left the kitchen. "Pain-kill," he was back after a bit with a small bottle in his hand. He set the bottle beside my elbow and walked to the sink for a glass of water.

I shook out four tabs and tossed them back, then drank most of the water Pap brought.

"Son, I know it's not my business, but I couldn't help noticing how you look at Sabrina."

"Yeah. You and everybody else in the Alliance," I acknowledged. Lifting my tea, I sipped the hot liquid while pointedly looking anywhere except at my father.

"I guess you'll figure this out on your own," he said. "I'm going to work. If you need anything, send a message."

"Hey, Bro," Travis and Trent appeared shortly after Pap left. "Kooper says he has new information on the small-time pirate attacks, including some vid-recordings for you to study today. You have to come to Headquarters to do it, though, because this isn't information he can transfer to your comp-vid."

"All right," I agreed, pushing my chair back to stand.

"No, eat breakfast first. Where's Dave?" Trent asked.

"Haven't seen him this morning," I said.

"I'm here." David walked into the kitchen and climbed onto a barstool. A kitchen comesula brought him a plate of food and coffee as he made himself comfortable. "I got the wakeup call from the boss," he grumbled as he lifted his cup to drink.

"We did, too—plus marching orders to bring Master Gage to Headquarters this morning," Travis said.

"Pain-kill?" I pushed the small bottle toward David, who took it without comment and dumped two tabs in his palm.

* * *

An hour later, the four of us walked into ASD Headquarters, located in Lissia. We were tagged with employee visitor passes, indicating we were field agents. We had Sabrina's weapons hidden in our clothing and sailed past security with barely a grunt from the personnel, there.

Travis sent mindspeech to Kooper advising him of that fact, which brought the Director out of his office and into a hallway to greet us, while wearing a huge smile.

"Come on," he motioned for us to follow him. "We have the vid images set up in a viewing suite. I think you may be as confused as I was when I saw them the first time."

The viewing suite had theater seating, so that anyone watching the vids had a clear view of the recordings. I sat on the second row with David. Travis and Trent took the row behind us while Kooper took a chair on the floor to operate the vid-projector.

"Here's the first one," Kooper announced. I settled into my seat to watch. At first, the camera recorded normal activity on a freighter ship—crew moving about, attending to duties and so on.

Until the lights went out. The hair on my arms rose in alarm; something was happening and the camera couldn't record it, as it was as much in the dark as the crew. I could hear shouting and a few screams of pain, but the camera had been effectively prevented from recording anything.

"This is odd, because the camera should have gone into infra-red mode and continued to record. It didn't," Kooper pointed out. "The crew who screamed were dead when the lights came on again, roughly half an hour later. By that time, everything had been stripped from their cargo hold and they'd been left to drift in the shipping lanes."

"What were they carrying?" Travis asked.

"Food—mostly packaged stuff," Kooper shrugged. "Things that wouldn't spoil for a while."

"Any records of it being re-sold elsewhere?" Trent asked.

"None. It could have been carried to a non-Alliance world and sold or traded there, but we have no records of it showing up again in either Alliance."

"Do we have images from other ships?" I asked.

"We do. All of them look like a replay of this first one."

"Was food their main objective?" Travis asked.

"Except for the few times medical supplies were taken. The reason I showed you this particular one," Kooper added, "Is that this ship is in port on Refizan right now. It regularly makes voyages between that world and two others. The crates stolen were from Refizani farms and such, that package their own food supplies. Two other ships from Refizan were targeted at different times, but both were attacked using the same methods."

"No indication from the sensors that another ship or ships were in the area?" Trent asked.

"None. The journey was normal every time, until the lights went out and they were boarded."

"Is there a way I can visit the ship on Refizan?" I asked. "I hope I can do what I did before, and recall images from the past."

"I thought you'd never ask," Kooper grinned. "I'll get us there; we've already set it up with the Captain and crew. They're waiting for us to arrive."

* * *

Refizan Space Port
Randl

"I'm pleased you've come to investigate this. Here's the manifest from that trip." Captain Len of the *Furrow* greeted us and handed a comp-vid to Kooper. He wasn't voicing his entire thoughts, however.

He'd been angry that the ASD hadn't thought it important enough to investigate before.

Captain Len's second-in-command blinked at me as I passed him in the narrow passage leading to the cargo hold; he wondered why a blind man would be accompanying the ASD Director and a hand-picked staff.

"I'd like a list of any employees on the ship during that attack who are no longer part of the crew," Kooper said as he studied the comp-vid. He already knew what they were carrying. He and I were more interested in crew members and whether any of them could have been involved with the piracy.

"I'll have it before you leave," Captain Len agreed. "Here's the cargo hold. As you probably already know, it was stripped, right down to the last splinter of every crate. Nobody came to look at it, then. I have no idea what you think you'll find two turns after the fact."

"Allow us to make that determination," Kooper held up a hand. "You may stay. All others must leave while we conduct our experiment."

"Experiment?" Captain Len didn't like the sound of that.

"Harmless, I assure you," Kooper assured him.

When the cargo hold was cleared of other crew members, Kooper nodded to me. I'd already chosen my spot; it was near the place where a crew member died. Taking a deep breath, I walked toward the selected area and placed my hands on the wall there.

The cameras couldn't see anything that happened.

The vision of what happened wasn't hidden from a blind man, however. I jerked when I saw the images after darkness enveloped

Chapter 17

the ship. I gasped again when I saw that Vrak was one of the six men who'd boarded the *Furrow* to steal its cargo.

* * *

Trent

This time, Randl included all of us in his visions. I felt as if my sight had been closed off to everything around me, sending me into a tunnel where I watched the events that took place in the cargo hold two turns earlier.

Two crew members were shot with laser pistols after the ship went dark, and six men, Vrak included, placed devices of some sort on the large crates that filled the ship's hold.

Those huge crates subsequently disappeared.

I think we're watching how three people disappeared on Pyrik, Kooper's mental voice was dry.

It didn't take long to remove the cargo—only a matter of minutes. The six men disappeared after that and the ship's lights came on, revealing two dead men and a scrambling crew.

I blinked at my surroundings, as if I'd been folded from one timeline to another, too abruptly for me to properly assimilate myself.

Captain Len stared at Randl, who removed his hands from the wall.

Somehow, Randl had included him in his vision.

"Randl, did you see anything else in those men?" Kooper asked, once his vision cleared.

"Vrak was in charge, as you've probably guessed," Randl replied. "They were taking the cargo to feed their people."

"Their people?"

"These pirates and their families."

"Where were they?"

"No idea; that was fogged. I was only able to read what was first and foremost in their minds—stealing food."

"I'll be wrapped in bacon and fried to a crisp," the Captain breathed.

"Doesn't sound particularly comfortable," Randl observed.

"Captain, the leader of those men has been dealt with and is now officially dead," Kooper informed Len. "We merely have to search for the others, now."

"I never thought we'd get anywhere with this," Len confessed. "Thank you for coming. You have my gratitude."

"Thank you for allowing us on your ship," Kooper spoke smoothly. "You've helped us a great deal, today."

Chapter 18

*B**each Palace, Le-Ath Veronis*
Randl
"They're holed up somewhere, we have no idea where, and they're stealing food to feed their people in order to avoid normal purchases and their subsequent transportation," Kooper said.

We sat on a wide patio outside Queen Lissa's beach palace, discussing what we'd learned aboard the *Furrow*. "If they're on a planet—say Pyrik, for argument's sake—hauling food in and out could raise suspicions, I suppose," Trent suggested.

"True. Like Randl said once before, they could be right under our noses and we could miss them easily," Kooper paraphrased my words.

"Or, perhaps they're in a place where nobody is supposed to be," Travis said. "Hauling supplies in and out could be a red flag."

"If they steal food and supplies, they hide their numbers," David pointed out.

"Also true," Kooper agreed.

"I didn't notice that the other five men had what Vrak did—that ability to record anything and everything with every cell of his body," I said. "They had the encroaching fog that we've seen before, but not the other. Perhaps only certain ones are selected for that."

"Supervisors, or chief bandits and pirate watchers?" David joked.

"Entirely possible," Kooper agreed.

"Maybe it's a progressive thing, too," I mused. "The older ones have the cellular recording ability. The younger ones may get there eventually—like the growing virus or whatever it is we've seen before."

"That's a frightening thought, but we do know Vrak's been around for a while," Kooper frowned.

"Director Griff?" I turned to Kooper.

"What is it, Randl?"

"May I see the gold coin from Vogeffa II again?"

"Of course. It's in evidence now, but I'll get it out for you. Take a break and have lunch; you've earned some time off. Don't forget dinner later on Avendor."

* * *

"You look fine, stop fretting," Pap told me later, after I'd dressed in a dark-blue knit shirt and cream pants. "It'll be warm there, so close to the equator on Avendor. They said dress casually."

"Who are these people, Pap?" I asked.

"I've met Merrill, he's one of the owners of NorthStar and one of Queen Lissa's mates. The others I haven't met, but they'll be there, too. Don't worry, you know most of the people invited tonight. It's just a meal, son."

"I know."

"It's because she'll be there, isn't it?"

"Part of the reason, yes."

Chapter 18

"Stop worrying and be yourself. Tomorrow you have to go to Harifa Edus, remember? I'd suggest holding back on too many drinks."

"I was planning on it," I sighed.

"Then I'll let our transportation know we're ready."

Transportation turned out to be Winkler, who grinned at Pap, David and me when he arrived in the entry shortly afterward. I lifted an eyebrow at him—the last time I'd seen him, he hadn't known who the father of Lissa's child was.

He was overjoyed to be a father, now that he knew.

"Congratulations," I dipped my head to him.

"Should have known I couldn't hide it from you," his grin widened. "Come on, we're expected pretty quick for appetizers and drinks."

David gave me a wink; his wife would be there to meet him. My shoulders sagged as Winkler folded us to Avendor.

* * *

"You come. Meet brothers," Bekzi was already there when we landed outside the huge villa. The others were walking up wide steps to enter the home. Bekzi wanted me to come with him.

After getting a glimpse of Sabrina, Travis and Trent just inside the door, I was willing to allow Bekzi to pull me away.

"This Nenzi's shop," Bekzi grinned after folding me elsewhere.

"We're not at NorthStar, now, are we?" I asked.

"EastStar," Bekzi confirmed. "Reah and Edward have space for us."

"Where did you find these?" I drew in a breath as I took in a huge, polished floor beneath a high roof, that housed at least fifty exotic vehicles. Many of them had actual wheels, which were meant to touch a road rather than hovering above it.

"We look in right places," Bekzi grinned. "Buy and restore, most times."

"This is exceptional work," I stepped forward to place my hand on the first vehicle. It was painted bright yellow with a tan, canvas roof. "The roof folds down?" I asked while stroking the smooth, polished metal exterior of the car.

"Yes. Ride open air. Nice."

"Hello." Seven more appeared close by; Bekzi's brothers, as he'd said. Soon enough, they were telling tales of this vehicle or that in their shortened speech, making me laugh as often as not with stories of successes and failures in vehicle restoration.

"What about this one?" I asked, touching the smooth, silvery-gray exterior. A small statue of a winged woman graced the hood of the vehicle, as Nenzi, Bekzi's brother, called it.

"Nineteen twenty-five Rolls Royce Phantom," Nenzi shrugged. "We convert to hover-car. Wheels for show, mostly."

"It's beautiful," I sighed, taking in the curved wheel-wells, front and back. Its windows were curved at the top, echoing curves elsewhere, while the chrome radiator cover, flanked by the round headlamps on either side, added to the elegance of the vehicle.

"You drive sometime," Nenzi promised. "We go back for dinner, now."

At least I was placed between Bekzi and Nenzi at the table, and enjoyed their company very much. Only upon occasion did my eyes stray to Sabrina, who sat between Travis and Trent.

Pap was close by, talking with two of Queen Lissa's mates—Rigo and Gavin. Both were asking questions about Vogeffa II, and Gungl in particular. It brought back my dream, and how the hooded man had spoken to someone there who'd had his back turned toward me.

I hadn't been curious enough about who it could be, I realized, and wished I could revisit the dream.

"You thinking about something," Nenzi observed.

"Yes. I'm sorry," I apologized to him.

"Not worry. It important, I think."

I couldn't help thinking it was important, too, but I couldn't say how, or why I hadn't really worried about it until now.

I heard our guest in the dungeon led a pirating party onto a Refizani ship, Queen Lissa sent to me.

I saw it, I confirmed. *I still couldn't read anything in him because of the fog on his brain, but I saw in the others that they wanted the food to feed themselves and others like them.*

That's what Kooper tells me. Is there anything else?

I've had some dreams, I confessed.

Ah. Let's discuss that after dinner, she said. *Dreams can be quite revealing, actually.*

A part of me felt nervous about telling her, while another part felt relief. If anyone could sort out dream from reality, perhaps she could.

That's how I found myself in a wide solarium later, which would surely present an amazing view of gishi trees across the landscape during the day.

Tonight, it showed a moon half-full, pouring its light from a cloudless sky.

"It's all right to speak in front of everyone here," Lissa reassured me. The two who'd discussed Gungl with Pap were there—Gavin and Rigo. Yes, I understood that Rigo was ancient, and had once borne the title Rigovarnus I, of Hraede.

The others were our hosts for the evening; Kiarra, Merrill and Adam.

They all belonged to a small race of defenders, who'd risked their lives countless times to save entire planets from the Ra'Ak. I'd seen mutated Ra'Ak on Bornelus. I understood their interest in what I had to say about that. After all, if a new race of those terrible creatures had evolved, they needed to have as much information as they could gather.

"Tell me about your dreams," Queen Lissa began as she made herself comfortable in a soft, curved chair.

I sat opposite her, while Adam and Merrill flanked me on the sofa I'd chosen. Rigo and Gavin chose to stand behind Lissa, while Kiarra took another chair adjacent to my sofa.

"I saw a hooded figure on Bornelus," I began. "I dreamed he stood on the edge of the deep hole where the concrete block had been. He raised his arms and it filled up with dirt—I can't say from where. Then, vines and creepers appeared, to cover the dirt. In the morning, I learned that the hole had been filled and vines and creepers lay over it, just as in my dream."

"Do you think it a prophetic dream? I know you have them at times," Merrill asked Lissa.

"It's possible. I'd say likely," she answered. "Did you get anything from this hooded figure?" she turned back to me.

"I have the idea it's a male, although I can't explain why I think that. It just feels right," I floundered. "I never saw past the hood over most of his face. I dreamed about him again later, and in that dream I saw him speaking to someone on the streets of Gungl. The one he spoke with had his back to me, so I couldn't see who that was, either. I was thinking about that dream during dinner, and wishing I'd seen something more in both of them."

"Do you think this is the one behind all this?" Adam asked.

"I feel that way, although I have no idea how to verify it."

"Tell us about the creatures on Bornelus," Kiarra said.

Chapter 18

"Those. Giant worms with scales, huge mouths and nasty teeth," I said. "Travis and Trent were the ones who said they resembled the Ra'Ak—I'd never seen one of those monsters before. Their descriptions fit these, though. If I hadn't had Travis' ranos rifle, we could have been in real trouble, there were so many of them."

"Living underground like earthworms," Kiarra blew out a frustrated breath. "How the hell did they morph into something like that?"

"Here's my question," Lissa interjected. "Do they have a humanoid form, like the Ra'Ak do?"

"There's a question that needs an answer," Rigo said. He wore a grim look as he considered that possibility.

"Did I miss anything?" Kooper walked into the solarium.

"Not much. Randl can fill you in later. Mostly what we have is a conundrum we can't solve at the moment," Lissa told him.

"Is there anything else to discuss?" Kooper asked. "If not, Randl needs his beauty sleep so he can be alert for New Fyris tomorrow."

"We can meet with him later, if new questions crop up," Lissa said, rising from her chair.

"Good. I'll get him back to Le-Ath Veronis." Kooper nodded in my direction. I rose and followed him out of the solarium.

* * *

Queen's Palace, Le-Ath Veronis
Sabrina

What were they waiting for? A sign from the heavens or something? I'd all but blatantly offered sex to Travis and Trent, but they were holding back for some reason. Sure, we'd gone for long walks, and had some interesting conversations, but they'd never gone past some great kisses and gentle hugs.

Those kisses promised so much more, but so far, more hadn't shown up. I'd kissed both of them outside my suite door, all but inviting them to spend the night, and they'd carefully seen me inside and shut the door behind them.

I wanted to scream in frustration. Maybe throw a few things.

If Randl were still speaking to me, I'd ask him about it. He'd carefully avoided me lately, and I wondered at that. I wasn't in pain, as he'd noticed the last time we'd really talked—I was frustrated and wanted a male perspective on why two other males were holding back.

It just didn't make sense, and Randl was the only one I'd be willing to discuss this with. I sure couldn't have it out with Travis and Trent—that would be embarrassing, on top of risking my heart if they told me the relationship had cooled on their side of things.

"Fuck." I raked fingers through my hair—I'd left it down for our dinner party, because it looked better with the dress I'd worn.

The dress was meant to convey that I was more than ready to move the relationship forward with the twins. Nothing had come of it, making me doubt myself at every turn.

"When Randl gets back from New Fyris tomorrow, we'll talk," I promised myself. Stalking into the bathroom, I removed the dress and my makeup before going to bed.

* * *

Randl

I'd pulled up the image of Phorde Gaster on my comp-vid after climbing into bed for the night. Time to study him more closely.

Quin was right—there was certainly something odd about Gaster. His records indicated that he was born on Tee'Marr, less than a day's travel by starship from Pyrik. Using the passkey, I searched for his birth records in Tee'Marr's databases.

Chapter 18

I found information, and a photograph of an infant. Yes, the infant's name was Phorde Gaster, whose age should now be sixty-seven.

What I knew from the baby's photograph was that this Phorde Gaster had died in his early forties.

For more than twenty years, someone else had been posing as Phorde Gaster.

Frantically, I searched through the real Phorde Gaster's records—school, work and so on.

Phorde Gaster's family owned a concrete manufacturing company, which they'd sold around the time of Phorde's death.

The new owner of that company was WildTree Industries.

Quin, are you awake? I sent.

I am, she replied quickly.

I need to see you, I said.

I'll have Wellend come for you, she replied.

Soon enough, the red-winged warlock was inside my suite while I was still shoving boots on my feet. After snatching my comp-vid off the bed, I nodded to Wellend, who transported me to Avii Castle.

* * *

Avii Castle

Quin

I'd never thought to search Gaster's birth records, or the records of his family's holdings. On the surface, and to most researchers, Gaster's life was plainly mapped out. His family had sold their business, and Gaster had gone to work for WildTree.

Except that the Phorde Gaster in the baby image wasn't the same person as the supervisor who worked for WildTree. That one I still felt unsure of, and Randl and I knew something was going on with him that we couldn't pinpoint, but it helped a great deal to know this wasn't the original Phorde Gaster.

Randl watched while I rustled my feathers in frustration and studied more photographs from Gaster's school days.

None of those were the same person as the WildTree supervisor visiting New Fyris the following day.

Kooper, we need you, I sent to him. This, I felt, was far too important to wait for the morning.

* * *

Randl

"How old?" Kooper lifted an eyebrow at me after studying the images on my comp-vid. Quin had asked him to come, although I'd arrived at the same conclusion she had—that this couldn't wait.

"The real one died at age forty-two, if my vision of him is correct," I said.

"So for twenty-five years or so, an imposter has been posing as him. I see that he's cut ties with his family," Kooper had pulled up information from the Gaster family, and there was enough correspondence between them to indicate the break between them and Phorde.

"This one—it's difficult to tell his age, because of the fog surrounding him," Quin said. "His name is Phorde Gaster—that's what his face and mind tell me. It's just that this Phorde Gaster," she indicated the baby's image from Tee'Marr's records, "Isn't that Phorde Gaster," she tapped the image of the WildTree supervisor. Quin had gone looking for the same information I had, and like me, had come away with nothing useful.

"I'll be going with you tomorrow, instead of Halimel," Kooper growled. "Look, go to bed—you need sleep before going to New Fyris tomorrow. I'll put somebody on this tonight. I want to know

Chapter 18

when this asshole goes to the bathroom and how big his turds are." Kooper disappeared while Quin and I laughed at his joke.

* * *

Queen's Palace, Le-Ath Veronis
Winkler

"This is what we're dealing with," Kooper set a comp-vid in front of me at breakfast the following morning.

I glanced at the information, taking several moments to re-read parts of it, to make sure I hadn't misread it the first time.

"This is an imposter?" I asked.

"Not only that, but WildTree owns the Gaster family's former business—a concrete manufacturing concern. Now, we figure the whole concrete block/sacrificing party happened roughly twenty or thirty years ago on Bornelus. Three guesses where that concrete came from and two won't be needed." Kooper was angry—I could see that easily enough.

"What about the hooded man that Randl saw in his dream vision?" I asked. I'd been clued in by Lissa the night before.

"An employee, perhaps, or someone pulling bigger strings? Who knows? I'm hoping we can get more information from Gaster when we see him."

"None of this is making the wolf happy," I frowned as I flipped through more information on Kooper's comp-vid.

"The snake wants to strangle the imposter," Kooper hissed. Yeah, the wolf and the snake wanted out.

Either way, I figured Gaster, or the one pretending to be Gaster, would be in Lissa's dungeon before the day was out.

"Do you have anyone working on the WildTree end of things?" I asked.

"All of the BlackWing crew, on every ship. I'm not sure I can trust anyone else with this right now."

"You think they've infiltrated the ASD?"

"Anything's possible."

"Yeah. Sit down, take a deep breath and eat. We'll handle what we can when we get to New Fyris."

* * *

Randl

I spent the night at Avii Castle, at Quin's urging. The whole thing was constructed of glass, and it intrigued me greatly.

Making a promise to myself to explore it later, I dressed for our trip to New Fyris and went to breakfast when a servant with multi-colored wings arrived at my suite to guide me to the King's private dining room.

My dreams during the night had been troubling ones—over and over, I'd envisioned meeting Phorde Gaster, the imposter, and when I took his hand, he'd exploded.

Like a loop in my head, the same thing occurred in the dream; until my dream self had taken charge and worked some magic, somehow, sending the imposter's exploding bits to Bornelus, where the concrete block had been.

This—I had no idea what to think of it, other than it had been a nightmare. I'd been terrified in the dream; I know that much. There wasn't any way I'd tell this dream to Queen Lissa—it was an impossibility.

Not that the imposter couldn't do what he'd done—I meant my part of it. Only taking charge of the dream had forced it away from me, and for that, I was grateful. Perhaps I should remember that in the future, if nightmares plagued me again.

"You look troubled," Quin said the moment I took a seat at the breakfast table.

"It's nothing," I waved off her concern.

"I had troubling dreams," she admitted.

Chapter 18

"What were they?" I lifted my napkin and dropped it on my lap, as was proper.

"Just a blur of things—like a terrible whirlwind," she said. "It was all I could see."

"Ah." *Here was a difference between male and female*, I told myself. Quin wasn't afraid to admit her dreams frightened her. I, on the other hand, refused to admit how troubling mine were—because it wouldn't seem manly enough.

Perhaps that was the trouble with Sabrina—she saw Travis and Trent as manly, while I appeared less than they. I didn't have the muscles or the tattoos, wasn't a dragon shapeshifter and certainly couldn't wield two blades at once.

I'd been feeling my way along in self-defense and the defense of others, while they strode right into any fight with no qualms.

They had a mysterious air about them, too, and I—I was an open book, as Morrett would say.

Besides, who'd want the blind man, when others who were whole and perfect were available?

Stop thinking about Sabrina and concentrate on New Fyris, I scolded myself. A plate of food was set in front of me, so I began to eat with determination.

* * *

Grand Master's Manor, Harifa Edus
Winkler

"Kooper is bringing Quin and Randl," I said. "We've learned a few things about Phorde Gaster in the last twelve hours or so, and the Director thinks his presence is warranted, to arrest Gaster properly."

"What has he done?" Lukas lifted his jacket off a chair and slipped into it. Fall had come to New Fyris, and the air would be noticeably cooler there.

"Nothing we can really pinpoint, other than he's not really Phorde Gaster."

"An imposter?"

"That's what I hear. The rest is rather complicated—I'll try to fill you in later."

"I'd appreciate that," Lukas huffed. He didn't like being in the dark any better than I did. I'd gotten some information from Kooper in a brief message, but he said to allow him to handle Gaster and crew, and to lend a hand if anybody tried to run.

Lukas and I could take care of that part. "Ready?" I asked.

"Yes."

I folded us to New Fyris.

* * *

New Fyris

Quin

Bel Erland had come to place a disguise before Randl and I left Avii Castle with Kooper. Nobody saw my wings except those who could see past the disguise. Randl and Kooper could see my feathers easily.

We landed in Amlis' private study in the castle. It bore great resemblance to the one he'd had when he lived on Siriaa. It didn't hold the best of memories for me. I'd been a lowly servant, then, working as a page for Amlis, because he thought I couldn't speak.

Don't think about the beating, I reminded myself.

Rodrik appeared stone-faced as Amlis rose from his chair to greet us—as he should. I was Queen of the Avii, and deserving of respect. A part of me still wanted to cringe in front of these, and there was no reason for that.

Another part wanted to lash out at them for their willingness to harm someone less than they. "Thank you for coming," Amlis dipped his head to Randl, Kooper and me. "I am having reservations now—as I should have had before."

"My Prince," a servant knocked on Amlis' open door. "Your guests have arrived, as have Grand Master Lukas and Master Winkler."

"Shall we?" Amlis gestured toward the door.

* * *

Randl

The difference in Amlis was shocking. Clear-minded and coherent—I'd never seen this Amlis before. Perhaps Quin had healed more than she thought or intended. Regardless, it was more than welcome, and the hate he'd hurled at me during our last meeting was noticeably absent.

He knew better than to look my way more than a few moments at a time, too, as if he were embarrassed by what I might see.

Focus, Randl, I warned myself. *An imposter is waiting downstairs.*

* * *

Mer'bali, Pyrik
Varok

My hand-picked team waited near the venue where Lebbon was scheduled to speak. The election was close, and an assassination now would ensure that O'Tunne won by default.

A crowd had gathered to see the candidate; most still waited their turn to go through security and be led to their seats. Soon enough, the martyrs I'd selected would perform their duty for the Prophet, and we'd be one step closer to our ultimate goal.

Microscopic cameras on clothing would ensure that the Prophet saw the martyrdom for himself. When next he visited, he would praise those who'd died for our cause.

All of us lived for that praise—to be noticed and thanked for our efforts. *Patience*, I reminded myself, as in my eagerness, I'd begun to stare at the crowd with pleasure, knowing they'd be dead soon and their candidate with them.

"More tea?" A server interrupted my thoughts as I sat at an outside table across the street from the venue.

"Yes, thank you." I even smiled at her while wishing her dead, too.

* * *

New Fyris

Randl

Kooper hadn't bothered to disguise himself. We passed through an area of dimness before reaching the square of light from a high window in Amlis' wide, marble-tiled entry.

Phorde Gaster and five others waited there for us, the light shining on them and revealing every flaw in those I could read. Gaster's imposter was still a closed book, and the fog on him had grown dark and dense.

I stopped short while still within the dimness. Kooper's hand dropped onto my shoulder and Quin stopped beside me. Amlis and Rodrik were behind us, with Winkler and Lukas behind those two.

Something's wrong, Quin sent to all of us.

Something *was* wrong.

Terribly wrong.

And not just here.

Chapter 19

*L*ee'Qee, Pyrik
V'dar

My mind was fed images from two places; Mer'bali and New Fyris. My soldiers called me *Prophet*, because I foresaw things. None knew of my beginnings, as it should be.

If Jett Riffler or Kooper Griff could find the slimmest of leads on my existence, they would expend all their efforts to find and destroy me.

As if I couldn't see it coming. I laughed humorlessly, startling two soldiers who stood nearby. Let them worry that I wanted something from them—perhaps their lives. I'd come to Lee'Qee to watch our victory in Mer'bali, never thinking that an opportunity would show itself on Harifa Edus, too.

The vision from New Fyris was dim, as if he stood in shadow, but I knew him. Director Griff was harder to locate than anyone I'd ever hunted before. This was an opportunity too good to miss, and I intended to take full advantage.

Let him come closer, I thought to myself. His death and that of Lebbon would command a feast this day.

I'd employed power to hide Lee'Qee from prying eyes long ago—someone else had done it before me. When I took charge of the forgotten city, only those I allowed knew of its existence.

When the Conclave resumed, I'd have Griff out of the way and Alliance leaders in a single place, waiting for my destruction.

It would bring me a great deal of pleasure to see them die.

Two deaths were on today's agenda. I smiled as a soldier watching the camera feed from the martyrs announced that everything was in place and merely waited for my command.

* * *

Harifa Edus

Randl

Whether the hooded figure knew I'd see past the fog when he activated the explosives hidden in Gaster's imposter I had no idea, yet for a brief moment, as I stepped forward to bring us into the light, I saw it.

Saw *him*.

Saw where he was and what else he'd planned.

I can't recall whether I shouted aloud or mentally, but I do know that I lifted my hands to ward off the blast.

In two places.

* * *

Mer'bali

Varok

I'd taken myself a safe distance away to watch the blast—no need to tempt fate as I wasn't scheduled to die that day.

I'd watched explosions before, as they happened and then vids of them later, slowing the images down so I could see them happening more clearly. I felt a rumble, as if the explosion had begun.

Abruptly, it stopped.

The Prophet's shout sounded in my head and I felt my body stretch, as if it were taffy pulled reluctantly away from a spoon. I had no time to wonder or question; it happened too quickly.

* * *

New Fyris

Winkler

Kooper and I threw up shields the moment the imposter exploded—except that he and the five with him exploded together, and then didn't.

Like a rubber band that had been stretched to its limit before popping back to its original size—that's what I recalled seeing before those six and Randl, who'd thrown up his hands in a defensive gesture, disappeared together.

"What the hell just happened?" Kooper cursed.

"Where's Randl?" Quin sounded close to tears.

* * *

Bornelus

V'dar

"Call the ships," I shouted at the soldiers I'd pulled away from Lee'Qee. The city was compromised and we'd never be able to go back.

He'd seen me—that nameless, faceless man whose vision had bored into mine for a moment, stripping plans away from me in the time it takes to blink.

The six from New Fyris and those martyrs dedicated to killing Lebbon in Mer'bali had been transported to Bornelus, too—by *him*. I'd barely thrown up a shield to protect myself and the others before their delayed explosion occurred.

Somehow, he'd accomplished that, and I was determined to learn it for myself, if it were possible to do so.

"The ships have been called," Varok replied to my order. I was clearly angered by the turn of events, so he knew not to approach me. Questions crowded his mind, however, and I was grateful he was too frightened of me to ask.

I had no real answers at the moment, but I intended to find them.

"I'll be back," I snapped. "Go to the designated place, best possible speed," I commanded.

"Of course." Varok bowed to me.

He wanted to know where *I* was going.

I was going back to Lee'Qee.

He would be waiting there for me; I was sure of it.

* * *

Lee'Qee, Pyrik

Randl

Under our noses, just as I'd said. This wasn't the time to gloat about being right. I had no idea what to do when he came back, because he surely would.

It's what I would do.

He hadn't known of my existence until now.

I'd seen him in my dreams. I'd seen more when my vision connected to him. His soldiers called him the Prophet; I'd gotten that much from him. As for his real name, I hadn't seen it—it was well-hidden. I'm sure he had a very good reason for that.

Just as I hoped to hide my name from him.

The thought made me laugh—I was about to die and I knew it. Whatever I'd done in New Fyris had been a fortunate accident, and I hadn't had time to analyze what it was, exactly, that I had done.

Chapter 19

Kooper could have died in the explosion—that was the Prophet's intention.

I'd not only interrupted that, but foiled the attempt to kill Haral Lebbon, the leading candidate in Pyrik's upcoming election.

I figured Lebbon would be less apt to go along with the Prophet's plans and ideas. He'd become a target, therefore, clearing the way for Lebbon's opponent.

I felt the planet groan beneath my feet as the heavy shield around Lee'Qee dissipated. For years uncounted, that shield had hidden Lee'Qee from prying eyes and held back the radiation poisoning from a nuclear accident, centuries earlier.

All of it was now making its way outward, and I had no idea what the effects the poisoning would have on the planet or its population. The six dump sites were microscopic next to this. Kooper and Jett would learn soon enough what Pyrik had hidden for so long.

I hoped the Conclave would be postponed indefinitely, and a new site chosen for a later date.

Twenty yards away, he appeared, still dressed in the robe and hood that covered his face.

I'd already seen past the hood—he couldn't hide from a mindsighted blind man who could see in the dark if he wanted.

Fine, flesh-colored scales served as his skin. Dark eyes saw much, although he wasn't blind. Like me, however, he could focus on what was around him with his mind. My hand went to the medallion around my neck, still hidden beneath my shirt.

Touch the stars, Zaria had engraved upon it.

Touch the stars, indeed.

* * *

V'dar

MindSighted

He stood there, waiting at the end of a broken street, a hand over his heart. Did he think that would protect him? That I couldn't blast the heart out of him and eat it if I wanted?

He'd won a round, because I hadn't been aware of his existence.

That existence would end here.

From where I stood, his eyes glowed silver in the light. What was that supposed to mean? I took a step forward, thinking to get closer so I could see his death more clearly. He closed his eyes, then, shutting off the silvery effect.

What the bloody hells was he doing?

No matter. His death belonged to me.

* * *

Randl

The stars exploded in my mind as I reached the proper place in my meditation. With each massive explosion, I breathed deeper, as if I were sucking in the essence of the universe about me. Before, when I'd reached out to them, it was only a half-hearted attempt, and I'd fallen asleep.

This—it took but a moment.

It took an eternity at the same time.

"Die, fool," the Prophet shouted.

I opened my eyes.

The blast he sent was designed to obliterate me and the abandoned city around me.

I slowed time and smiled.

* * *

Le-Ath Veronis, ASD Headquarters

Travis

"Bloody, fucking Lee'Qee," Kooper pounded his fist on the desk which held the vid-monitor.

Chapter 19

We'd watched it in real time, then Kooper replayed the vid again and again, to make sure he hadn't missed anything.

Nothing would change, no matter how many times I watched. The two men faced each other on a street full of broken concrete and neglect. The blast the hooded one sent—as if it were a simple thing for him to do—was blinding in its brightness.

Kooper slowed the image of the blast, which showed Randl, putting up his hands at the last moment.

The subsequent explosion rocked the abandoned city and destroyed everything within a twenty-mile radius.

I felt numb.

Somewhere nearby, Sabrina wept as Trent held her. David and Terrett had turned their backs on the vid-screen after the first viewing.

I hoped we were drawing the wrong conclusions, but in my mind, if one had survived, then the other likely survived as well.

Perhaps it was better to believe both were dead. Ultimately, to think that someone with the kind of power the hooded man wielded could die in his own blast was more comforting than thinking he was still alive and plotting revenge, somewhere.

I'd already attempted to send mindspeech to Randl.

There was no reply.

"Message from Director Riffler," a flunky held out a comp-vid to Kooper. I didn't fail to notice that his hand shook as he did so.

Kooper took the device without a word and read Jett's message.

"Teeg and Ildevar say the Conclave has been postponed until next year, and will be held on Campiaa. Pyrik has been quarantined and its population is rushing to get inoculations against radiation sickness."

"How the hell could anyone survive in that poisoned mess while hiding from everyone for years?" Mom and Winkler had arrived, although Winkler was the one to speak.

"No idea. It would have altered them somehow, I think." Kooper raked fingers through his hair. He was resigning himself to the fact that Randl was likely dead.

"You know the filth behind all this took Lee'Qee's residents elsewhere," Mom pointed out. "We have to find them before they continue with their plans. We've only interrupted them for now."

"I understand that." Kooper sat heavily on the chair beside the desk.

"Word from BlackWing VII," the flunky was back with a second comp-vid.

"Well, looks like their jumping off place was Bornelus," Kooper read the message, then tossed the comp-vid onto the desk, where it rattled against the first. "BlackWing VII says dozens of ships appeared in Bornelus' orbit, then left shortly afterward. No idea where they came from or where they went—they were shielded too well and only dropped their shields to load passengers. VII was too far away to do anything about it."

"Great. They're holed up in another place like Lee'Qee, and nobody will find it," Mom fumed.

"We've started an investigation into WildTree and the other logging concerns after the events in New Fyris," Kooper said. "If there's a connection, or anything else to find, we'll get to it. Quin's willing to work overtime with images and such."

"Because we don't have Randl anymore." Winkler's voice was flat. He was suffering, too, he merely hid it better than some of us.

"Honey?" Mom came to me and touched my arm.

"Mom, I think they're both alive," I blurted. "That's a really good thing and a really bad thing at the same time."

Chapter 19

"I'm not going to question your assumption," Mom sighed. "Because I'm worried about the same thing."

* * *

Vogeffa II

V'dar

It made sense in a twisted sort of way that I'd land here—where I was born. My father was dead; my mother, too. There was nothing here for me, except a place to recuperate from the blast in Lee'Qee.

I'd never been affected this way by any attack before, and felt extremely weak and ill as a result. How he'd accomplished that, I had no idea.

While I recovered—however long that might take, I'd begin making plans to hunt the bastard and destroy him.

Yes, I was sure he'd survived, just as I had. Where he'd landed, I had no idea. Perhaps he'd landed on the planet of his birth, as I had.

Time to begin looking for those things—as soon as I found food and a comfortable bed.

The outskirts of Gungl taunted me as I slowly hobbled down its fractured streets, searching for a suitable roof and sustenance.

* * *

Randl

Where the fuck was I? I'd awakened in a strange place, in a strange bed, half-frozen and feeling drained of strength.

"You're in the mountains of Falchan," an unfamiliar voice informed me. "Winter is coming, so get used to the cold."

Turning my head on the soft pillow, I found a dark-haired man sitting on a chair beside my bed. "Salidar DeLuca," he introduced himself. "It's five years earlier than the time you were blasted away from Pyrik. I was asked to instruct you in the ah, finer arts of warfare."

"By whom?" I turned my face toward the ceiling, which was made of finely-carved wooden beams. Wolves, dragons and eagles were engraved in detail along each beam.

"A friend," Salidar shrugged. "She said you needed an edge when you went back to work, six years from now."

"Zaria," I sighed.

"She said you'd know."

"Yeah."

The End